THE CASE OF THE BORROWED BRUNETTE
THE CASE OF THE BURIED CLOCK
THE CASE OF THE FOOTLOOSE DOLL
THE CASE OF THE LAZY LOVER
THE CASE OF THE SHOPLIFTER'S SHOE
THE CASE OF THE FABULOUS FAKE
THE CASE OF THE CROOKED CANDLE
THE CASE OF THE HOWLING DOG
THE CASE OF THE FIERY FINGERS
THE CASE OF THE HAUNTED HUSBAND
THE CASE OF THE MYTHICAL MONKEYS
THE CASE OF THE SHAPELY SHADOW
THE CASE OF THE GLAMOROUS GHOST
THE CASE OF THE GRINNING GORILLA
THE CASE OF THE NEGLIGENT NYMPH
THE CASE OF THE PERJURED PARROT
THE CASE OF THE RESTLESS REDHEAD
THE CASE OF THE SUNBATHER'S DIARY
THE CASE OF THE VAGABOND VIRGIN
THE CASE OF THE DEADLY TOY
THE CASE OF THE DUBIOUS BRIDEGROOM
THE CASE OF THE LONELY HEIRESS
THE CASE OF THE EMPTY TIN
THE CASE OF THE GOLDDIGGER'S PURSE
THE CASE OF THE LAME CANARY
THE CASE OF THE BLACK-EYED BLOND
THE CASE OF THE CARETAKER'S CAT
THE CASE OF THE GILDED LILY
THE CASE OF THE ROLLING BONES
THE CASE OF THE SILENT PARTNER
THE CASE OF THE VELVET CLAWS
THE CASE OF THE BAITED HOOK
THE CASE OF THE COUNTERFEIT EYE
THE CASE OF THE PHANTOM FORTUNE
THE CASE OF THE WORRIED WAITRESS
THE CASE OF THE CALENDAR GIRL
THE CASE OF THE TERRIFIED TYPIST
THE CASE OF THE CAUTIOUS COQUETTE
THE CASE OF THE SPURIOUS SPINSTER
THE CASE OF THE DUPLICATE DAUGHTER
THE CASE OF THE STUTTERING BISHOP
THE CASE OF THE ICE COLD HANDS
THE CASE OF THE MISCHIEVOUS DOLL
THE CASE OF THE DARING DECOY
THE CASE OF THE STEPDAUGHTER'S SECRET
THE CASE OF THE CURIOUS BRIDE
THE CASE OF THE CARELESS KITTEN
THE CASE OF THE LUCKY LOSER
THE CASE OF THE RUNAWAY CORPSE
THE CASE OF THE RELUCTANT MODEL
THE CASE OF THE WAYLAID WOLF

The Case of the
Moth-Eaten
Mink

Erle Stanley Gardner

BALLANTINE BOOKS • NEW YORK

Foreword

Captain Frances G. Lee, a seventy-year-old woman who has donated her life and her fortune to legal medicine, police work and scientific crime detection, is a character so fabulous that the most colorful creations of the mystery writer seem drab in comparison.

Several years ago she first invited me to attend one of the seminars on homicide investigation which are given under her auspices at the Harvard Medical School in Boston.

At this seminar my attention was attracted to one of the younger instructors, Dr. Russell S. Fisher, a man who had a thorough command of his subject, who had the knack of imparting information, and who, above all, had a manner of quiet sincerity. He was modest, almost to the point of self-effacement; yet the calm confidence with which he went about his work showed that he had faith in himself.

I am interested in mysteries, murders, police detection and in crime, but above all, as a writer, I am interested in people. I like to try to classify people and try to "read character."

There are those who claim that it is impossible to "read character." What these skeptics overlook is that as a man establishes the daily contacts of his life, he is, to a large extent, treated according to his character and his worth. It is quite possible that the man's character may not show in any particular stamp of features; nevertheless by his bearing, his manner, and the tone of his voice, a careful observer can tell a great deal about that individual and how he is accustomed to being treated by those who know him well.

The man whose opinions are consistently ignored will either make his remarks apologetically, or try to offset the effect he feels his words will create by clothing himself in a synthetically positive manner, which is so patently assumed it fools no one.

The man who is suspect of carrying tales or double-crossing will always be on the defensive. The man whose opinions are good but not quite good enough will keep on talking long after he has made his point, trying to bolster up his ideas in the face of the expected refusal.

I have known people who are very expert at this sort of character reading, and it is a hobby with me to study these things. So I made it a point to study Dr. Fisher, and the more I saw of him the better I liked him.

During the next eighteen months, Captain Lee invited me to attend two more seminars, and each time I noted Dr. Fisher's development with increased pleasure.

Then came a time when Maryland decided it must put up really adequate appropriations and quit playing around with homicides and murders, and put its ten-year-old Medical Examiner System on a solid footing. They wanted a man to head it who was thoroughly competent.

I knew generally that the five-man commission in Baltimore had decided to get the very best man available in the field. The position carried a salary which they felt would attract a man of top caliber.

Captain Lee is by way of being godmother to most of the state police organizations on the Atlantic Coast, and it was my good fortune to accompany her on a friendly tour of the state police, starting in New Hampshire (where she herself holds the title of Captain) and moving on down, state by state, until we came to Virginia.

The Maryland bigwigs in state and city police administration and crime detection went out of their way to honor Captain Lee, and I was included in the invitations. I caught a glimpse of real Southern hospitality, outstanding, it seems to me, because it is essentially founded upon sincerity and a recognition that friendships constitute the true wealth in life. Money may be desirable, but it is distinctly secondary.

It was a warm evening. There were mint juleps in frosted glasses, and a dinner served so efficiently, yet so unostentatiously, that one was inclined to take it as much for granted as the ice and the mint. Then, over the after-dinner coffee, the conversation gravitated toward the new position which was open, and I realized that these people had deferred naming the man who was to be Chief Medical Examiner until they could have a heart-to-heart talk with Captain Lee.

It came out of a clear sky so far as Captain Lee was concerned. She starting thinking out loud, checking over persons who were available, and then said, "There's a young man who I think would fit in perfectly. He's young, he's at Harvard, and he's going to go places. He's competent, conscientious, and he has a lot of innate executive ability. His name is Dr. Russell S. Fisher."

And then she turned to me and said, "You know him, Erle. What do you think of him?"

I agreed with her estimate in as few words as possible. It was her party. I was watching, listening and learning.

There was quite a bit of talk during the next ten minutes.

It was very apparent that the sponsors of this Maryland program felt that it was a matter of the greatest importance that everything get off to a good start. In fact, to a large extent their own reputations were at stake. They needed a man who was really outstanding.

Captain Lee gave them her ideas about Dr. Fisher. There was some thoughtful puckering of brows. Captain Lee's recommendation went a great way, but one gathered that Dr. Fisher was going to be investigated up one side and down the other. And then they started asking questions.

During my years as a trial lawyer I have learned to appreciate what an art it is to extract definite information by short, pertinent, searching questions, and I pushed my chair back from the table so I could more thoroughly enjoy what was taking place.

There were seven or eight of the top-flight men gathered at this dinner, and they had brains. They had brains enough to work together, to co-ordinate each other's efforts, and for ten or fifteen minutes Captain Lee was subjected to a cross-examination about Dr. Fisher that was an intellectual treat to an ex-trial lawyer who had enjoyed a wonderful dinner, who was basking happily in the glow of Southern hospitality, and who was listening to as shrewd a group of men as it had ever been his good fortune to see in action.

And then one of the men asked a highly pertinent question. "This Dr. Fisher," he said, "he is young. We'll concede from what you say, Captain Lee, that he has a competent grasp of the subject. Now, suppose he comes in here as Chief Medical Examiner and a murder case breaks where he goes on the stand and is subjected to cross-examination by some of the best attorneys in the country, who are, perhaps, trying to confuse him, trying to get him to shade his conclusions, or perhaps even trying to browbeat him and ridicule him. Is he the type of man who can go through an experience of that kind and maintain his dignity, who can rely on his knowledge, who can keep his temper and handle the situation simply through his competency and his knowledge?"

I was looking down at the tablecloth, waiting for Captain Lee to answer, thinking to myself that the person who asked that question had shown by the question itself that he had a keen insight into the technique of cross-examination.

There was a silence. I wondered if Captain Lee might be a little dubious. I glanced up at her, and saw that everyone was looking at me. For the first time I realized that the question had been addressed to me as an attorney.

It caught me by surprise so that I blurted out the two-word answer that told them exactly how I felt about Dr. Fisher. I said, "Hell, yes."

They took some little time to investigate Dr. Fisher. Their findings were favorable, and they offered him the position. Dr. Fisher accepted, and the choice has been a particularly happy one.

In the years that have ensued, the Chief Medical Examiner's Office of Maryland, located in splendidly equipped offices and laboratories provided by the city of Baltimore, has been the subject of discussion in many a gathering. No matter where you go throughout the United States, when you discuss legal medicine and the efficiency with which unexplained deaths are checked, homicides investigated, and facts placed in the hands of the prosecuting attorney, you find that Baltimore and Maryland rank high up in the top grouping of the top brackets.

Too few people realize how many murders go undetected because of ignorance, incompetence, or lack of proper investigative facilities on the part of those who are called upon to make medical (or medicolegal) investigations.

Too few people realize how frequently cool, calm efficiency on the part of a medical examiner can aid in the cause of justice.

There is one case which will illustrate my point, and which will, I think, prove to the reader Baltimore's wisdom in seeking the best brains available in this particular field of investigation.

A few months ago, a young white man, accompanied by three friends, was operating his car on the streets of Baltimore. Another car, driven by a colored lad, cut them off at a corner.

There was ill feeling. The white driver speeded up and forced the colored boy's car to the curb.

The colored boy got out of the right-hand front door of his car and stood on the sidewalk ready to defend himself.

The driver of the pursuing car jumped out of the door on the left-hand side, hurried around the car and approached the colored boy.

Witnesses said that the colored boy hit the white boy with his fist. The white boy promptly collapsed to the curb, unconscious. He was rushed to a hospital and died six hours later without regaining consciousness.

The colored lad was arrested and charged with manslaughter. The newspaper took up the case and racial feeling began to flare up.

Then Dr. Fisher performed an autopsy. He found something that a less skillful man would have missed. He found the cause of death was due to a ruptured aneurysm in that portion of the brain known as the "Circle of Willis." There was no indication that the man had been struck. It was evident that a congenital aneurysm had ruptured under the influence of increased blood pressure due to anger.

So the Medical Examiner requested that the police start checking up on those who had *seen* the blow struck.

Then a peculiar thing developed.

Confronted with the findings of the Medical Examiner it turned out that no one really had seen a blow struck. The witnesses had been "pretty sure a blow was struck since the white boy fell just as a fight was starting."

A careful reconstruction of the scene of the crime showed that some of the witnesses simply were not in a position to have seen the blow even if a blow had been struck. In view of the findings of the Medical Examiner it was proven that the man had died from natural causes, probably superinduced by his own anger.

And so I set forth an authentic example showing the responsibilities of a medical examiner, and one of the reasons why Maryland and Baltimore are ranked among the top areas in this work, feeling that you readers of mystery stories who, like myself, are interested in all the puzzling manifestations of crime and crime detection, will find it interesting. And I dedicate this book to my friend:

RUSSELL S. FISHER, M.D.
Chief Medical Examiner
State of Maryland

ERLE STANLEY GARDNER

Cast of Characters

PERRY MASON—Came up with a double portion of trouble the night he stopped in at Morris Alburg's restaurant 1

DELLA STREET—As Mason's secretary, she had a good chance to examine the mink 1

MORRIS ALBURG—needed a lawyer—the very best—to get him out of the mess he found himself in 1

DIXIE DAYTON—A terrified waitress who ran so fast she forgot the mink 8

LIEUTENANT TRAGG—Co-operated with Mason, but it was much against his better judgment 26

PAUL DRAKE—Head of the Drake Detective Agency. The one time he regretted that Mason's business was his bread and butter. 28

GEORGE FAYETTE—A solitary diner—obviously his mind wasn't on his steak 30

MAE NOLAN—Claimed Morris Alburg wasn't a boss one could get enthused about 44

ROBERT CLAREMONT—A dedicated cop who was taken for a ride 58

THOMAS E. SEDGWICK—Suspected bookmaker and cop killer. When the heat was put on, he made himself scarce 62

SERGEANT JAFFREY—In charge of the Vice detail. The tie-in with Claremont's murder brought him into the case 103

MINERVA HAMLIN—Night switchboard operator at the Drake Agency and a most efficient young woman .. 111

FRANK HOXIE—A hotel like the Keymont had use for a man of his particular talents 123

HAMILTON BURGER—Barrel-chested district attorney who clothed himself in an air of unctuous dignity 189

Chapter 1

It had been a hard, grueling day. Perry Mason and his secretary, Della Street, had finished taking a deposition. The witness had been cunning and evasive, his lawyer brimming with technical objections, and all of Perry Mason's skill was needed finally to drag forth the significant facts.

The lawyer and his secretary, entering Morris Alburg's restaurant, sought the privacy of a curtained booth in the rear. Della sighed her relief, glanced at Mason's rugged features, said, "I don't know how you do it. I'm like a wet dishrag."

Morris Alburg made it a point to wave the waiter aside and himself take the order of his distinguished customer.

"Hard day, Mr. Mason?" he asked.

"A bear cat," Mason admitted.

"In court all day, I presume?"

Mason shook his head.

"A deposition, Morris," Della Street explained, indicating her shorthand books. "I took check notes."

Alburg, not understanding, said, "Uh-huh," vaguely, and then asked, "Cocktails?"

"Two double Bacardis," Mason ordered, "a little on the sour side."

Morris passed the cocktail order on to the waiter. "I have some nice fried chicken," he suggested. "And the steaks are out of this world."

He raised a thumb and forefinger to his lips.

Della Street laughed. "Are you going ritzy on us, Morris? Where did you get *that*?"

"The steaks?"

1

"No, the gesture."

The restaurant proprietor grinned. "I saw a guy do that in a restaurant scene in the movies," he confessed. "Then you should have seen the junk he brought on, steaks you could look at and tell they were tough like shoe leather."

"Then never mind the gestures," Mason told him. "We want two thick steaks, medium rare, lots of lyonnaise potatoes, some buttered bread, with—" He glanced expectantly at Della Street.

Della nodded.

"Garlic," Mason said.

"Okay," Morris Alburg said. "You'll get it. *The best!*"

"Tender, juicy, medium rare," Mason said.

"The best," Alburg repeated again, and vanished, letting the green curtain drop back into place.

Mason extended his cigarette case to Della Street and held a match. The lawyer took a deep inhalation, slowly expelled the smoke, and half-closed his eyes. "If that old goat had only told the truth in the first place, instead of beating around the bush," he said, "we'd have been finished in fifteen minutes."

"Well, you finally got the truth out of him."

"Finally," Mason admitted. "It was like trying to pick up quicksilver with your bare fingers. You'd ask him a question and he'd run all over the place, twisting, turning, evading, throwing out red herrings, trying to change the subject."

Della Street laughed and said, "Do you realize there was one question you asked him exactly twelve times?"

"I hadn't counted the times," Mason said, "but that was the turning point. I'd ask the question, he'd try to lead me off on some other conversational channel, and I'd wait until he'd finished, then ask the same question over again, in exactly the same words. He'd try new tactics to shake me off. I'd nod attentively as though I were taking it all in, and inspire him to new heights of verbal evasion. Then, when he'd finished, I'd ask him the same question in exactly the same words."

The lawyer chuckled reminiscently.

"That was what finally broke him," Della Street said. "When he caved in after that, he was your meat."

Morris Alburg came back with the cocktails, glowing pink and cool in the big goblets.

Mason and Della Street touched glasses, drank a silent toast.

Morris Alburg in the door, watching them, said, "The way you talk with your eyes," and shrugged his shoulders.

"Mr. Mason gets tired of talking with his voice, Morris," Della Street said, slightly embarrassed.

"I guess that's right, I guess lawyers talk," Morris Alburg said hastily, trying to cover the fact that his observation had been too personal.

"Our steaks on the fire?" Mason asked.

Morris nodded.

"Good?"

"The best!" Morris grinned. Then, with a gesture that was like a silent benediction, he backed out of the booth and the curtain fell in place.

Mason and Della Street were undisturbed until, the cocktails finished, Alburg reappeared with a tray on which were stacked hot plates, platters with sizzling steaks, lyonnaise potatoes, and french bread toasted a delicious golden-brown, glistening with butter and little scrapings of garlic.

"Coffee?" he asked.

Mason held up two fingers.

Alburg nodded, withdrew, and returned with a big pot of coffee and two cups and saucers, cream and sugar.

For a few minutes he busied himself, seeing that water glasses were filled, that there was plenty of butter. He seemed reluctant to leave. Mason glanced significantly at his secretary.

"I don't get it," Mason said. "Taking our order was a fine gesture of hospitality, Morris, but bringing it is gilding the lily."

"I got troubles," the proprietor said with a sigh. "I guess

3

we all got troubles. These days nobody wants to work except the boss. . . . Skip it. You folks came here to forget troubles. Eat."

The green curtain once more fell back into place.

It was as Mason was finishing the last of his steak that Alburg came back to the doorway.

Della Street said, "Oh-oh, Morris has a problem, Chief." Mason glanced up.

"Now ain't that crazy," Alburg commented.

"What's crazy?" Mason asked.

"This waitress I've got—nuts, absolutely nuts."

Della Street, watching him, said jokingly, "I think it's a legal problem, Chief. Better watch out."

"You're damned right it's a legal problem," Morris Alburg exploded. "What are you going to do with a girl like that?"

"Like what?" Mason asked.

"She came to work five days ago. Today is the first of the month, so I'm going to pay her. I tell her so. I have the check ready. She looks like she sure needs the money. Then a little while after you two came in, she takes a powder."

"What do you mean, a powder?" Mason asked.

"She walks out the back door. She doesn't come back."

"Perhaps her nose needed powder," Della Street said.

"Not in the alley," Morris Alburg said. "She went out through the alley door. She dropped her apron in the alley right after she got through the door, and she traveled. Mind you, no hat, no coat, and you know what it's like outside, cold."

"Perhaps she didn't have a coat," Della Street said.

"Sure she's got a coat. She left it in the closet. Once upon a time it was one swanky coat. Now it's moth-eaten."

"Moth-eaten?" Perry Mason asked, puzzled. "What sort of a coat?"

"The best."

"What's that, Morris?" Della asked.

"Mink—the best—moth-eaten."

4

"Go on," Mason invited. "Get it off your chest, Morris."

"Me," Morris Alburg said, "I don't like it. That girl, I'll betcha, is wanted by the police."

"What makes you think so?"

"The dishwasher watched her out of the alley window. She dropped the apron to the ground and then she started running. She ran like hell. . . . All right, here I am with her check for five days' wages, her fur coat, a restaurant full of customers, and some of them mad like crazy. I thought she was waiting on some of the tables, and everything was all right. Then I heard the bell start to ring—you hear that bell ring, ring, ring?"

Della Street nodded.

"That bell," Alburg said, "is what the cook rings when an order is ready to go on the table. He's got stuff stacked out there for orders that this Dixie girl took and didn't do anything about. I thought she was waiting on the table. She's gone. So what? The food gets cold, the customers get sore, and this girl runs like an antelope down the alley. What kind of mess is that?"

"So what did you do?" Mason asked.

"I made each of the other girls take an extra table, then I got busy myself," Alburg said. "But ain't it something? Five days she works, and then she goes out like a jackrabbit."

Mason pushed the dishes aside. Despite himself, interest showed in his eyes.

"You told her she had a check coming?"

"I told her. I wanted to give it to her half an hour ago. She was busy. She said she'd pick it up later on."

"Then she didn't intend to leave," Mason said, "not then."

Alburg shrugged his shoulders.

"So," Mason went on, "when she left in a rush it must have been that someone came in who frightened her."

"The police," Alburg said. "She's wanted. You must protect me."

"Any detectives come in?" Mason asked.

5

"I don't think so. . . . She just took a powder."

Mason said, "I'd like to take a look at the coat, Morris."

"The coat," Morris repeated. "That's what's bothering me. What am I going to do with the coat? The money—well, that belongs to her. She can come and get it any time. But the coat—suppose it's valuable? Who's going to be responsible for it? What am I going to do?"

"Put it in storage someplace," Mason said. "Let's take a look at it."

Alburg nodded, vanished once more.

Della Street said, "She must have seen someone coming in, perhaps a detective—perhaps . . ."

"Wait a minute," Mason said. "Let's not get the cart too far ahead of the horse, Della. We'll take a look at the coat first."

Alburg returned, carrying the coat.

Della Street gave an involuntary exclamation. "Oh, what a shame! What a terrible shame!"

It was quite evident, even from the doorway where Alburg held the coat, that it was moth-eaten. The fur had little ragged patches in the front which were plainly visible, places where smooth, glossy sheen became ragged pin points. The damage might not have been so noticeable upon a less expensive fur, but on the mantle of that rich coat, it stood out clearly.

Della Street arose from the table, pounced on the coat, turned it quickly back to look for the label, and said, "Gosh, Chief, it's a Colton and Colfax guaranteed mink."

"I suppose she picked it up cheap somewhere," Alburg said.

"I don't think so," Mason told him. "I think a great deal can be done to recondition that fur. I think there are places where new skins could be sewed in. . . . Yes, look. . . ."

"Why, certainly," Della Street said. "It's only moth-eaten in two or three places there in the front. New skins could be put in and the coat would be almost as good as new. No secondhand dealer would have sold a coat like that in that

6

condition. He'd have fixed it up and sold it as a reconditioned coat."

"The waitress owned this coat?" Mason asked.

"Owned it or stole it," Alburg said. "Perhaps it's hot and she didn't know what to do with it so she left it in a closet for a few weeks, and the moths got into it."

"Perhaps some boy friend gave it to her and then ducked out so that she got the idea it might have been stolen," Mason observed thoughtfully. "In any event, it's a mystery, and I like mysteries, Morris."

"Well, I don't," Morris said.

Mason inspected the coat carefully, paying particular attention to the stitching on the side.

"Think the label's phony?" Alburg asked.

"The label's genuine," Mason said. "It might have been taken from another coat and sewn in this one . . . Wait a minute, here's something! This sewing is fresh. The stitches are a little different in color from those other stitches."

His fingers explored the lining back of the place where he had found the fresh sewing. "There's something in here, Morris."

Mason looked at the restaurant proprietor, then hesitated.

"You're the doctor," Alburg said.

Mason suddenly became wary. "There are certain peculiar circumstances in connection with this case, Morris."

"Are you telling me?"

Mason, said, "Let us assume that this coat was originally purchased by this young woman. That means at one time she was quite wealthy, comparatively speaking. Then she must have gone away hurriedly and left the fur coat behind. She wasn't there to take care of it, there was no one else on whom she wanted to call or on whom she dared to call to take care of it."

"And then?" Della asked.

"And then," Mason went on, "after an interval, during which the moths got into the coat, she returned. At that time she was completely down on her luck. She was desperate.

She went to the place where the fur coat was located. She put it on. She didn't have money enough to go and have it restored, or repaired, or whatever you call fixing up a fur coat.''

"She was broke, all right," Morris Alburg said.

"She came to this restaurant and got a job. She must have been hard up or she wouldn't have taken that job. Yet when the pay check is all made out and she knows she has only to ask Morris for it, she suddenly gets panic-stricken and runs out, leaving the fur coat behind her, also the check for her wages.''

Morris Alburg's eyes narrowed. "I get it now," he said. "You're putting it together so it's just plain, like two and two. She's been in prison. Maybe she poured lead into her boy friend during a quarrel. Maybe she beat the rap, but was afraid to be seen with her fur coat. She . . .''

"Then why didn't she store it?" Della Street asked.

"She didn't want anybody to know she was mixed up in this shooting. It was something that she did, and they never identified her . . . Wait a minute, she may have been picked up for drunk driving. She gave a phony name and wouldn't let anybody know who she was. She drew a ninety-day sentence in the can, and she went and served it out—serving under some phony name. Take this name she gave me— Dixie Dayton. That's phony-sounding right on the face of it. . . . She's been in jail.''

Della Street laughed. "With an imagination like that, Morris, you should have been writing stories.''

"With an imagination like I've got," Morris said ruefully, "I can see police walking in that door right now—the trouble I'm in—a crook working here. If she's wanted they'll claim I was hiding her. . . . Okay, so I've got friends at headquarters. So what?''

"Keep it up," Della Street laughed. "You're certainly dishing it out to yourself, Morris. You'll be having yourself convicted of murder next—being strapped in the death chair in the gas cham . . .''

"Don't!" Morris interposed so sharply that his voice was like the peremptory crack of a pistol. "Not even to joke, don't say that."

There was silence for a moment, then Alburg regained his self-control, nodded his head emphatically. "That's the story," he said. "At one time she was rich. She got tangled up. Maybe it was marijuana. That's it. She went to a reefer party, and she was picked up. Six months she got, right in the can. That's why the fur coat was there in the closet, neglected all the time she was in jail. Then, when she got out, the moths were in it. . . ."

"And then," Mason said, smiling, "when she went in she was wealthy, when she came out she was broke."

Alburg gave that frowning consideration. "How come?" he asked.

"Don't ask me," Mason told him. "It's your story. I'm just picking flaws. If she was a wealthy society dame who got picked up at a reefer party, and served six months, how does it happen that when she came out she had to get a job as a waitress?"

"Now," Alburg said, "you're really asking questions."

"Tell us about how she left," Mason invited. "Just what did happen, Morris? We want facts now, no more of your imaginative theories."

Alburg said, "She simply walked out, just like I told you. I heard the bell ring a couple of times, the bell the cook rings when food is taken off the stove and ready to be picked up. You don't like to hear that bell ring because it means the waitresses are falling down on the job."

"How many waitresses?" Mason asked.

"Five waitresses, and I have a man who handles the trade in the booths on this side. He's been with me a long time. The booth trade is the best because you get the biggest tips."

"All right, go on, what about the waitress?"

"Well, after I heard the bell ring a couple of times I went back to investigate. There was this stuff on the shelf by the stove—food that was getting cold. I start for the waitresses to bawl them out. Then one of the customers asked me what was taking so long. I asked him who was waiting on him; he tells me what she looked like. I knew it was Dixie. I went around looking for her. She's nowhere. All the food on the shelf was for Dixie's tables.

"I sent one of the girls to the powder room. 'Drag her out,' I say. 'Sick or not, drag her out.' She wasn't there. Then the dishwasher told me he'd seen her. She went out the back door and ran down the alley.

"Well, you know how things are. When an emergency comes up you have to take care of the customers first, so I started the girls getting the food out to the tables, made them take an extra table apiece, and . . . well, then I came in here to pass my troubles on to you."

"Did this waitress make friends with the other girls?"

"Not a friend. She kept her lip buttoned."

"No friends?"

"Didn't want to mingle around. The other waitresses thought she was snooty—that and the mink coat."

"Well," Mason said, "I gather that . . ."

A waiter pulled aside the green curtain, tapped Alburg on the shoulder, and said, "Beg your pardon, Boss, but the police are here."

"Oh-oh," Alburg said, and glanced helplessly over his shoulder. "Put 'em in one of the booths, Tony. I can't have people around the restaurant seeing me being questioned by the police. . . . I knew it all along, Mason, she's a crook, and . . ."

"The other booths are all full," the waiter said.

Alburg groaned.

"Tell them to come on in here," Mason said.

Alburg's face lit up. "You won't mind?"

"We've gone this far with it, and we may as well see it through," Mason said.

Alburg turned to the waiter. "Plain-clothes or uniform?"

"Plain-clothes."

"Bring 'em in," Alburg said. "Bring in a couple of extra

chairs, Tony. Bring in coffee and cigars, the good cigars— the best.''

The waiter withdrew. Alburg turned to Mason and said, ''That's awfully nice of you, Mr. Mason.''

''Glad to do it,'' Mason said. ''In fact, I'm curious now. What do you suppose they want?''

''What do they want? What do they want?'' Alburg said. ''They want that dame, of course, and they want the mink coat. Even if it isn't hot they'll take it as evidence. Two weeks from now the cop's sweetie will be wearing it. What'll I do with it? I . . .''

''Here,'' Della Street said, ''put it over the back of my chair. They'll think it's mine.''

Alburg hastily draped the mink coat over the back of Della Street's chair. ''I wouldn't want to hold out on them,'' he muttered, ''but I don't want them finding that mink coat here. You know how that'd look in the paper. 'Police find a stolen mink coat in the possession of a waitress at Alburg's restaurant,' and everyone immediately thinks it was stolen from a customer. I . . .''

The curtains were pulled back. The waiter said, ''Right in here.''

Two plain-clothes men entered the booth. One of them jerked his finger at Alburg and said, ''This is the fellow.''

''Hello,'' the other one said.

''Sit down, boys, sit down,'' Alburg said. ''The booths were all crowded and I was just talking with my friend in here, so he said . . .''

''That's Mason, the lawyer,'' one of the plain-clothes men said.

''That's right. That's right. Perry Mason, the lawyer. Now what seems to be the trouble, boys? What can I do for you?''

Mason said, ''Miss Street, my secretary, gentlemen.''

The officers grunted an acknowledgment of the introduction. Neither one offered his name. The smaller of the two men did the talking.

The waiter brought two extra chairs, coffee and cigars.

"Anything else I can get for you?" Alburg asked. "Anything—?"

"This is okay," the officer who was doing the talking said. "Tell him to bring in a big pot of coffee. I like lots of cream and sugar. My partner drinks it black. Okay, Alburg, what's the pitch?"

"What pitch?"

"You know, the waitress."

"What about her?"

"The one that took a powder," the officer said. "Come on, don't waste time stalling around. What the hell's the idea? You in on this?"

"I don't get it," Alburg said. "Why should you come to me? She was working here. You fellows spotted her, and she spotted you, so she ran out."

The officers exchanged glances. The spokesman said, "What do you mean, spotted us?"

"She did, didn't she?"

"Hell, no."

"Then why did she leave?" Alburg asked.

"That's what we came to see you about."

"Well, then, how did you know she left?"

"Because somebody tried to make her get in a car that was parked down the alley. She wouldn't do it. The guy had a gun. He took two shots at her. She started to run, got as far as the street, and was hit by a car that was trying to beat the light. The guy who was in the car that struck her wasn't to blame. The signal light at the corner was green. The man in the other car, who pulled the gun, backed the length of the alley and drove away fast."

Morris Alburg ran his hand over the top of his head. "Well, I'll be damned."

"So we want to know what about her, what happened. She had her purse with her. It shows her name is Dixie Dayton, and she works here. She's been identified as a waitress who came running out of the alley. We found a waitress's apron lying in the alley outside the back door. The dishwasher says she took it on the lam. She grabbed her purse as she went by, but didn't even stop to take off her apron until she got outside. . . . Now, tell us about her.''

Morris Alburg shook his head. ''I just told Mr. Mason all I know about her,'' he said. ''She came to work. She seemed to need the money. I had her pay check ready. She . . .''

''What's her real name?''

''Dixie Dayton—that's the name she gave me.''

''Sounds phony.''

''It did to me, too,'' Alburg said, ''but that was her name and that's the way the check is made out.''

''Social Security number?''

''Oh, sure.''

''What is it?''

''I can't remember it. It's on the back of the check.''

''We'll take a look. What made her run out?''

''Now you've got me,'' Alburg said.

The police seemed to feel that finishing their coffee was more important than making a check-up.

''Anybody see what frightened her?''

''I don't think so.''

''Find out.''

Alburg got up from his chair, went out into the restaurant.

Della Street smiled inquisitively at the officers. ''My, you certainly got on the job fast,'' she said.

''Radio,'' one of the men explained. ''How do you folks get in on this?''

''We don't,'' Mason said. ''We just finished eating. We were visiting with Morris. He told us about the waitress taking a powder.''

''How did he find it out?''

''Orders began to stack up, food started getting cold, people started complaining about the service.''

Alburg came back and said, ''I can't get a line on what scared her except it was . . .''

''What table was she waiting on?''

''She had four tables,'' Alburg said. ''She had started out

13

with a tray. It had three water glasses and butter. We know that much for certain. More, we don't know."

"*Three* glasses?" Mason asked.

"That's right."

"That's our clue," the officer said. "Usually people dine alone, in pairs, or four. A crowd of three isn't usual. That tells the story. She had three people at one of her tables. She started out to take the order and recognized them, or they recognized her."

Alburg nodded.

"Where are the three?"

"They're still here. I wish you wouldn't question them though."

"Why?"

"Because they got sore. They had to wait for service and they're mad."

"That's all right," the officer said, "we're going to question them."

"Can't you do it quietly?"

"Oh, to hell with that stuff," the officer said. "Someone tried to kill this babe. She was frightened by the persons at that table. We're going to shake them down. They'll be damned lucky if we don't take them down to headquarters. Come on, Bill, let's go."

The officers finished their coffee, scraped back their chairs.

Alburg followed them out, protesting halfheartedly.

Mason looked at Della Street.

"The poor kid," Della said.

"Let's take a look," Mason said.

"At what?"

"At the three people."

He led the way, selecting a place from which they could see the table to which Morris Alburg escorted the officers.

The officers didn't bother to put on an act. It was a shakedown and everyone in the restaurant knew it was a shakedown.

14

The party consisted of two men and a girl. The men were past middle age, the girl was in the late twenties.

The officers didn't even bother to draw up chairs and pretend they were friends. They stood by the table and made the shakedown. They made it complete. They demanded drivers' licenses, cards, and any other means of identification.

Other diners turned curious heads. Conversation in the restaurant quieted until virtually everyone was staring at the little drama being enacted at the table.

Mason touched Della Street's arm. "Notice the lone man eating steak," he said. "Take a good look at him."

"I don't get it."

"He's sitting at a table all by himself, the chunky individual with the determined look. He has rather heavy eyebrows, coarse black hair, and . . ."

"Yes, yes, I see him, but what about him?"

"Notice the way he's eating?"

"What about it?"

Mason said, "He's eating his steak with strange regularity, swallowing his food as fast as he can. His jaws are in a hurry but his knife and fork are disciplined to a regular rhythm. He wants to get the job finished. Notice that he's one of the few men who are paying absolutely no attention to what is going on at the table where the three are being questioned by the officers."

Della Street nodded.

"He is, moreover, sitting within ten feet of the trio. He's in a position to hear what's being said if he wants to listen and yet he's just sitting there eating. Notice the way his jaws move. Notice the way he keeps an even tempo of eating. He doesn't want to seem to be in a hurry, and he doesn't dare walk out and leave food on his plate, but he certainly wants to get out."

"He certainly is shoveling in the grub," Della Street agreed.

They watched the man for several seconds.

"Does he mean something?" Della Street asked.

"Yes."

"What?"

Mason said, "Nine chances out of ten the police have the cart before the horse."

"I'm afraid I don't understand."

"Look at it this way," Mason said. "The waitress ran away just after she had filled three glasses with ice water, just after she had picked up three butter dishes with squares of butter on them, and proceeded as far as the serving table near the door to the kitchen."

Della Street nodded.

"Therefore," Mason said, "it is quite obvious that she had left the kitchen knowing she had to serve three people at a table."

"Naturally." Della Street laughed. "Three water glasses and three butter dishes mean three at a table."

"And what happened?" Mason asked.

"I don't see anything wrong with the police theory," Della Street told him, frowning. "As she got a better look at the three people seated at the table, she saw that she knew one or all of those people, and there was something in the association that filled her with panic, so she decided she was going to clear out fast."

"How did she know there were three people at the table to be waited on?"

"She must have seen them when she went after the water glasses."

"From what point did she see them?"

"Why, I don't know. She must have— She must have seen them walk in."

"Exactly. She couldn't have seen them from the kitchen."

"But she could have seen them when she emerged from the kitchen carrying an order to some other table."

"Her tables were all grouped together," Mason pointed out. "There they are, the four tables, in that cluster. Now if she had first seen the three people while she was waiting on

16

one of the other tables, she'd have been near the one where the three are sitting.''

''Oh, I see,'' Della said, ''then you don't feel that she left hurriedly because she got a closer look at the three people when she emerged from the kitchen.''

''That's what the police think,'' Mason said, ''but the facts don't bear out that theory.''

Della Street nodded.

''Therefore,'' Mason said, ''why not assume that the three people meant absolutely nothing to her; that she saw them come in when she was delivering an order of food to another table; that when she returned to the kitchen she picked up a tray, put three glasses of water and three squares of butter on that tray, and started for the table. It was then, for the first time, she noticed someone who had just entered the restaurant, someone who did mean something to her.''

''You mean the man eating the steak?''

''It could very well be the man eating steak,'' Mason said. ''In a situation of this kind, where a girl is completely terrified over something, and dashes out the back of the restaurant into the alley, the assumption would be that she was more likely to have been terrified by one man who was looking her over, than by a social party that was wrapped up in its own problems and its own entertainment.

''Now then,'' Mason went on, ''if that is the case, any individual who suddenly pushed back his plate, with food still on it, would arouse the suspicions of the police.''

Della Street nodded.

''On the other hand, if a man bolted his food hurriedly, the police might also become suspicious.''

Again she nodded.

''Therefore,'' Mason said, ''if the individual who was responsible for the flight of Dixie Dayton saw the police in the restaurant asking questions, he would be inclined to try to get out as quickly as he could *without doing anything to arouse suspicion*.

''Therefore, Della, we should notice this man who is

eating with such studied rapidity. Let's watch to see if he orders dessert, or has a second cup of coffee. If he glances at his watch, acts as though he had an appointment, casually calls the waitress, gives her bills and doesn't wait for his change . . ."

"Good heavens, Chief, he's doing all those things now," Della Street exclaimed, as the heavy-set man pushed his plate back, glanced at his wrist watch, tilted up the coffee cup, draining the last dregs of the coffee, and held up his finger to get the attention of the waitress.

The voice in which he said, "I have an appointment. Please get me a check. I won't care for dessert, thank you," was distinctly audible.

"Do you," Mason asked Della Street, "suppose you could play detective? Slip out there, Della, and see what happens to that man when he gets outside. Perhaps you can get the license number of his automobile. Follow him if you have the chance—but don't run any risks. There may be some element of danger if he thinks you're on his trail. He'll perhaps suspect a man, but a good-looking woman might get away with it. I'd like to know a little more about that fellow. . . . It would be better if we both went, but the police will want to check up with me before they leave. They're a little suspicious. My presence was too opportune."

"I'll give it a try," Della Street said, and then added, "You think there's a lot more to this than what Morris told us, don't you?"

"Yes," Mason said, giving her the keys to his car.

"What about the mink coat?"

Mason hesitated.

"If the police are asking questions," Della went on, "they'll find out about the fur coat and then they'll want it."

"Well, let them have it," Mason said. "After all, they're trying to clear the case up to the best of their ability."

"I was just wondering about Morris Alburg. He's looking to us, and he certainly didn't want the police to know about that coat."

18

Mason said abruptly, "Okay, Della. Go ahead and wear it."

Della slipped into the coat, stood poised near the entrance to the booth.

"You don't think he's spotted you, do you, Della?"

"I doubt it. It's hard to tell about him. He doesn't seem to look around, doesn't seem the least bit curious about what's going on, and yet he gives you the impression of being completely, thoroughly aware of every move that's made."

Mason said, "He's getting ready to go now. Don't take any chances, Della. Just sail on out as though you were a working girl who had just treated yourself to a good meal and were on your way home."

"A working girl in *this* coat?"

"A working girl wore it before you did," Mason reminded.

"Darned if she didn't," Della Street admitted. "And look where she is now. Well, here I go, Chief."

"Now, remember," Mason said, "don't try to push your luck too far. Just get the license number of the automobile. Don't try to play tag. You *might* get hurt. We don't know what this is all about yet."

Della Street snuggled her neck back against the luxury of the fur collar, then, with chin up, eyes fixed straight ahead, marched demurely out of the restaurant.

Mason, standing back by the corner of the booth, watched the police conference at the table draw to an end, saw the chunky man pause briefly at the checking concession, exchange a ticket for a heavy overcoat and a dark felt hat, then push his way out into the night.

Morris Alburg led the officers back to the booth.

"What happened to the jane who was here with you?" one of the officers asked.

"Went home," Mason said. "I'm on my way myself, Morris. I was only waiting long enough to pay the check."

"There isn't any check," Alburg said. "This is on the house."

"Oh, come," Mason protested. "This . . ."

"It's on the house," Alburg said firmly.

His eyes flicked to Mason's with a quick flash of meaning.

"What did you find out over there?" Mason asked.

"Hell," one of the officers said, "the whole situation is screwy. This gal just took a powder, that's all. Those three certainly didn't have anything to do with it."

"Who are they?"

"Out-of-town people; that is, two of them are. The girl's here in town. Same old story. The girl is employed as a secretary in the sales department in one of the firms here. These two guys are out-of-town buyers. They're trying to get a party organized. That is, they were. I guess they're scared to death now."

"What sort of a party?" Mason asked.

"They were asking this girl if she had a friend. The girl phoned her roommate. The trio were just killing time, having dinner, and waiting to go places and do things until the other girl joined them.

"Now we've thrown a scare into the guys and they're filled with a desire to get the hell back to their hotel, and write reports. They're shivering so hard it's a wonder their shoes don't shake off."

"What about the girl?" Mason asked.

"She's okay. She didn't know the waitress here—is absolutely positive of it. She got a look when the waitress put down the tray with the three glasses of water on it. . . . The girl is a nice enough kid, but she's been around. She's secretary in the sales department. We'll check her tomorrow if we have to, up where she works."

"And what frightened the waitress?" Alburg asked.

"How the hell do we know?" the officer said impatiently. "She may have seen a boy friend outside, or she may have thought she did, or she may have got a telephone call. Anyhow, we'll investigate. Tomorrow somebody will check in at the hospital, see how she's getting along, and if she's conscious she'll answer questions. Nothing else we can do here."

Morris Alburg's face showed relief. "That's the way I feel about it," he said. "Nothing here that frightened her. It must have been a phone call. . . . People don't like police to come in and ask questions about who they're taking to dinner. I've lost three customers right now."

"We don't like to do it," the officer said, "but in view of the circumstances, we had to find out who they were. Okay, Alburg, be seeing you."

The officers went out. Alburg turned to Mason, wiped his forehead. "The things a man gets into," he moaned.

Mason said, "Della went out to get some information for me. She took the fur coat along. I didn't know whether you wanted the officers to see it."

"Of course I didn't want them to see it. I saw Miss Street go out. She was wearing the coat. I'm tickled to death. I wanted those officers out of here quick. I didn't dare seem too anxious. Then they'd think I was trying to cover up something, and then they'd stick around, stick around and stick around. You are my lawyer, Mr. Mason."

"Anything you want *me* to do?" Mason asked. "I thought, perhaps, you had something in mind from the way . . ."

"Keep that fur coat," Alburg said. "If anybody shows up looking for the waitress, asking questions about her, about her check, about anything, I'll send them to you. You represent me all the way. How's that?"

"What do you mean by 'all the way'?"

"I mean all the way."

"You shouldn't be involved in any way," Mason pointed out. "If you didn't know her, and . . ."

"I know, I know," Alburg interrupted. "Then there'll be nothing to do. You don't do it and send me a bill. That'll suit you, Mr. Mason, and it'll suit me. But if anything happens, you're my lawyer."

"All right," Mason said tolerantly. "If you don't want to tell me, you don't have to."

"Don't have to tell you what?"

"What you're not telling me."

"What makes you think I'm not telling you something?"

"Because I haven't heard you say it—yet."

Morris threw up his hands. "You lawyers! You don't take nothing for granted. Detectives are different. Lawyers I'm afraid of. A while back I hired detectives. A good job they did, too."

"Why detectives, Morris?"

"I had trouble. Anybody can have trouble. Then I want detectives. Now I want a lawyer. The best!"

"Fine," Mason said, smiling at the other's nervousness. "And now, Morris, since this is on the house, I'm going back and have some of your apple pie a la mode while I'm waiting for Della Street."

"She's coming back?" Alburg asked.

"Sure," Mason said. "She just got out so the fur coat could get out of the door without having the officers ask a lot of questions."

"I am glad to see them go," Alburg said. "You know, they could have saved me customers. The way they shake those people down, everybody is talking. I've got to go back now. I circulate around the tables, and reassure everybody."

"What'll you tell them?" Mason asked.

"Tell 'em?" Alburg said. "Tell 'em any damned thing except the truth. . . . I have to tell so many lies I get so I can pull lies out of the air. I'll say these people parked their automobile and some drunk ran into it. He smashed in the rear end. Police were trying to find out who the car belonged to and whether to make charges against the drunk. That's why they were looking at driving licenses."

Mason grinned. "That doesn't sound very convincing to me, Morris. I doubt if it will to your customers."

"It will by the time I get done with it," Morris said.

Mason went back to the booth, waited an anxious ten minutes, then the curtain was pulled to one side and Della Street, with the fur coat wrapped tightly around her, her face some-what flushed from exercise in the cold air, said, "I drew a goose egg."

"Sit down," Mason invited, "and tell me about it."

"Well," Della Street said, crestfallen, "I guess I'm one heck of a detective."

"What happened, Della?"

"He went out to the street, started walking down the side-walk, suddenly hailed a cruising taxicab and jumped in.

"I pretended to show no interest until he had got well under way, but I got the cab's number. Then I ran out and desperately tried to flag down a taxi."

"Any luck?"

"None whatever. You see, he had walked for about half a block and picked up a cruising taxi. He had all the luck. Of course, he timed it so that he would."

Mason nodded.

"When I tried it, the luck was all bad. Some people came out of the restaurant and wanted a cab, and the doorman ran out with his whistle. Naturally the next cruising cab passed me up in order to do a favor to the doorman. Your car was in the parking lot."

"Did you lose him?" Mason asked.

"Wait a minute," she said, "you haven't heard anything yet. I ran to the corner so I'd have a chance on cabs going in two directions. I waited and waited, and finally a cab came down the cross street. I flagged it and jumped in.

"I told the driver, 'A cab just went down Eighth Street and turned right at the corner. I want to try and catch it. I don't know where it went after it turned right, but give this bus everything you have and let's keep going straight on Eighth Street in the hope we can overtake him.'

"The cab driver gave it the gun. We went tearing down the street, slued to the right at the corner, took off up the cross street, and the cab driver said to me, 'Do you know this cab when you see it?' and I said, 'I got a look at the number. It's 863.' "

"Then what happened?" Mason asked, as Della Street stopped talking.

Della Street made a little gesture of disgust. "I was in cab 863."

"What?" Mason exclaimed.

"That's right. What that man had done was to pick up the taxicab, go to the corner, turn the corner, go about two-thirds of a block, pay off the cab and get in his own car that had been parked there at the curb all the time."

"Oh-oh," Mason said, "then he must have known you were following him."

"I don't think he did, Chief. I think it was just a blanket precaution he was taking to make certain that he wouldn't be followed. Of course, when he got in the cab he was able to watch the street behind him. That's why he walked in the opposite direction from that in which he wanted to go. In that way he was able to make certain that anyone who was following him would have had to follow by car."

Mason chuckled. "At least we have to hand it to him for being clever, and the fact that you tried to follow the cab you were already in gives it an interesting, artistic touch."

"I hate to have him make a monkey out of me," Della Street said.

"He didn't necessarily make a monkey out of you," Mason said. "He made one out of himself."

"How come?"

Mason said, "This waitress ran out because she was frightened by someone or of someone. We had no way of knowing what it was that frightened her, or who the person was who frightened her. Now we know."

"You mean he's given himself away?"

"Sure. The fact that he resorted to all that subterfuge proves that he's the man we want."

Mason stepped to the door of the booth and motioned to Morris Alburg.

"How many of your customers are regulars, Morris? What percentage?"

"Quite a few repeats."

Mason said, "Now, as I gather, a man and a woman, or a foursome, might straggle in here on the prowl. They'd either have heard the place recommended or they might have been just looking for someplace to eat, and came on in."

"That's right."

"On the other hand," Mason went on, "a lone diner, a man who came in here and ate by himself, would be pretty apt to be a regular customer."

"Yes, I'd say so."

"I wonder if you could tell me the name of that chunky man with the rather heavy eyebrows, who sat over at that table right over there, the one that's vacant now."

"Oh, him? I noticed him," Alburg said hastily. "I can't tell you; I don't know. I don't think he ate here before."

"Take a good look at him?"

"Not so much. Not his face. I look at the way he acts. You have to be careful about a man by himself: maybe he tries to make a pick-up and gets in bad. If he don't make trouble we do nothing; if he's drinking, if he paws women, we do something. That's why we watch single men. This one I watch—he minds his own business. I wish the police would mind theirs."

Mason nodded.

"Why did you ask?" Alburg asked suddenly.

"I was just wondering," Mason said, "just trying to figure out who he was."

"Why?"

"I thought I'd seen him someplace."

Morris Alburg studied Mason's face for a few seconds. "The hell of it is," he said solemnly, "you and me try to fool each other. We don't either one get to first base. We both of us know too damn much about human nature. It is what you call no percentage. . . . Good night."

Chapter 2

Mason stopped at a public telephone within a block of Morris Alburg's restaurant and rang Lieutenant Tragg on the Homicide Squad.

"Perry Mason, Lieutenant. Would you do something for me?"

"Hell, no," Tragg said.

"Why not?"

"Because it'd get me in trouble."

"You don't even know what it is yet."

"The devil I don't. If it wasn't something that was so hot you didn't dare to touch it with a ten-foot pole, you'd never call on . . ."

"Now wait a minute," Mason said. "Keep your shirt on. This is doing a good turn for a girl, a girl who was struck by a motorist who probably wasn't to blame. The girl was running from a man who was trying to make her get into the car with him. Some witnesses say he had a gun, and . . ."

"That the one out by Alburg's restaurant?"

"That's the one."

"What's she to you?"

"Probably nothing," Mason said, "but I have a feeling that girl may be in danger. Now here's what I want. She's probably at the Receiving Hospital. I don't know how serious her injuries are, but I'm willing to pay for a private room and special nurses."

"The hell you are."

"That's right."

"Why all the philanthropy?"

"I'm trying to give the girl a break."

"Why?"

"Because I have a feeling that if she goes into a ward in a general hospital she'll get herself killed."

"Oh, come now, Mason. Once a patient gets in a hospi . . ."

"I know," Mason interrupted, "it's purely a screwy notion on my part. I'm dumb. I have a distorted idea of what goes on. I've seen too many contracts lead to lawsuits. I've seen too many marriages terminate in divorce courts. I've seen too many differences of opinion that have resulted in murder. . . . A lawyer never gets to hear the details of a normal, happy marriage. He never gets to see a contract that terminates without a difference of opinion, and with both sides absolutely satisfied. So what? He becomes a cynic. . . . Now, the question is, will you help me see that this girl is taken out of the Receiving Hospital and placed in a room where no one, absolutely no one, except an attending physician, knows where she's located?"

"What else?" Tragg asked.

"That's all."

"Why?"

"Because I feel uneasy about her."

"You know who she is?"

"I've never seen her in my life. That is, not to recognize her. I may have had a brief glimpse of her when I entered Morris Alburg's restaurant. I just happened to be there when the thing happened."

"She's not your client? You don't have any interest in her?"

"None whatever. I did tell Morris Alburg that I'd take care of any matters pertaining to her affairs that might come up, and told him to refer anyone to me who . . ."

"Okay," Tragg said. "It's a deal. I'll handle it privately and send the bill to you."

"Thanks," Mason told him, and hung up.

Back in Mason's car, the lawyer said, "Now, Della, if I can get you out of that mink coat long enough, I want to explore the place where there was fresh sewing in the lining. I felt there was something under there."

"I'm certain it's just a little padding." Della Street laughed. "Tailors sometimes have to help out a girl's figure."

"This didn't feel like figure help to me," Mason told her. "Out of that coat, girl, and let's have at the Morris Alburg mink-coat mystery."

She wriggled out of the coat.

Mason parked the car, turned on the dome light, and with his penknife clipped away at the stitches in the coat, opening up a fold in the lining of the garment.

Mason inserted his index and second finger in its opening and scissored out a small piece of pasteboard.

"Now what in the world is that?" Della Street asked.

"That," Mason said, "seems to be a pawn ticket on a Seattle pawn shop, pledge number 6384-J, which can be redeemed at any time within ninety days on paying the amount of an eighteen-dollar loan, a handling charge, a storage charge and one percent per month interest."

"How dreadfully unexciting," Della Street said. "The poor girl had to hock her family jewels to get out of Seattle and she chose that method of making certain she didn't lose the pawn ticket."

Mason said, "Eighteen dollars' worth of jewels, Della? You wrong the family. We'll drive up to the Drake Detective Agency, and ask Paul Drake for the name of his Seattle correspondent. We'll rush the ticket up there by air mail and redeem the pawned article. That will at least give us eighteen dollars' worth of something and a few hundred dollars' worth of information. Then we can sell the article even if we can't sell the information."

"Suppose the information turns out to be something you don't want?" Della Street asked.

"Then I'm stuck with it," Mason said, "but by that time we'll know a lot more about Morris Alburg."

Chapter 3

It was around nine-thirty when Perry Mason unlocked the hall door to his private office, and found Della Street arranging piles of freshly opened mail on his desk.

"Hi, Della, what's new?" Mason asked, crossing over to the hat closet and placing his hat on the shelf.

"Morris Alburg telephoned."

"What did he want?"

"An insurance agent wanted to see the waitress."

"You mean Dixie?"

"That's right. He represents the company that carried insurance on the car that hit Dixie as she ran out of the alley."

"Fast work," Mason said. "Too fast."

"What do you mean by that?"

"They want to rush through a settlement, getting proper releases, and . . . No, they don't either."

"It would certainly look like it."

Mason paused, standing by the corner of his desk. He ran the tips of his fingers over his clean-shaven jaw, frowned down at the papers on the desk without seeming to see them, and said, "That's a new one."

"I don't get it. I thought insurance companies always did that."

"They used to," Mason said. "Some of them still do, but for the most part insurance companies are pretty ethical now. If there's a claim against them they want to see that a reasonable and fair compensation is paid.

"But here's a case where a girl runs out of the back door of a restaurant and into an alley, dashes right in front of an oncoming car, which, of course, hit her."

Della Street said, "I still don't see what you're getting at."

"Simply this," Mason said. "The driver of the car that hit her couldn't have been negligent unless there's something we don't know anything about. He was driving his car along the road, apparently going at a reasonable rate of speed. He was probably intent on making the traffic signal at the corner, but he had the right to expect that everyone on the street would be using it in a safe and prudent manner. All of a sudden this girl darts out from the curb, running in blind terror, and jumps right in front of him."

"Perhaps he had been drinking."

"The records indicate that he stopped his car almost at once. There's nothing to show that he had been drinking, yet within a few hours here comes a man from the insurance company wanting a settlement. . . . What did Morris Alburg tell him?"

"Told him to come up and see you, that you were taking care of everything pertaining to Dixie Dayton's affairs."

Mason laughed and said, "I'll bet that answer gave the fellow something to think of."

"You don't think he'll come up here?"

Mason laughed and said. "I hardly think he wants to deal with an attorney. He— Wait a minute, Della. There's just a chance that this is simply an attempt to find out where the girl is. That man may be simply— Did he give Morris Alburg a name?"

Della Street nodded. "George Fayette."

"How long ago did Morris call?"

"A little after nine."

The phone on Della Street's desk gave a jingle. Della Street picked up the receiver, said, "Yes, hello, Gertie. . . . Who is it? . . . Just a moment."

She cupped her hand over the transmitter and said to Mason, "He's here."

"Who?"

"George Fayette."

30

Mason grinned. "Go on out and bring him in, Della. Let's not let him have a change of heart and get away. I want to see what he looks like, and I want to ask him a few questions."

Della said into the telephone, "I'll be right out, Gertie," and hung up.

Mason settled himself in the chair behind his desk, and Della Street walked out to the reception room to escort George Fayette into Mason's private office.

A moment later she was back alone.

"What happened?" Mason asked sharply. "Did he leave?"

Della Street carefully closed the door, said, "Chief, it's the same one."

"What do you mean?"

"The man I was trying to follow last night, the man who sat alone at the table. . . ."

"You mean he's out there now, supposed to be representing an insurance company that carried insurance on the car that hit Dixie Dayton?"

"That's right."

Mason grabbed the telephone. "Get the Drake Detective Agency on the line right away, Gertie. Get Paul Drake if you can. Tell Mr. Fayette I'll see him in just a minute. Don't let him hear you. Tell him I'm on a long-distance call."

Mason looked at his wrist watch. "Telephoning may be a waste of time, Della. Paul's office is just down the corridor. Perhaps you'd better go and . . ."

"Wait a minute. . . . Gertie says Paul's on the line."

Mason said, "Hello, Paul, Perry Mason."

"Well, well, well, how are you . . ."

"Hold it, Paul, this is a rush job."

"What is it?"

"There's a man in my office. He has given his name as George Fayette. I don't know whether that's his real name or not. I doubt very much if it is. I want that man shadowed. I

31

want to know who he is, I want to know where he goes, I want to know what he does."

"Okay, how much time do I have?"

Mason said, "I'll stall him along as much as possible, but I have an idea that five or ten minutes is all I can count on. Now, Paul, he's about thirty-five years old, he's about five feet seven inches tall, but he must weigh pretty close to a hundred and eighty-five. He's dark and has bushy eyebrows—and he may fool you. He'll seem to be completely engrossed in his own affairs, and yet he'll be wary as the devil."

"I know the type," Drake said. "We'll handle him."

"I'm very much interested in getting the license number of his automobile," Mason said, "and finding out who he is, all of that stuff."

"Okay. You think I'll have ten minutes?"

"Better figure on five," Mason said. "I feel quite certain I can hold him here for ten minutes, but he *may* not like the looks of the thing, figure on stalling, and start out."

Drake said, "I'll have a man waiting to ride down in the elevator with him. Be sure I have at least five minutes, Perry."

Mason hung up, said to Della Street, "Now, Della, go out and stall him for a minute. Smile sweetly at him, tell him that I'm talking long distance on a call that just came in from the East; that you'll let him know as soon as I've finished. Then go over to Gertie's desk and tell her to wait until you cough. When she hears you cough she can say that I'm finished with my call. Get it?"

"Uh-huh. When do I cough?"

"When he begins to get restless. Hold him as long as you can. We want time. If you see he's getting nervous, cough."

"I'm on my way," she said, and glided out through the door to the outer office.

The door had hardly closed before Della Street jerked it open once more.

"Chief, he's gone!"

"What? When?"

"Gertie says the minute she started to put through your call to Paul Drake's office, he got up, smiled reassuringly at her, said, 'Be back in a second,' and stepped out in the corridor. He . . ."

Mason jumped up so violently that his desk swivel chair was hurled back against the wall. He rounded the desk, jerked open the door of his private office, said, "Come on, Della. Tell Paul! Let's go!"

Mason sprinted to turn in the corridor, looked down toward the elevator. There was no one in sight.

He dashed to the elevator and frantically jabbed at the bell button.

Della Street, running on tiptoes behind him, detoured into the office of the Drake Detective Agency.

A red light flickered on and off, then glowed steadily. A cage came to a stop. Mason jumped in, said to the elevator operator, "Run it all the way down to the ground floor, buddy. Don't stop. It's important. Let's go."

The elevator operator threw the control over, and the cage dropped rapidly.

"What's the matter?" he asked.

"Want to catch a guy," Mason said.

The cage came to a smooth stop. The door slid open. An angry elevator starter said, "What's the idea, Jim? You . . ."

"I'll take the responsibility," Mason said, and dashed across the lobby to the street.

He looked up and down the street, saw no immediate trace of the man he wanted but recognized that the crowded sidewalk offered a perfect opportunity for anyone to mingle with the pedestrians and vanish.

Mason moved to the curb, looked down the street to see if a taxicab had recently pulled away from the curb, spotted one at the corner waiting for a stop light, and ran down halfway to the corner before the signal changed and the cab glided away.

33

Back at the entrance of the building, Mason saw Paul Drake, Della Street and one of Drake's operatives standing by the door.

"No dice," Mason said. "Not here. Let's cover parking lots. Della, you know him. Take Drake's operative and cover the parking lot down the street. Paul and I will take the one across the street. If you see him, stop him."

"How?" Della Street asked.

"Stop him," Mason said to Drake's operative. "I don't give a damn what you do. Pretend he ran over your toe, hit you, or anything else; just stop him. Claim he smashed a fender on your car. Demand to see a driver's license."

"Get tough if I have to?"

"Hell, yes," Mason said. "Come on, Paul."

Paul Drake and Mason ran from the curb, threaded their way through traffic, regardless of the angry protest of horns, and crossed over to the parking lot across the street.

"If he came in his own car," Mason said, "we'll catch him one place or the other. Watch here, and get everyone who's coming out, Paul. I'll signal Della."

Mason moved over to the curb, waved a signal, then said, "Come on, Paul, let's take a look through and be sure he isn't just sitting in a car."

Five minutes later Mason acknowledged defeat. He walked back across the street to where Della and the operative from Drake's office were waiting, and said, "Well, I guess we're licked. I still don't see how he could have got down and vanished into thin air, but in that time . . ."

"The taxicab?" Drake asked.

"I *think* it was empty. I don't think he could have made it, Paul. I had my elevator operator shoot all the way down without stops. I sprinted out to the curb. Remember, if this man had been ahead of me . . . Oh, well, let's go talk to the elevator operators and see if they know anything."

They entered the building.

One by one they checked the elevator operators as they brought their cages down. The fourth and last operator listened to their story, said, "My gosh, Mr. Mason, I remember him perfectly. He didn't go down, he went up."

"Up?" Mason said.

The operator nodded. "I remember there was both a down and an up signal on your floor, because just as I picked him up the cage going down stopped and the door slid back, but there was no one waiting to go down. What he'd done was to press both the up button and the down button. . . . Of course, sometimes fellows will do that when they want to go up. They'll mechanically press the down button and then remember and change it to the up button, and . . ."

"Not this guy," Mason said. "He knew he was hot. He wanted to get away fast. He pressed both buttons and took the first cage that stopped. He wanted to get off that floor, Paul, there's a damned good chance he's still in the building."

"How was he dressed?" Drake asked.

Della Street said, "He had on a dark, double-breasted suit, a red and blue necktie, white shirt."

"A hat?"

"He had a black hat last night, and— Yes, I'm quite certain there was a black hat on the chair beside him."

Mason said to Drake, "Go on upstairs, Paul. Put one of your girls at my switchboard. Gertie saw him. Get her down here. He may have gone up a few floors, got off and just waited around, figuring he'd outwait us. We know now that he couldn't have been ahead of us. I'll go ask the girl at the cigar stand."

Drake said, "A couple of minutes more and I'll have another operative here. Let's check at the cigar stand, Perry."

The girl who was running the cigar stand and magazine rack flashed them a smile. "What was all the rush?" she asked.

Mason said, "Trying to find someone. I wonder if you might have noticed him."

She shook her head and said, "Not unless he's a regular tenant. People stream past here all day, and . . ."

"This man must either be in the building, or must have come out very shortly after I left," Mason said. "He may, or may not be wearing a black felt hat, a dark, double-breasted suit, blue and red necktie, about thirty-five years old, five feet seven inches tall, weighs about a hundred and eighty-five. His most noticeable feature is a pair of bushy eyebrows."

"Good heavens!" she exclaimed.

"What's the matter?"

"Why, he got off the elevator just after your secretary and Paul Drake and the other man reached the street."

"Go on," Mason said.

"He didn't seem to be in a hurry at all. He was just sauntering out of the building when he abruptly veered over here to the counter and started looking at a magazine."

Mason exchanged glances with Paul Drake, said, "You see what happened, Paul? He saw Della Street standing out at the curb so he swung over and buried his face in a magazine."

"Then he bought a cigar," the girl said, "and when you and Mr. Drake ran across the street he went out of the door and turned to the right. . . . I guess the only reason I noticed him was because I was so interested in seeing you dash across the lobby, and then your secretary and Mr. Drake and this other man came running out. Naturally, I wondered what was happening. He . . ."

"Come on, Paul," Mason said. "Della, Paul and I will grab the first taxi and go up the street. You take the next one that comes along, go to the corner and turn right. We'll keep circling around the blocks, watching pedestrians and seeing if we can pick him up."

"What is this?" Drake asked. "A murder?"

"Not yet," Mason said grimly.

"What'll we do if we find him?" Drake's operative asked.

"Tail him," Mason said. "Don't try to stop him now. But one way or another, find out who he is."

Mason went to the curb, and by luck found a cruising cab almost immediately. He and Drake jumped in and went four blocks up the street, then turned right a block and came back down on a parallel street.

"Like hunting for a needle in a haystack," Paul Drake said.

Mason nodded, but with his eyes intent on the sidewalk, studying the pedestrians, said, "Go slow. After you get down to the next street, turn right and then go five blocks on the cross street, then turn and start threading back and forth along the cross streets. Just keep moving."

"Are you the law?" the driver asked.

Mason said, "Don't worry about who I am. Just watch your driving and keep your eye on the meter."

"No rough stuff," the driver said.

"No rough stuff," Mason promised. "Just keep your eyes on the road and your hands on the wheel."

They cruised slowly up and down the various streets until finally at a corner they picked up the cab in which Della Street and Paul Drake's operative were also cruising.

"Blow your horn," Mason said. "Get the attention of the people in the other cab. . . . That's right."

Mason flashed a signal to Della Street when she looked up at the sound of the horn.

She slowly shook her head.

Mason gestured back toward the office, turned and settled back against the cushions. "That's it, Paul," he said. "We give the guy the benefit of the first trick—actually, the first two tricks."

"Who is he?" Drake asked.

"That's what I was hiring you to find out."

Drake asked, "Am I hired?"

"You're damned right you're hired," Mason told him.

"How strong do you want me to go?"

"Shoot the works. I'm tired of having some cheap crook make a monkey of me."

"He may not be cheap."

"Perhaps, but I'll give you ten to one he's a crook. Della will give you all the information we have. You take it from there."

Chapter 4

Back in Mason's office the lawyer said, "Get Lieutenant Tragg on the line, Della. We'll see what he knows. Perhaps we can interview the terrified waitress and solve at least part of the mystery."

Della Street put through the call, then said, "Hello, Lieutenant, how are you today? This is Della Street. . . . What's that? . . . Well, Mr. Mason wants to talk with you. Just hang on, please."

Della Street nodded to Perry Mason. Mason picked up his telephone, said, "Hello, Lieutenant, how are you?"

"What kind of a deal did you get me in on?" Tragg asked.

"What do you mean?"

"Getting that girl in a private hospital with special nurses . . . The next time I pull any of your chestnuts out of the fire, you can . . ."

"Whoa, back up," Mason said. "What's eating you now?"

"You know damned well what's eating me," Tragg said, irritably. "You knew that if we handled the matter ourselves we'd have it so she couldn't take a powder. You pretended that you wanted her to be completely safe and then put her in a position where she could . . ."

"You mean she's gone?" Mason asked.

"You're damned right, she's gone."

"Tragg, I give you my word the thing was on the up and up. It was just as I outlined it to you."

"Yeah," Tragg said sarcastically. "Just wanted to co-operate with the good old police force, didn't you, Mason?"

"Look here, Tragg," Mason said, "have I ever pulled a fast one on you?"

"*Have* you?" Tragg said. "You've pulled so many fast ones on me that . . ."

"I may have been on the other side of the fence a time or two," Mason said, "but have I ever asked you for your co-operation on anything in order to take advantage of you?"

"Well—no."

"And I won't," Mason said. "This is as much news to me as it is to you, and it bothers me. How did she work it?"

"Nobody knows," Tragg said. "She was there one minute, and five minutes later she was gone. She was lying apparently asleep. The special nurse stepped down the hall for a sandwich and a cup of coffee. She said, of course, that she'd only been out of the room five minutes. It probably was around half an hour. The patient was resting easily and sleeping, and the nurse was looking in and out."

"How seriously was the patient injured?"

"Apparently she was just knocked out. Possibility of a concussion, some bruises, a couple of broken ribs that were taped up, and some scratches and abrasions. The doctor wanted to keep her under observation for a while."

"What about clothes?" Mason asked.

"Oh, hell," Tragg said, "her clothes were in the closet. She put 'em on and walked out."

"What about money?"

"She didn't have a dime. The contents of her purse had been inventoried and left at the desk."

"How could she have got away from the hospital without taxi money?"

"You asked me," Tragg said. "What do you think I am, a mind reader? I'm telling you what happened."

"Well, it's all news to me," Mason told him. "Now then, just to show you I'm on the up and up with you, I'll put all of my cards on the table, if you want. I'll tell you everything I know about the case, and . . ."

"Not me," Tragg said, "not me. I've got enough on my

mind. Turn it over to Traffic Department. . . . I just tried to do you a favor, that was all.''

"You did, and thanks a lot."

"Don't mention it."

"You don't want me to keep you posted if there are any further developments?"

"I was doing you a favor," Tragg repeated. "I don't give a damn where she goes or what she does. As far as I'm concerned, she could have got up and walked out of the front door any time. It just made me look like something of a sucker, that's all. . . . When the case gets to murder, call me up. I'm in Homicide, remember?"

"I'll remember," Mason said, and hung up.

Chapter 5

It was late afternoon when Paul Drake tapped out a code knock on the door of Mason's private office.

Mason nodded to Della Street, who opened the door.

"Hi, Paul," she said. "How's the sleuth?"

"Fine. How's tricks?"

Drake entered the office, placed one hip on the round of the arm of the overstuffed leather chair, balanced himself in a posture which indicated his intention of making this a flying visit.

"How busy are you, Perry? Got time to listen to something?"

Mason nodded.

Della Street indicated the pile of unsigned mail.

"Go ahead," Mason said, "talk. And I'll sign letters while you're talking. Have you read these, Della?"

She nodded.

"All ready for my signature?"

Again she nodded.

Mason started signing letters.

Drake said, "There's something screwy about this case, Perry."

"Go ahead, Paul, what is it?"

"I don't know."

"How do you know there's something screwy?" Mason asked, his pen dashing off signatures as Della Street handed him one letter after another then blotted the signatures as Mason signed.

"The police are interested."

"They should be."

"Not from anything we know, Perry. It's a deeper interest than that."

"Go ahead. What seems to be the angle?"

"Well, in the first place, you gave us a pawn ticket on a Seattle hock shop."

Mason nodded.

"Know what that was?"

Mason shook his head and said, "It was an eighteen-dollar item. That was the amount stamped on the back of the ticket, and I figured that eighteen dollars plus one per cent a month, plus . . ."

"I know," Drake said. "You figured you couldn't go wrong as far as value was concerned. Now I'll tell you what the article was."

"What was it?"

"A gun."

"Any good?"

"Apparently so. A thirty-eight Smith and Wesson special."

"You picked it up?" Mason asked.

Drake shook his head. "The police did."

"What police?"

"The Seattle police."

"How come? You had the pawn ticket, didn't you? I wanted you to mail it to Seattle, and . . ."

Drake said, "When the police went to Alburg's cafe last night, they naturally asked Alburg what he knew about the girl. Alburg told them he didn't know a damned thing, that she'd applied for a job as waitress, that she needed money, that it was the first of the month, and . . ."

"I know," Mason said. "He told me all that."

"The officers looked around a bit and found this girl's handbag had been picked up by the ambulance driver and taken to the hospital. Just as a matter of routine they made an inventory."

"That was the traffic detail?"

"Yes—traffic accidents."

"Go ahead."

"They found lipstick, keys that don't mean anything yet, a compact, and a ticket on a Seattle pawn shop."

"Another one?"

"That's right."

"So what did they do then?"

"Sent a teletype to Seattle. The police went around to investigate. That pawn ticket was for a diamond ring. The pawnbroker remembered her. He said she'd hocked a gun at the same time. The police took a look at the gun. Then things began to happen."

"What sort of things, Paul?"

"I can't find out for sure, but it touched off a lot of activity down here. Police began to go places and do things. Alburg's restaurant is crawling with detectives."

"Where's Morris Alburg?"

"Lots of people want to know," Drake said.

Mason quit signing mail. "I'll be darned," he said.

Drake said, "Alburg could just be out on business."

"What else, Paul?"

"Alburg never told the police anything about the fur coat, but one of the waitresses did. She told the police that Alburg had given the fur coat to you, and that your secretary had worn it out."

"Observing brats, aren't they?"

"Uh-huh," Drake said. "And apparently there's a certain amount of friction and jealousy on which I think we may be able to capitalize."

"How come?"

"I think Alburg is giving you a bum steer."

"Alburg is?" Mason asked. "Good Lord, Paul, I'm doing this for Alburg."

Drake nodded.

Della Street blotted the last of the letters, took them out to the stenographic room to be folded and mailed, then returned and seated herself at her secretarial desk.

Drake said, "One of the waitresses is named Nolan, Mae

Nolan. She just *might* have had an idea that Morris Alburg was noticing her a little bit.''

"Does he play around with his waitresses?''

"Apparently not,'' Drake said. "And that may be part of the trouble. However, there are a lot of angles to be considered. There are certain tables that are choice, as far as tips are concerned, others that aren't so good, and stuff of that sort.''

"It goes on a basis of seniority?''

"It goes on a basis of favoritism,'' Drake said. "At least the girls seem to think so.''

"What about this Mae Nolan?''

"She's in my office. I've just taken a statement from her. I thought perhaps you'd like to talk with her.''

"Sure thing,'' Mason said. "If Morris Alburg is cutting any corners with me, we'll show him where he gets off.''

"Well, you talk with this girl and then see what you think,'' Drake said.

"All right, bring her in.''

Della Street said, "I can run down and get her, Paul, if you and the chief want to talk.''

"Not that,'' Drake said. "But I'm sure lazy, Della. If you'll do the leg work, it'll help. . . . She's in my office. The girl at the telephone desk knows her. Just tell her to come on down here.''

"I'll introduce myself?'' Della Street asked. "That is, is there any reason why she wouldn't know that . . .''

"None whatever,'' Drake said, "not as far as I'm concerned.''

"Sure,'' Mason said. "Go ahead, Della.''

"You have that Seattle pawn ticket?'' Mason asked.

"Our Seattle correspondent has it,'' Drake said. "They telephoned as soon as they'd contacted the pawn shop. He found the pawnbroker running around in circles, acting as though he'd been caught sucking eggs.''

"Wasn't his nose clean?''

"It was supposed to have been, but something was bothering him. Under the circumstances my Seattle man didn't tip his hand once he found out the police had the gun.''

Mason reached for a cigarette. ''Want one, Paul?''

Drake shook his head. ''Not now.''

Mason was just lighting up when they heard the sound of quick steps in the corridor, and Della Street, escorting a young woman into the office, said, ''This is Mr. Mason, Miss Nolan.''

''How do you do, Mr. Mason.''

Mae Nolan was an artificial blonde, somewhere in her thirties. Her face was held in the lines of perpetual good nature, but the blue eyes above the smiling mouth were swift in their appraisal, and cold in their scrutiny.

''Sit down,'' Mason invited.

''Thank you,'' she said, with her best company manner.

Drake smiled indulgently and said, ''No need to mince around any, Mae. Just tell Mr. Mason your story.''

She flashed him an angry glance, and said, ''I wasn't mincing around.''

Mason said, ''I think you misunderstood Paul Drake, Miss Nolan. He merely was referring to the fact that you could get right down to brass tacks. He wasn't referring to your manner, but pointing out there was no need for any verbal detours.''

''Oh, thank you,'' she said, smiling at Mason, and batting her eyelashes. Then, swiftly turning to Paul Drake, said, ''I've been nervous and upset today. What with one thing and another, I haven't had a chance to get much sleep. We go on at six o'clock and work until twelve-thirty in the morning, right straight through.''

''Pretty tough job?'' Mason asked.

''Sometimes.''

''The tables fill up pretty well?''

''Well, of course, it varies. On Saturday night we're packed jammed. Then on Monday night there isn't quite so much business. But, of course, every night during the rush hour everything is jammed. Then things taper off around ten o'clock except on Saturday night. Then there's about an hour when things quiet down, but they start off again with a rush as soon as the theaters are out.''

"Certainly must be a job," Della Street said sympathetically, "being on your feet all the time like that."

"You don't know the half of it, dearie," Mae Nolan said, turning to Della Street. "You have a cinch in a job like this. Gosh, I— Oh, well, never mind. You folks aren't interested in my troubles. . . . It isn't the work so much as it is the people who are unappreciative, the people who bawl you out for their own mistakes. . . . A man will order roast beef and forget to tell you that he wants it rare. Then afterwards he'll swear that he told you he didn't want it unless it was real rare, and . . . Oh, what's the use?''

"I thought you asked them how they wanted it when you took the order," Della Street said.

Mae Nolan flashed her a cold glance. "I just used that as an illustration, dearie.''

"You were going to tell us something about Dixie Dayton," Paul Drake said.

"Oh, was I?''

"I thought you were.''

"I don't know whether I should go around shooting my mouth off. I don't know what there is in it for me.''

"Probably nothing," Mason said.

She studied him thoughtfully. "You come to the place every once in a while. I've waited on you.''

Mason nodded.

"And," she said, "you're a good tipper. . . . Most of the time you sit in the stalls though, don't you?''

"I like privacy," Mason said. "When I eat I like to relax, and when I'm out in the main dining room I'm recognized occasionally . . .''

"*Occasionally?* You should hear what people say about you when you eat out there. I know how you feel. I don't blame you. . . . I don't think I've waited on you over twice in all the time I've been there. I suppose one of these times

I can get the privilege of waiting on the booths, if I stay there long enough. I'll probably drop dead in my tracks before that waiter who's in there now ever lets go.''

"As I remember it, you're a very skillful waitress," Mason said. "If I gave you a large tip, I can assure you it was because the service was more than satisfactory.''

"Well, thank you ever so much for those kind words. We don't hear them too often. Like I was saying, when you're out in front people crane their necks all over and there's a lot of whispering. Then when I go to other tables to get the orders, people will beckon me to lean over closer, and say, 'Isn't that the famous Perry Mason over there at that other table?' and I'll nod, and then you know what they want to know, Mr. Mason?''

"What do they want to know?" Mason asked, winking at Paul Drake.

"They want to know who's that woman with him.''

"And what do you tell them?" Mason asked.

"And then," she said, "is when I draw myself up and tell them it's none of their business.''

"You were going to tell us about Dixie," Paul Drake interpolated.

"Oh, *was* I?—that may be what *you* thought, but . . .''

Mason turned to Paul Drake and said, "You know, Paul, there's something funny about that Dixie Dayton.''

"In what way?" Drake asked, catching Mason's eye.

"Well, she somehow didn't seem to fit in," Mason said. "I don't know just how to express it but I had the idea that perhaps Morris Alburg was giving her the breaks.''

"Well, that's the way I understood it," Drake said. "Of course, Mae, here, evidently doesn't want to discuss it any more.''

"I think I've shot off my big mouth all that's good for me," Mae Nolan said.

Mason ignored her, and continued to Paul Drake: "Of course, I've known Alburg for quite a while, and if he was giving Dixie Dayton any favors you can be pretty certain that it was because she was in a position to earn them—I mean in a business way. I think by the time you check into her past history, you'll find that she had waited tables in some of the real swanky spots over the country, and that Alburg knew that and . . ."

Mason was interrupted by a loud, brazen laugh from Mae Nolan.

The lawyer turned to her and raised inquiring eyebrows.

"What a hot detective *you* turned out to be," she said, and then, raising her hand, made the gesture of one shooing a fly away from her face. "That girl a waitress? Phooey! Whatever she had on the ball that appealed to your friend, Morris Alburg, wasn't anything she displayed during working hours. Not *that* girl."

"Bad?" Mason asked.

"Bad? She stunk."

"But I can't understand it," Mason said, his voice showing that he was puzzled. "Alburg is such a keen businessman."

" 'Keen businessman'?" she repeated. "Where do you get that noise? He may be a keen businessman when it comes to running the kitchen and putting the prices on the menu so that he's damned certain he won't lose any money, but don't kid yourself that he's a businessman when it comes to handling waitresses. My Gawd, I've seen girls twist him right around their fingers, just absolutely right around their fingers."

"Indeed?" Mason said.

"You can bet your bottom dollar. I've waited tables ever since I was knee-high to a grasshopper, Mr. Mason, and I've yet to find the man running a joint who couldn't be handed a line of taffy by a good-looking, up-and-coming hustler."

Mason made his voice sound all but incredulous. "Do you mean to tell me that Morris Alburg could be taken in by . . ."

"Could he? Say, I guess you don't know Morris very well. And that Dixie girl was the girl that did a job on him, too."

"A fast worker, eh?"

"Well, I don't know how fast she was, but she certainly was thorough."

"Apparently she'd known him before," Drake said.

Mason slowly shook his head.

"What are *you* shaking your head about?" Mae Nolan demanded. "Why, Morris Alburg knew her. . . . Say, you're not talking to me! When she came walking into the joint Morris Alburg was having one of his spells of efficiency. He wanted 'more this' and 'more that' and 'more the other,' and then he looked up and saw that girl coming toward him, and his jaw fell open and his eyes bugged out like he was seeing a ghost."

"What did he say?" Mason asked.

"He took a step or two back, and then his face broke into a smile, sort of a dubious smile, and he put out his hand and came forward, and that was when this Dixie pulled her first fast one."

"What do you mean?"

"She spoke right up before he had a chance to say anything and she said, 'Are you the proprietor here? Well, I understand you're looking for a waitress, and I'm looking for a job.' "

"Then what happened?"

"Then Mr. Alburg sort of caught himself and straightened up and said, with dignity, 'Well, if you'll step into one of the booths there in back, I'll talk with you in a few moments. Right now I'm busy giving instructions to my waitresses about how to handle the business. I'm expecting a heavy night tonight. Just step right in there and sit down.' "

"And she did?" Mason asked.

"Gave us girls one of those patronizing smiles and swept on past us to the booth at the farthest end of the line," Mae Nolan said.

"Then what happened?"

"Then Mr. Alburg went into the booth and was in there for—oh, I guess ten or fifteen minutes."

"Then what?"

"Then he came out and introduced Dixie to the rest of us girls and told us he was going to put her on as a waitress."

"That was about a week ago?"

"Just a week ago, yes."

"And then what?"

"Well," Mae said, her manner thoughtfully judicial, "she had waited tables somewhere, but not very long, and it wasn't a really high-class place. She wasn't good at it. She made too many trips back to the kitchen, she didn't space them so she could kill two birds with one stone, and she got terribly tired. And every time she did, Mr. Alburg would fix things so that people who came in went to the other tables."

"Did she lose tips that way?"

"She lost tips and she got out of work, but, if you ask me, Mr. Alburg was making it up to her in some way because she'd flash him one of those graceful, gooey smiles whenever he'd steer customers over to the other tables and let her take it easy during the rush hour."

"You other girls didn't mind that?" Mason asked.

"Oh, we didn't care. We'd have taken on the extra work for the extra tips, but what made us sore was the fact that when business was light and some person would come in who was a regular customer and was known as a good tipper, Mr. Alburg would steer him over to Dixie's table. Now that isn't right. If a man's going to run a place like that, he should run it on a fair basis. If he wants to have friends, he can have them on the outside. We don't care what he does, just so he's fair to us girls in working hours."

"You girls commented on this among yourselves?" Mason asked.

"Not so much. Morris doesn't like for us to have those huddles. When he sees us talking together he manages to break it up, one way or another; puts us to work doing something. That way we keep pretty much to ourselves."

"Then you haven't talked this over with the other girls?"

"Not to speak of."

"Then it may be your imagination."

"What is?"

"What you've been telling me about his favoritism."

"Don't be silly," she said. "I guess I've been in this racket long enough to know when I'm getting a runaround and when I'm not."

Mason took a wallet from his pocket, took out a crisp twenty-dollar bill and handed it to her. "I'm sorry," he said, "that I haven't been at your table lately, Miss Nolan. Perhaps you would accept this by way of an apology and in lieu of the tips I would have left if I had been there."

"Say, now," she said, "that's what I call being real decent. You really are okay, Mr. Mason, and remember, any time you come in if you sit at my table you'll get the best any place, but—well, thank you."

She folded the bill, pulled up her skirt without any pretense of modesty, and inserted the bill in the top of her stocking.

"Anything else?" Paul Drake asked.

Mae Nolan slowly pulled down her skirt. "Well, now," she said, "this is a little different. It's always a pleasure to do what I can for a couple of good sports. . . . I suppose you know Mr. Alburg gave her that fur coat?"

"Alburg did?" Mason asked.

"That's right."

"He certainly didn't let on to me that he had," Mason said. "I can't believe that he'd . . ."

"Well, he did all right. He went out and got it for her."

"Where?"

"That's what we've been asking ourselves, Mr. Mason. Some of the girls think he got it out of a closet in his apartment. He might have been keeping it for her."

"But he's the one who got it?"

"I'll say. He went out and when he came back he had a bulky brown paper parcel under his arm. He took it into the kitchen. The next thing we knew, one of us went into the little girls' room and here was this same brown paper all stuffed into the wastebasket. . . .

"And Dixie Dayton cried all that afternoon. We couldn't figure out why she was crying until we saw her flash this mink coat. And then we saw the moths had got into it.

"That's just like Morris Alburg. He'd been keeping it for her, all wrapped up in paper. He never thought to put any moth balls in with it.

"My Gawd, that coat set somebody back a chunk of dough at one time. Personally, I don't think Dixie was classy enough to promote it. *I* think it was stolen."

"Well," Paul Drake said, "I guess that's a piece of news. Anything else?"

She thought for a minute or two, then said, "I guess that's all. I've got to go. Thanks for the buggy ride."

She gave them a dazzling smile, got up and stretched, smoothed her skirt over her hips.

Drake got up and held the door open. Mae Nolan flashed another glance at Perry Mason, smiled and batted her eyelids several times, then, with a slightly exaggerated hip motion, swept from the office only to turn suddenly and say, "Hey, wait a minute. You aren't going to tell Mr. Alburg anything about this, are you?"

Mason shook his head.

"Thanks," she said.

The door closed. Della Street picked up a newspaper and made fanning motions to clear the atmosphere of the perfume.

Mason cocked a quizzical eyebrow. "I didn't notice it was as bad as that, Della."

"You wouldn't," she said.

"No?"

"No. Not with those legs and the way she bats her eyes. Personally, I wouldn't take the word of that little tramp for anything."

"A lot of it could be imagination," Mason said, "but not all of it. Let's see if we can get Alburg on the phone, Della."

"On the private line?"

Mason nodded.

"Ten to one you draw a blank," Drake said.

Della Street went over to her desk, said to the girl at the switchboard, "Give me an outside line, Gertie," and then, with swift, competent fingers, dialed the number of Alburg's restaurant.

"I want to talk with Morris Alburg," she said. "This is Mr. Mason's office. . . . What's that? . . . When? . . . When do you expect him? . . . Well, ask him to call Mr. Mason as soon as he comes in, will you?"

She hung up and said to Mason, "He went out about two hours ago and hasn't been back."

"Anyone know where he is?"

"Apparently not. They said they didn't know where we could reach him, but they'd have him call as soon as he came in."

The interoffice phone on Della's desk exploded into a series of three short, sharp rings.

Della Street turned to Perry Mason. "Lieutenant Tragg is on his way in. That's a code signal I fixed up with Gertie—"

The door from the outer office pushed open. Lieutenant Tragg, in plain clothes, stood surveying the room. "Hello, folks," he said. "Are you busy, Mason?"

"Heavens, no," Mason said. "I just rent the office so I'll have a place to work up a private handicap on the races. I used to try doing it down on the street corner, but the traffic noises tended to distract me, so I got this place up here."

Tragg walked in, closed the door behind him, said, "Don't feel so put out, Mason. I always give Gertie a chance to let you know I'm on the way, and hesitate long enough so you can hide anything you want to ditch, but it's beneath the dignity of the law for me to wait in anybody's outer office."

"I know," Mason said sympathetically. "The taxpayers' money has to be conserved, even at the expense of the taxpayers' time."

54

"Exactly," Tragg said, settling himself into a chair and tilting his hat back on his head.

He studied Mason thoughtfully, then said, "I might have known that if I started pulling any chestnuts out of the fire for you I'd get my fingers burnt."

"Are they burnt?" Mason asked.

"Well, they're feeling pretty hot. I hope I don't raise a blister. I could have got them burnt off."

"I don't get it."

"Neither do I. I came in to find out."

"I'm afraid I can't tell you."

Paul Drake got up, said, "Well, I'll toddle along and see how the overhead is clicking in my office."

"Don't let me frighten you away, Drake."

"Just away—not frightened," Drake said, and flashing Mason a glance, eased out of the exit door.

Tragg drew a cigar from his pocket, clipped the end, looked at Mason shrewdly and lit up. "How's business?"

"Too much business, not enough money."

"I know," Tragg sympathized. "Some days when you don't make even a measly thousand dollars. . . . What's your tie-up with the Alburg case?"

Mason said, "I was in the restaurant when all the excitement took place. I eat there once in a while. Alburg asked me a few questions."

"What questions?"

Mason smiled at Tragg and said, "I can't remember, Lieutenant."

Tragg inspected the end of the cigar to see that it was burning evenly, gave Mason a grin and said, "You know, Counselor, I like you."

"Thanks."

"That's where the trouble comes in."

"What trouble?"

"My trouble. There are those down in the department who don't like you."

"No?"

"No. They think you're on the other side of the law."

Mason said, "The law gives a man the right to have counsel and . . ."

"Save it," Tragg said. "Someday a luncheon club may want you to make a speech and I'd hate to have you use up all your material."

"I'm just rehearsing."

"You don't need rehearsal. You do all right when you ad lib. In fact sometimes you're too good. . . . What about the fur coat?"

"What fur coat?"

"The one Della wore out of the restaurant last night."

Mason turned to Della Street with mock sternness. "Della, have you been shoplifting again?"

She nodded, contritely. "I can't help it, Chief. It's that awful impulse. Everything goes black, and when I come to, there I am standing on a corner in a fur coat with the price mark still on it, and I know that my amnesia has been playing tricks on me again."

Tragg clucked and sadly shook his head. "Poor kid," he said to Mason, "it's something she really can't control. It's an occupational disease. It comes from working for you."

"No, it doesn't," Della Street said quickly. "It's hereditary. It came from my paternal grandfather's side of the family—old Captain Street, the pirate. He used to take what he wanted whenever he could find a cutlass handy."

"Why don't you try going to a psychoanalyst?" Tragg asked.

"I did. He told me that my conscience was at war with my inherited impulses. And so whenever I wanted to take anything I blacked out so I wouldn't know what I was doing. It was what he called a defense mechanism."

"Offer any cure?" Tragg asked.

"He wanted me to lie on a couch and tell him about my early life."

"It didn't help?" Tragg asked.

"Not a bit."

"Well," Tragg said, "I'm going to give you a treatment of my own that *may* cure you, Della."

"What is it?"

"I'm going to give you twenty minutes to get that fur coat in my possession."

"Which fur coat?" Mason asked.

"The fur coat she wore out of Alburg's restaurant last night."

"Well, now, let's see," Mason said. "Was that the Hudson Bay rabbit, or the clipped beaver cat, Della?"

Lieutenant Tragg interrupted. "It was the 'mink stole.' "

"A mink stole?" Mason asked, genuinely puzzled.

"Perhaps that is the wrong use of grammar," Tragg said. "I should have said the 'mink stolen.' "

Della Street glanced at Perry Mason.

"Stolen from whom?" Mason asked.

"That I can't tell you, yet."

"Come again when you can."

"No, I want the coat, Mason."

Mason lit a cigarette and settled back in his chair.

"You could get in bad over this thing," Tragg told him.

Mason asked politely, "How was the elevator service coming up, Tragg?"

"Lousy."

"It frequently is this time of night. The fellows who can clear up their desks early leave their secretaries to handle the last-minute rush of stuff, and start streaming out of the building and getting in their cars so they can beat the traffic rush going home."

Tragg nodded.

"So that sometimes you have to wait awhile for an elevator. And yet, Tragg, people do put up with that inconvenience. They come all the way downtown and pay for a parking lot for their car. Then they put up with all the inconvenience of the elevators and come up here to see me just to ask me to protect their rights. You know, after a person has gone to all that trouble, I feel that I really should give him at least a run for his money.''

"Anybody ask you to protect her rights on the fur coat?"

"If I answered that question," Mason said, "you'd probably ask me another.''

"I'd ask you *two* more."

"I thought so."

Tragg said, "So I'm going to tell you something.''

"Go right ahead."

"Ever hear of Robert Claremont?''

Mason shook his head.

"Don't remember reading about him?''

Again Mason made a gesture of negation.

"Bob Claremont," Lieutenant Tragg said, almost musingly. "A pretty darned nice kid. I worked on that case. A fine, clean-cut, upstanding young chap who had always wanted to be on the force. That was his ideal. The war came along and put a crimp on his ambition for a while, and then he was discharged and used the schooling he had coming to study up a lot of stuff about police science so he'd be a better cop. . . . Can you imagine that, Mason, a fellow going to school day after day, studying. So many people think of cops as being beetle-browed gorillas who go around smacking citizens on the head with night sticks, collecting payoff from the bookies . . .''

"And then retiring to ranches down in Texas," Mason interrupted.

For a moment Tragg frowned. Then he said, with repressed anger in his voice, "That's the hell of it, Mason. That's what gives the decent cop a hard row to hoe, a few rotten apples in the barrel. Citizens don't remember the story of the cop who gave his life trying to stop a hold-up. All they can remember is the cop who has the bad memory and can't recall for the life of him the name of the bank in which he deposited the last hundred thousand dollars.''

"I was only kidding," Mason said.

"I'm not kidding," Tragg told him. "You have any idea

58

what it means to be a cop, Mason? You're off duty. You go to a market or a service station or a liquor store. The door opens. Three men stand there with sawed-off shotguns. It's a stick-up.

"If you were a citizen you'd reach for the ceiling. Your friends would make a hero out of you because you didn't faint. But you're a cop. You reach for the ceiling and the hoodlums would frisk you and take your gun and badge. The angry citizens would swamp the department with letters of protest.

"So you go for your gun. You haven't a chance in a million. You're off duty. You're at a disadvantage, but you have the tradition of the force on your shoulders. You take your one chance in a million. You go for your gun. You brace yourself against the bite of the slugs in your guts so you can squeeze the trigger a couple of times before you cash in.

"Then citizens make wisecracks about oil wells in Texas."

"Okay," Mason said. "There are cops and cops. You're on the square, Tragg. I didn't mean you when I talked about the millionaires. You told me to save my line for a luncheon-club speech when I tried to talk about the lawyers. I've let you talk about the cops. Now tell me about Claremont."

"Bob became a rookie. He went ahead rapidly. Everybody liked him. He was alert, on the job every minute of the time, and if anyone had told him there was corruption anywhere on the force, he'd have smeared the guy. The force was his ideal. It represented the law, standing guard over the helpless."

"What happened to him?" Mason said.

"No one knows exactly. Apparently he saw something about an automobile that made him suspicious. He must have stopped the car to question the driver. Why he would have done it, no one knows. He wasn't on traffic, and he wouldn't have stopped a car for a routine shakedown. There was definitely something about the car that aroused his suspicions."

"Go ahead," Mason said.

"There must have been at least two men in the car, and

perhaps more," Tragg said, "because they undoubtedly surprised him and forced him to get into the car with them."

"Why would they do that?" Mason asked.

Tragg shook his head.

"Go ahead," Mason invited.

"As nearly as we can put things together," Tragg said, "he was forced into the car. They made him lie down on the floor. They took his gun away from him, and then they drove about ten miles out of town. And then while he was still lying down on the floor of the car, they pushed the gun against his head—a contact wound. Ever see a contact wound, Mason?"

Mason raised his eyebrows.

Tragg said, "They're not nice to look at. The gun is held right against the head. The bullet goes in and so do the gases from the gun. When the gases get inside the head, they keep on expanding."

"Go ahead," Mason said, "but don't torture yourself, Lieutenant."

"Hell, I can't get over it," Tragg said bitterly. "You should have talked with the guy's wife, and his two kids, a couple of fine upstanding children who looked like their father with steady, honest blue eyes. The older one was old enough to know what had happened. The younger one wasn't."

"And the wife?" Della Street asked.

Tragg looked at her for a moment, then tightened his lips and said, "She knew what had happened, all right. . . . A darned nice girl. She and Bob Claremont had been in love for years, but the war came along and he went overseas. You know what it means, praying for someone every night, looking for a letter from him in the mail, dreading the delivery of a telegram, hating to hear the phone ring. . . . All right, she went through that, so did a lot of other people. That's war. Her man came back to her. Lots of men didn't come back.

"She was lucky that far. He came back on leave. They got married. He never did see his son until the war was over. The boy was over a year old then. . . . Then Bob started studying, studying so he'd be a credit to the profession. He had an idea law enforcement was a career. Used to claim that the scientific investigator would be as important in the public eye as the lawyer or the doctor. Spent all of the money he could get hold of buying books on crime detection, criminology, legal medicine, and that sort of stuff.''

"You said it was a contact wound?" Mason said.

"One of them was. The others weren't. It was the contact wound that caused death. Then they went on and emptied the gun into him just to make sure. Or else because one of the guys was trigger-happy and liked to hear the bullets thud.''

"Then what happened?" Mason asked.

"Then," Tragg said, "they dumped him out."

"Right where he was shot?" Mason asked.

"Nobody knows where he was shot," Tragg said. "Apparently it was in a speeding car. They dumped him. They didn't even bother to stop the car—just opened the door and let him hit the pavement and roll over and over like a sack of meal, leaving little splotches of blood every time he hit. The car kept on going.''

Tragg puffed thoughtfully at his cigar for a moment, then said, "We saved the bullets, of course. . . . Now here's a funny one. We've got a man in Ballistics who has been collecting a bank of specimen bullets. Every cop has to fire a bullet from his gun into a tube of cotton waste. The bullets are saved and filed.

"So we had test bullets from Bob Claremont's gun. We compared them with the fatal bullets. They matched. Bob had been shot six times with his own gun."

"Well?" Mason asked.

Tragg shook his head. "It couldn't have happened that way. Bob Claremont wouldn't have knuckled under and let them take his gun. That's why I was telling you about cops, Mason. Even if there's only one chance in a million, a cop has to take it. If there's no chance at all, a cop goes out fighting—Bob Claremont's kind of cop.

"They wouldn't have found six shells to have shot at him from his own gun. He'd have fired a shot or two—if he'd stopped an auto to shake it down."

"What about his gun?" Mason asked.

"It never showed up. That's strange. Ordinarily they'd have tossed the gun out before they'd gone a hundred yards. Remember the gun was empty. It was an officer's gun and it was hot."

"You searched, of course?"

"Searched?" Tragg said. "We combed the sides of that road—every inch of it. Then we got mine detectors and looked around through the tangled weeds."

"And found nothing?"

"Not a thing."

"I presume," Mason said, "you're telling me the story for some particular reason?"

"For a particular reason," Tragg said. "Bob Claremont was murdered September seventeenth—a year ago. . . . Believe me, Mason, we turned everything upside down. We had one suspect."

"Who?" Mason asked.

Tragg hesitated.

"Don't tell me if you don't want to," Mason said. "I was just trying to get a picture of the case."

"No, I'll tell you," Tragg said. "I'm putting all the cards on the table, because this may be awfully damn important, Mason. The suspect was a fellow by the name of Sedgwick. His name was Thomas E. Sedgwick, and he was making book. Claremont was on to him. Claremont was hoping to get the goods on him, and run him in. Claremont hadn't learned all of the angles yet. That is, he knew them but he didn't want to use them. He wouldn't work through stoolies. He wanted to get evidence himself. He was working on Sedgwick at the time he was bumped off.

"We wanted to round Sedgwick up for questioning on the murder, not that we had anything specifically on him, but we knew that Claremont was working on him."

"Go ahead."

"And," Tragg said, "we couldn't find Sedgwick. He had vanished, disappeared, swallowed his tail, gone. We'd like very, very much to know where Thomas E. Sedgwick is."

"You didn't have anything else on him," Mason asked, "only the fact that this officer had been working on Sedgwick . . . ?"

"Sedgwick had a cigar counter," Tragg said. "He was doing a pretty good business. He was doing a damned good business, when you put everything together. And the night Claremont was killed, Sedgwick left town. The next day there was a new chap in the cigar counter. Said that Sedgwick had sold out to him for a thousand dollars, and had a bill of sale to prove it. Said that he had been negotiating with Sedgwick for a purchase for a week or ten days, that at two o'clock in the morning Sedgwick had called him on the phone, told him that if he wanted to put up a thousand dollars in spot cash, the cigar business was for sale, lock, stock and barrel, lease, good will, cigars on hand, inventory, everything.

"The fellow jumped at the chance. Sedgwick wouldn't take his personal check. He had to have cash. The guy finally raised the cash, and about four o'clock in the morning the deal was consummated. Sedgwick signed the bill of sale in front of witnesses, and that was the last anyone has ever seen of Thomas E. Sedgwick. Needless to say, the guy who bought the place sold cigars, that was all; just cigars. It was a good location. He sold cigars and he kept his nose clean. If he'd ever given us a chance to take him down to headquarters the boys would have worked him over. He never gave anybody the chance. We tried everything on him. We tried stoolies. We tried spotters. We tried everything we could think of. Hell, the guy was clean."

"What happened to him?" Mason asked.

"He stuck around the place for about two months, then he sold it out to another guy who had a police record. That guy started making book and we flattened him so damn fast he never knew what hit him."

"But no Sedgwick?"

"No Sedgwick."

"I suppose this is leading up to something," Mason said.

"Last night," Tragg said, "there was this mix-up down at Alburg's place. A waitress got terrified and ran out through the back alley. Someone threw a gun on her. She didn't react the way the gunman probably expected she would act. She didn't get in the car. She screamed and made a dash for the mouth of the alley.

"Sometimes things are funny that way. A man has a gun and it's a symbol of power. The average person is deathly afraid of a gun. He looks down the big black hole and sees the wicked little bullets grouped around the cylinder, and his knees buckle. . . . The more you know about guns the more you realize that it isn't the gun that's dangerous—it's the man behind it. Some men can shoot a gun, some men can't. A few men who pack rods couldn't hit a man-sized target at a distance of fifteen feet, without stopping to take careful aim, and even then they might miss. Shooting a gun just by the feel of the weapon takes a little practice."

"Go on," Mason said.

"Whoever was driving that car hadn't figured on the fact that the open door gave him a pretty narrow target. His first shot missed. He didn't expect to have to shoot. When the waitress jumped forward she got out of the line of fire. The driver stepped on the throttle to speed up so he could get abreast of her. When he did that, the right-hand door jerked back shut. The fellow fired a second bullet, and, according to the story of witnesses, that bullet, which was fired just as the door was swinging closed, went through the right-hand door of the car.

"The girl screamed and gained the street. The bullets had missed her. A motorist knocked her down. The mouth of the alley was blocked by stalled traffic, by gawking pedestrians.

"The man in the car really knew his way around with an automobile. It isn't an easy job to back an automobile at high speed. There wasn't any room in the alley to turn around.

64

The man was trapped. He had to get out of there fast. He could have abandoned the car and mingled with the pedestrians, but for some reason he didn't dare do that. He threw the car into reverse and went backing out of the alley just as fast as the reverse gear could propel the car backwards.''

"You found that out?" Mason asked.

"We found that out," Tragg said. "A couple of witnesses saw the car backing up. They assumed that the driver was going to get out. The driver never got out. The car picked up speed. It went back in a straight line, without any wobbling or weaving. You know what that means, Mason. That means the man was an expert. The ordinary motorist doesn't get to drive like that. A man who's accustomed to running a squad car might do it, and a fellow who had been educated in the bootlegging or the dope-running business could do it. That's part of their stock in trade, taking a car and whipping it around alleys and through traffic faster than other people can drive."

"All right," Mason said, "let's come to the payoff."

"The payoff," Tragg said, "is that you asked me as a special favor to see that this woman was put in a private hospital. I did it. In a private hospital she had a better chance of walking out. She walked out. She took a powder, vanished."

"Am I responsible for that?" Mason asked.

"I'm damned if I know," Tragg said. "Wait until you get the punch line."

"What's the punch line?"

Tragg said, "Naturally, when she took a powder like that we became interested. It was a traffic department case. They went around to Morris Alburg's place. They asked questions. Alburg didn't seem to be trying to cover up particularly, but he certainly didn't know much about this particular woman. He certainly was dumb."

Mason nodded. "Go ahead."

"However," Tragg said, "the boys found the waitress's purse. They looked in it. There was a pawn ticket on a Seattle pawn shop. The boys got in touch with the Seattle pawn shop detail and they went down and picked up the article that was on the ticket. It was a diamond ring, flanked with two small emeralds, a pretty good job. She'd got a hundred and a quarter on it. It was worth a thousand.''

"And?'' Mason asked.

"And,'' Tragg said, "naturally the boys got to asking questions, getting a description, finding out anything they could, and the pawnbroker remembered that there had been two transactions made at the same time. She'd pawned the diamond ring, and she'd pawned a gun.

"We didn't have the pawn ticket for the gun so the Seattle police didn't know about it, but the pawnbroker remembered it. He got the gun and the Seattle police telephoned a description down to us, just in case. They gave us the serial number.''

"And?'' Mason asked.

"And,'' Tragg said, "it was Bob Claremont's gun—the gun that had been missing ever since the night someone jerked it out of Bob Claremont's holster, held it against his head, pulled the trigger and snuffed out his life, then fired five more shots into his twitching body, and callously dumped him out of the car like a sack of meal.''

Tragg stopped talking. He looked at the end of his cigar, seemed surprised to find that it had gone out, took a match from his pocket, scraped it into flame on the sole of his shoe, rotated the cold cigar carefully while he nursed the end into flame, then dropped the match into an ashtray, settled back in the overstuffed leather chair and started smoking, apparently concentrating on his thoughts and the aroma of his cigar.

Mason and Della Street exchanged glances.

There was a thick, ominous silence in the office.

Mason pinched out his cigarette, started drumming slowly on the edge of his desk, using only the tips of fingers, making almost no sound.

Tragg kept on smoking.

"When did you find this out?" Mason asked at length.

"About half an hour before I started up here."

"Where were you during that half-hour?" Mason asked.

"Where the hell do you suppose? I was trying to find Alburg."

"And where is Alburg?"

Tragg shrugged his shoulders, made a little gesture with spread palms and went on smoking.

"And just why are you telling me this?" Mason asked.

"For one thing," Tragg said, "I like you. You've cut corners before. You've managed to get away with it because they were cases where you were in the right. If you'd been in the wrong you'd have been lashed to the mast. As it was, you wormed out. You're smart. You're damned smart. You're logical, you're a two-fisted fighter. You stick up for your clients. . . . You've never been in a case before where an officer was killed in the line of duty. Take my advice and don't get in one. Things happen in cases of that sort. You could get hurt. You will get hurt."

Tragg ceased talking, went on smoking his cigar. Then he turned to Mason and said, "I want that fur coat."

Mason gave that problem frowning consideration, while his fingertips once more drummed on the edge of the desk.

"Do I get it?" Tragg asked.

Mason, still drumming with his fingers, said, "Let me think it over for a minute."

"Take your time," Tragg said. "This isn't tiddlywinks you're playing."

There was an interval of silence. Della Street's apprehensive eyes were on Mason's granite-hard face.

Abruptly Mason stopped drumming. "No question about it being the same girl?" he asked.

"Sure, there's a question," Tragg said. "There's a question about everything. That's one of the reasons I wanted to talk with Alburg again. . . . But the girl who pawned that ring was the same girl who pawned Bob Claremont's gun."

Mason resumed drumming with his fingertips, then said

abruptly, "The thing that I simply can't understand, Tragg, is why the hell she would do anything like that. Whoever killed Claremont knew that gun was hot as a stove lid. That gun would put somebody right in the gas chamber. The lawyer doesn't live who could get an acquittal in the case of the person who showed up with Claremont's gun. Not if there is the faintest scintilla of other evidence to hang anything on."

"Are you telling me?" Tragg said.

"How much did she get for the gun?"

"Eighteen dollars."

"In good shape?"

"Just as perfect as the day Bob Claremont kissed his wife and kids good-by and put it in his holster for the last time."

Mason said, "The murderer simply wouldn't have been that dumb, Tragg."

"The murderer was that dumb. I'll tell you something else, Mason. It's hard to get fingerprints from a gun. Don't be kidded by what you read in stories. Ninety-five times out of a hundred you can't find a fingerprint on a gun. But we found one on this. It had been out in the wet somewhere and someone had touched the rough inside of the frame with a wet finger. Then rust formed on the lines of moisture."

"And do you know whose fingerprint it is?" Mason asked.

"It's the print of Thomas Sedgwick's right index finger," Tragg said.

Mason abruptly turned to Della Street. "What did you do with the fur coat, Della?"

"I took it to a safe place."

"Where?"

"A fur storage place."

"Where's the receipt?"

"In my purse."

"Give it to Lieutenant Tragg."

Della Street opened her purse, took out a blue pasteboard ticket, handed it to Tragg.

Tragg got up, flicked ashes from his cigar and said, "Thanks."

"Just a minute," Mason said. "We want a receipt."

"Write it out," Tragg said to Della Street.

"Let me see the ticket, please."

Tragg gave her the ticket. Della Street sent her fingers flying over the typewriter keyboard, whipped the paper out from the roller, and gave it to Tragg to sign.

Tragg twisted the cigar over to one corner of his mouth so the smoke wouldn't get in his eyes as he bent over and scrawled his name on the sheet of paper.

Slowly, as though debating something with himself, he took a cellophane-covered photograph from his pocket. It was mounted on Bristol board and showed a young, ambitious face, a face with good features, keen eyes that held a humorous twinkle, a mouth that was firm without being coarse, cruel or hard, a good chin, straight nose, and a well-shaped forehead surmounted by wavy black hair.

"Good looking," he said.

"I'll say!" Della Street exclaimed. "Who is he?"

"He isn't. He was. Look at the youthful purpose, the square-deal eyes. . . . Hell, I'm getting too sentimental to be a cop."

"Bob Claremont?" Mason asked.

"Bob Claremont," Tragg said, and walked out.

Chapter 6

At nine-thirty Perry Mason dropped into Drake's office.

"Nothing yet, Paul?"

"Nothing yet," the detective said.

"Find out anything about Fayette?"

"I can't be sure about the Fayette," Drake said, "but there was a George Fayette arrested for making book about five years ago. It could have been the same one."

"Could have been," Mason said. "What happened to the case?"

"Nothing."

"What do you mean, nothing?"

"Just that. The man was arrested, booked, released on bail and then nothing happened. The case has simply evaporated into thin air."

"How much bail?"

Drake grinned. "A hundred bucks."

"Looks like a fix," Mason said.

"Could be, all right. You know how those things are."

"Can you find out where he lives or anything about him?"

"Not a thing."

"What kind of a bond?"

"One of the bail bond brokers—a fellow who has property worth about twenty thousand dollars, with a mortgage of twenty-five thousand on it, and he's written about five hundred thousand dollars in bail bonds giving that piece of property as security."

"Can you prove it?" Mason asked.

"Hell, no," Drake said, grinning. "You wanted me to look up Fayette. If you want me to expose the bail bond racket you'd better get me five assistants, ten bodyguards, a suit of armor, and hunt yourself a cyclone cellar. I'm just giving you glittering generalities.''

"All right," Mason said. "I've been hoping Alburg would call me. I wrote him a letter and sent it by special messenger to his place. It was left with the cashier. I told her if Morris phoned in I wanted him to know that letter was there, and for him to arrange to have it delivered to him.''

"What did you tell him, Perry?''

"Lots of things. And I told him to call me at any hour of the day or night. I gave him this number and told him to call me here if I wasn't at my office—to call me the very moment he got this letter no matter what time it was . . . Let me use your phone.''

Mason picked up the phone, gave Drake's operator the number of Morris Alburg's restaurant, and when the line answered, said, "Mr. Alburg, please.''

"He isn't in.''

"Mason talking. When will he be in?''

"I don't know, Mr. Mason.''

"Let me talk with the cashier.''

"Just a moment.''

When a woman's voice came on the line, Mason said, "This is Perry Mason, the lawyer. I left a letter there for Mr. Alburg. That is, I sent it out by messenger, with directions that if Mr. Alburg came in or communicated with his office he was to . . .''

"Yes, Mr. Mason. I think he has it.''

"Has what?''

"The letter.''

"Has he been in?''

"No. He— Well, you see, he isn't going to be in tonight. He telephoned and—well, several people have been looking for him.''

"*Several* people?'' Mason asked.

"*Several* people,'' she said. "They're waiting around here.''

"I understand," Mason said.

"I told him," she said, "that quite a few people were looking for him, and I also told him that I had this letter from you, which was supposed to be very important. So he asked me to hop in a taxicab and leave the letter at a cocktail bar. He said he'd pick it up later."

"He didn't say how much later?"

"No."

"If you should hear from him again make certain he has that letter. Tell him it's the most important move in his schedule right now. Tell him to read that letter and to call me."

"I will, Mr. Mason."

"One other thing," Mason said, "when do you go off duty?"

"One o'clock."

"Where do you live? What's your telephone number?"

"Mr. Mason!"

"Don't be silly," Mason said. "This is important. What's your telephone number?"

"Exford 3-9827."

Mason wrote it down. "I may have to call you," he said. "Be sure to have Morris get in touch with me. Good-by."

Mason hung up the telephone, said to Paul Drake, "Morris Alburg is going to call me at this number. Now, as soon as he calls in I want you to have your switchboard operator call the unlisted number at my apartment and put me on the line with Alburg's call. Can your switchboard handle that?"

"Sure."

"Tell your switchboard operator that it's very, very important. I want to be sure that call comes through without any trouble."

"When's it coming in, Perry?"

"Sometime tonight—I hope. It may be any minute now."

"When are you leaving for your apartment?"

"Right now."

"I'm buttoning things up here myself, and going to call it a day. My night switchboard operator is new, but very competent. She comes on at midnight. The girl who's on the switchboard now is a wizard. I'll see both of them are posted and on their toes. You'll get the call switched through to you the minute it comes in."

"That's fine," Mason said. "I'm on my way."

"I'll ride down with you," Drake told him.

Drake paused at the switchboard to relay Mason's instructions, then accompanied the lawyer to the parking lot.

"How strong do you want me to go on this Fayette business?" Drake asked.

"Plenty strong," Mason told him. "Keep plugging away checking records. If you have someone who knows his way around you might ask him about Fayette."

"I should turn up something tomorrow if he's around town at all, particularly if the Fayette who was picked up on that bookmaking charge is the one I think he is. . . . Well, I'll be seeing you."

"There won't be any trouble about that call coming through, will there, Paul?"

"Hello, no. It'll be a matter of routine. My switchboard operators will be watching for it."

Mason glanced at his wrist watch as he started the car; it was nine-forty-two.

By ten Mason was ensconced in his apartment, trying to interest himself in a magazine. By ten-forty-five, frowning with annoyance, he started pacing the floor. At eleven-ten he picked up a book. At eleven-thirty he threw the book to one side, undressed and went to bed. It was more than an hour before he could go to sleep. At first he slept fitfully, then weariness overcame him.

Mason was deep in slumber when the unlisted telephone by the side of his bed jangled into noise. At the third ring the lawyer managed to waken sufficiently to pick up the instrument.

"Hello," he said.

A crisp feminine voice said, "Mr. Mason, I'm sorry to disturb you, but those were your instructions."

"Oh, yes, this is Drake's office?"

"That's right. Mr. Alburg is on the other phone. He said he was calling you in accordance with a letter."

"Put him on. Can you connect these lines?"

"Yes, sir. Just a moment. I'll plug them across the switchboard."

There was the click of a connection, then Mason, somewhat irritably, said, "Hello, Alburg. This is going to cost you a lot of money. Why the hell didn't you call me earlier?"

Alburg's voice, sounding strained and hoarse, said, "I couldn't."

"Why not?"

"I can't tell you."

"All right, you're calling me now," Mason said. "What's the low-down on this thing? Was the story the way you gave it to me or were you acquainted with . . ."

"No names please," Alburg said.

"Oh, for heaven's sake," Mason said angrily, "aren't you where you can talk? If you aren't, get to a phone where you *can* talk. I want to get this thing straight. I'm . . ."

"Look, Mr. Mason, I'm in trouble, lots of trouble," Alburg said. "I need you bad. Now get this, Mason, money is no object. I'm in something awful deep. I'll tell you about it when I see you."

"When's that going to be?" Mason asked.

"As soon as you can get here."

"As soon as *I* can get *there*?" Mason exclaimed.

"That's right," Alburg said. "I want you here."

Mason said, "If it's really important, I'll see you at my apartment. If it isn't, you can come to my office at nine-thirty tomorrow morning. But if . . ."

"Now listen, Mason," Alburg said, his voice low but filled with apprehension. "This is the worst. This is one hell of a case. I have to see you. We have to make a lot of talk. I don't go to your apartment. I don't go to your office. I don't go nowhere. I don't leave this room. Instead, you get here quick. You have to come. I write you a letter. I write you before you write me. My letter has a check for one thousand dollars. That's retainer. There's more where that comes from. A good fee for you—the best!''

''Why can't you leave that room?'' Mason asked.

''I'm hot.''

''Why can't it wait until I get to my office in the morning?''

''Tomorrow maybe I am not around any more.''

''All right,'' Mason said wearily, ''if you'd played fair with me and given me the low-down on this thing, perhaps you wouldn't have been in such a jam.''

''I'm in a jam before I ever see you, Mason.''

''Where are you?''

''The Keymont Hotel, room 721. The place is not high-class. It's a joint. Don't stop at the desk. Walk by the desk like you had a room. Don't speak to anybody. Take the elevator, come up to the seventh floor, go to 721. The door is unlocked. I'm there.''

''All right.''

''And, Mason—''

''Yes?''

''Make it snappy, yes?''

''All right,'' Mason said. ''I'll be there.'' He hung up the telephone, kicked the covers off, telephoned the garage to have his car brought out in front and left with the motor running, rubbed exploratory fingers over the slight stubble on the angle of his jaw, jumped into his clothes, hastily knotted his tie, started for the door, then returned to pick up his overcoat, paused to ring the desk and make certain his car was waiting outside, then dashed for the elevator.

The night clerk looked at him curiously, said, ''Must be something of an emergency, Mr. Mason.''

''Must be,'' Mason said, and glanced at the clock over the desk. It was two-fifteen.

The lawyer glanced at his wrist watch to verify the hour shown by the clock on the wall, walked over to the revolving door, and out into the crisp, cold air of early morning.

The night garageman was seated in Mason's car at the curb. He nodded to the lawyer, opened the door and got out.

Mason slid in behind the steering wheel, noticed that the heater was already warming up the interior of the cold car.

"Thanks a lot, Jake," he said.

"Yes, sir."

He glanced at the dial on the gas tank.

"I filled it up when you brought it in last night," the night man said. "You instructed me to see that it's always kept full and . . ."

"That's fine," Mason told him. "I never know when I may have to go someplace in a hurry."

"This looks like one of those times."

"It does for a fact," Mason admitted. He slammed the door and sent the car purring smoothly away from the curb.

It took Mason about fifteen minutes to reach the Keymont Hotel. At that hour of the morning there were plenty of parking spaces and Mason parked his car, locked it and entered the lobby.

It was a shabby lobby with well-worn chairs and a musty atmosphere. Entering the place after his brief sojourn in the crisp night air, Mason was all the more conscious of the stale odor of decay. The empty chairs arranged in an orderly row seemed hopelessly incongruous. In keeping with the atmosphere of the place, they should have been occupied by seedy men sitting quietly, reading newspapers, or just staring off into space.

The clerk looked up as Mason entered the lobby, followed the lawyer with his eyes, until Mason had reached the elevator shaft.

"Someone you wanted to see?" the clerk asked, as Mason jabbed the button on the elevator.

"Me," Mason told him.

"You mean . . ."

"That's right."

"You're registered here?"

Mason said, "Sure. And you'd better call me at seven-thirty in the morning . . . No, wait a minute, I've got to make a couple of calls first. I'll wait until I get to the room and then give you a ring when I find out what time I want to be called. I may be able to sleep later than seven-thirty.''

The elevator rattled to a stop. Mason pushed back the door. It was, at this hour of the night, on automatic, and Mason jabbed the last button, which was for the eighth floor. He waited what seemed an interminable interval until the elevator, swaying and rattling, came to a hesitant stop.

Mason slid back the door, closed it and walked down the corridor to a red light which marked the location of the staircase. He took the stairs down to the seventh floor, located room 721 and tapped gently on the door.

There was no answer.

Mason waited a few moments, then tapped again, this time more insistently.

There was still no answer, no slightest sound from within the room.

Mason tried to doorknob. It turned and he opened the door a crack. The light was on.

Mason, standing in the hallway, pushed the door with his foot, swinging it wide open.

The room was empty, but seemed to have been recently occupied since there was a distinct odor of fresh cigarette smoke.

Mason cautiously crossed the threshold.

It was the standardized room of a cheap hotel. The thin carpet was worn through the pattern in a well-defined trail from the door around the bed to the window. There was a washstand and mirror over in the corner, and the carpet in front had been worn through almost to the floor.

Mason's eyes made swift inventory.

He saw the imitation-leather-bottomed rocking chair, the two straight kitchen chairs with cane bottoms, the square table which looked as though it had been primarily designed to hold a white glass pitcher and bowl before running water had been installed in the room.

Mason left the door open, and took two swift but cautious steps to the door, pulling it toward him to make sure no one was standing behind it. He walked over to another door and disclosed a narrow closet. The next door showed a toilet and a shower jammed together in a room scarcely the size of a good-sized closet.

Having satisfied himself there was no one there, Mason went back and closed the door. This time he gave the room a more careful survey.

It was illuminated with a reddish glow from a glass bowl which hung from the center of the room and was supported by a chain of brass-colored links, through which ran electric wires down to the single bulb.

The bed was an iron bedstead with a thin mattress, carefully covered, however, with a smooth but somewhat threadbare white bedspread. A reading lamp was clamped to the head of the bed.

Mason noticed the indentation near the head of the bed where someone had evidently been sitting. Then he noticed another indentation near the center of the bed.

The lawyer stooped so that he could see this indentation to better advantage.

It looked very much as though someone had thrown a gun onto the bed. The gun had been picked up, but it had left an imprint in the white spread.

Something the color of gold, glittering in the light, caught Mason's eye. He stooped and picked up a lipstick.

The lipstick was worn flat, and from little ridges at the edges looked as though it might have been drawn across some hard surface.

The lawyer searched the room carefully, studied the lipstick once more, then turned up the small square table. On the underside had been lettered in lipstick, *"Mason Help 262 V 3 L 15 left."*

Mason was standing looking at the lipstick and the message on the bottom of the table when he heard a faint squeaking noise from across the room. The knob of the door was slowly turning.

Hastily thrusting the lipstick into the side pocket of his coat, Mason put the table back into position, and was standing poised thoughtfully, one foot on the chair, in the act of taking a cigarette from a cigarette case as the door slowly, cautiously opened.

The woman who stood in the doorway was about twenty-five years of age, with a good figure, raven-dark hair, large dark eyes, and olive skin, against which the vivid red of her mouth was a splash of crimson.

She drew back with a quick intake of breath, half a scream.

Mason, regarding her with calm, steady eyes, said nothing.

The woman hesitated in the doorway, then slowly entered the room. "You— Who *are* you?"

"Is this your room?" Mason asked.

"I—I came here to meet someone. Who are you?"

"I came here to meet someone. Who are you?"

"I—I don't have to give you my name."

Mason, watching her, said slowly, "My name is Perry Mason. I am an attorney. I came here to meet a client. The client told me he was registered in this room. Now, tell me whom you expected to meet."

"Oh, thank heaven! *You're* Mr. Mason. Where's Morris? I'm Dixie Dayton. I came here to meet Morris Alburg. He telephoned me that you were coming, but he said he'd be here with us. He said he was going to have you represent me, so I want to tell you frankly . . ."

Mason seated himself, gestured her to a chair. "Now, wait a minute," he said, "it may not be that simple."

"What do you mean?"

"In the first place, you *may* have had a wrong impression of what Mr. Alburg wanted to say to me."

"No, I didn't, Mr. Mason. I know it was that, honestly it was."

"In the second place," Mason said, "regardless of what anyone might say, I might not want to represent you."

"Why? Morris—Mr. Alburg will pay you whatever it's worth."

"What makes you think he will?"

"He promised me he would."

"You might be guilty of something."

"Mr. Mason, don't let them pull the wool over *your* eyes."

"I'll try not to," Mason said, "but after all, I have to pick and choose my cases. I can't possibly take all the work that's offered to me. I have to know a good deal about the facts in any given case before I commit myself. And I frequently turn down cases."

She dropped down to the floor at his feet. "Mr. Mason, if you only knew what it meant; if you only knew what I'm up against."

Mason said nothing.

"Mr. Mason, tell me, how much do you know? How much has Mr. Alburg told you?"

"Not very much," he said.

She said, "All right, I'll tell you the truth, Mr. Mason. I'll tell you the facts in the case."

"I may not be free to listen," Mason told her. "At the moment I'm not free to receive any confidential communication from you. If you tell me anything I can't treat it as a professional confidence."

"Oh, don't be so cagey," she said. "After all, why should you and I sit here and spar with each other? Let's get down to brass tacks."

She quickly reached up and took his hand in hers. "I suppose I'm being terribly impulsive and you must think I'm a ninny, but I'm in an awful jam, Mr. Mason, and you're going to have to get me out."

"I've already explained to you," Mason said, "that I can't talk with you, and I'd prefer not to listen until after I've seen Morris Alburg. I have to know where I stand before I . . ."

"Oh, Mr. Mason," she wailed. "Please—I'm going to put my cards on the table for you, Mr. Mason."

"I can't even let you do that at the moment," Mason said.

She sat silent for a few minutes, thinking. She still held onto his hand. Gripping it, she said, "You mean so much to me, Mr. Mason. I can't begin to tell you what it means to have you working on the case."

"I'm not working on it."

She met his eyes with laughing challenge and said, "Yet."

"Yet," Mason told her, half-smiling.

"And you certainly are one cautious lawyer."

"I have to be."

She lightly kissed the back of his hand. "For the moment that will have to serve as a retainer," she said. "You stay right there. I'm going to see if I can't get a line on Morris Alburg. You just wait here and I'll bring him within fifteen minutes, and then we'll get started right."

She walked quickly across the room, opened the door and vanished.

Mason came out of the chair almost at once, hurried to the telephone, and gave Paul Drake's private, unlisted number.

It seemed minutes before Mason heard Drake's sleepy voice.

"Wake up, Paul," Mason said. "This is important. Get it, and get it fast."

"Oh, Lord, you again," Drake said thickly. "Every time I try to get a little sleep . . ."

"Forget the sleep," Mason barked into the telephone. "Snap out of it. I'm up here in the Keymont Hotel, room 721. There's a brunette girl, about five feet two, who weighs one hundred and fifteen, age twenty-five or twenty-six, olive skin, large round eyes, a vivid red mouth, up here with me— that is, she will be here inside of a minute or two, and . . ."

"Well, congratulations," Drake said. "You sure do get around!"

"Can the wise stuff," Mason snapped. "Get hold of some

operatives and send them up here. . . . First, I want a woman, if you can find one, to make the original contact. Try and have her in the corridor when this girl leaves the room. You'll have to work fast, Paul. The woman can put her finger on this girl and identify her so that the men who are on the outside can pick her up when she leaves. I want her tailed and I want to find out where she goes."

"Have a heart, Perry," Drake begged. "It's three o'clock in the morning. Good Lord, I can't pull people out of a hat. It'll take me an hour or two to get anybody on the job. I'll have to get someone out of bed, get him dressed, give him time to get down there . . ."

"Who's at your office?" Mason asked.

"Just a skeleton crew. I keep a night switchboard operator, a night manager, and there's usually one man available . . ."

"The switchboard operator," Mason interrupted, "man or woman?"

"Woman."

"Competent?"

"Very."

"Get her." Mason said. "Shut off the switchboard for an hour. It's a slack time in the morning so you won't miss any business. Get that woman up here. Do it now. You only have a few minutes, so get busy. Close up your office for an hour if you have to, but be prepared to shadow this girl the minute she leaves the hotel."

Mason didn't wait to hear Drake's expostulations. He slammed up the receiver and went back to the chair where he had been sitting.

Taking a white handkerchief from his pocket, he used a corner to wipe off the stain of lipstick from the back of his right hand. Then, moving the table to an inverted position, he used another corner of the handkerchief to wipe off a small sample of the lipstick from the bottom of the table.

Restoring the table to its original position, he took the gold-plated lipstick container from his pocket and very carefully touched the end of the lipstick to still another portion of the handkerchief. With his fountain pen he made marks on the handkerchief opposite each of the stains—*1, 2* and *3*. Then he folded the handkerchief, put it back in his pocket and settled back once more in the chair to wait.

It was a long wait.

At first Mason, watching the minute hand on his wrist watch, counting the minutes, kept hoping that time would elapse before the young woman returned so that Drake's operatives could get on the job. Then after fifteen minutes he frowned impatiently, and began to pace the floor. There was, of course, the possibility that he was being stood up, being put in a position of complete inactivity at a critical period by a deliberate ruse.

He had been certain that it was Morris Alburg who had called him. He was at the place Alburg had designated as a rendezvous. There was nothing to do except await further developments—or go home.

Abruptly and without warning the doorknob turned. The door opened with careless haste, and the brunette girl appeared on the threshold. Her cheeks were flushed, her eyes shining with excitement. It was apparent that she had been hurrying as fast as she could.

At the sight of Mason she abruptly relaxed. "Oh, thank heavens you're still here! I was so terribly afraid you wouldn't have had enough confidence in me to wait."

Mason raised his eyebrows.

"I didn't intend to be so long. I was afraid you'd walk out on me."

"I wasn't going to wait much longer at that. What was the idea?"

"I *had* to see Morris. That was all there was to it. I simply had to see him. I knew that."

"And you've seen him?" Mason asked.

"Yes. I have a note for you."

She thrust her hand down the front of her blouse, pulled

out a note, crossed the room rapidly and pushed it into Mason's hands. "Here, read this."

The note was typewritten.

MR. MASON:

Dixie tells me that you came to the room in the hotel all right, but won't talk with her and are waiting for me to give you an okay.

I gave you an okay over the telephone. I told you I had sent you a letter with a check in it for a retainer, and that I wanted you to represent me and represent Dixie. It's a bad mess. Dixie will tell you all about it.

I want you to consider Dixie, the bearer of this note, just the same as you consider me. She is your client. I have turned to you for help because I need help. I need it bad and I need it right now. I was hoping I could wait in that room until you arrived, but I simply had to go out on this angle of the case that I'm working on. I don't dare to tell you what it is because I don't want to put you in an embarrassing position.

Now please go ahead and help us out of this mess. You'll be paid and well paid.

Yours,

MORRIS

The body of the note had been typewritten, the signature was a scrawl in pencil. It could have been Morris Alburg's signature. Mason tried to recall whether he had ever seen Alburg's signature and couldn't remember any specific instance.

The young woman radiated assurance. "*Now* we can talk," she said.

Mason said nothing.

"Well—*can't* we?"

"I want to know why Morris Alburg isn't here," Mason said. "He promised to meet me here."

"But he had to change his plans."

"Why?"

84

"Because he's busy doing something that's terribly important."

"What?"

"Protecting me—and also himself."

She drew up a chair, sat down, said, "Mr. Mason, when can one person kill another person—and be justified?"

"In self-defense," Mason said.

"Does a person have to wait until the other one is shooting at him?"

"He has to wait until he is attacked, or until a reasonable man under similar circumstances would think that he was in great bodily danger or threatened with death."

"And then he could shoot?"

Mason nodded. "That's generally the law of self-defense. There are a lot of various qualifications about the man's duty to retreat and about who provoked the conflict in the first place. But that's the general rule."

"Now, then," she said, "suppose you knew that a cold-blooded, deliberate, efficient killer was on your trail and was going to commit murder. Wouldn't you have the right to kill him first?"

"Under the circumstances I've mentioned," Mason said.

"I know," she said, "but suppose you knew a man was out to kill you. Suppose he was watching your place, sitting in a car, a machine gun in his lap, and you managed to sneak out of your back door without his knowing it. Couldn't you take a rifle and blow the top of his head off without being guilty of murder?"

Mason shook his head.

"Why not?"

"Because under those circumstances," Mason said, "you'd have had a chance to call up the police and ask for protection."

She laughed scornfully. "Trying to get police protection from a man like the one I'm talking about is like asking the police to protect you against smallpox or the bubonic plague . . . Why, the man would simply slip through the fin-

85

gers of the police like nothing at all and you'd be dead before morning.''

"You asked me to tell you what the law was. I've told you. I don't make the law, I study it.''

She said, ''That's exactly the same thing Morris told me, but I wouldn't believe him. It doesn't sound fair to me, but that's what he said the law was, and so he said that you wouldn't approve of what he's doing.''

"What *is* he doing?''

"Ever hear of George Fayette?''

"Why, do you know him? I'd like to find out something about him.''

She laughed bitterly. "Lots of people would like to find out something about him. He's a killer.''

"Go ahead,'' Mason invited.

"And right at the moment he's trying to kill Morris and me.''

"Why?''

"That's one of the things I'd like to know. I presume because I'm Tom Sedgwick's girl friend.''

"And who is Tom Sedgwick?''

"He's someone the police are looking for. They're trying to frame a murder on him.''

"So they want to kill you and Morris Alburg?''

"That's right.''

"Why? That doesn't make much sense.''

"You act as though you didn't believe me.''

"I'm not certain that I do.''

"Listen, you can't argue with facts. Fayette tried to have me killed there in that alley back of Mr. Alburg's restaurant.''

"Just what happened then?'' Mason asked.

She said, ''Fayette was on my trail, intending to kill me. He came walking into that restaurant with just one thought in mind, and that was to frighten me into running out into the back alley.

"If I'd had one lick of sense I'd have known that was

86

exactly what he wanted. Even a man with Fayette's pull and brass could hardly expect to shoot a woman down in a public restaurant and then just get up and walk out of there.

"And yet he's done things that have been just as crazy as that—and got away with them, too. But somehow you don't stop to think when you see George Fayette looking at you. It's like reaching up to put your hand on a rock and finding a rattlesnake coiled there."

"Go ahead," Mason said as she stopped. "I'd like to know exactly what happened."

She said, "I dashed out of that restaurant, and that's exactly what Fayette wanted. He had an accomplice in a car waiting for me.

"All Fayette had to do was to sit tight and appear to be innocently enjoying his dinner, and I'd rush right into the jaws of his trap."

"And just what did happen when you reached the alley?"

"Well, the accomplice tried to force me to get into the car with him. I was just too plain panic-stricken to co-operate. And I guess that upset everyone's plans. It had never occurred to anyone that I wouldn't fold up like an accordion and march right into that car like a good little girl.

"As it was, I did the unexpected. I started to run.

"By the time the man managed to take a shot at me I was out of the line of fire through the open door. He stepped on the throttle to catch up with me, and the lurch of the car jerked the door back so it closed. He fired again, and the bullet went clean through the car door.

"By that time I was just running in blind panic. I dashed out into the street, and right in front of an oncoming car.

"Well, that's virtually the entire story. I regained consciousness in a hospital, and I knew, of course, that where I was would be a matter of public record, and Fayette could find me without any trouble. So I got up and explored the private room in which I'd been placed. I found my clothes in the closet. I was pretty wobbly on my pins, but I dressed and got out of there. Of course I got in touch with Morris at once.''

''And what did Morris do?''

''He fixed me up with an outfit and gave me a chance to hide. . . . But, of course, Morris was pretty much upset because he realized Fayette was after him at the same time.''

''So Alburg is taking steps to remove Fayette?''

''I probably shouldn't have told you that. In fact, I'm not going to tell you that. I'm simply telling you that right at the moment Morris is busy on a matter of the greatest importance and he isn't going to have any opportunity to get in touch with you until—well, I'd say for three or four hours at the most, but he's written you this note so that you'll understand.''

''All right,'' Mason said, ''what do you want me to do?''

''That's rather difficult to say. You're not very cooperative. You're still suspicious.''

''Do you blame me for that?''

''Yes.''

Mason laughed.

''Morris—Mr. Alburg wrote you a note, didn't he?''

''No.''

''What do you mean by that?''

''The signature is a scrawl. I'm not at all certain it's his. I'm not familiar with his signature.''

''It's his. I saw him sign it.''

''It's just a scrawl.''

''He was in a hurry. He had things on his mind.''

''The note is typewritten. He could have written it in his own hand a lot easier than tapping it out on a typewriter and it would have been a lot faster.''

''How do you know? Perhaps he writes faster on a typewriter than with pen and ink.''

''Don't be silly,'' Mason said. ''Whoever typed this note tapped it out laboriously with two fingers.''

''Perhaps Mr. Alburg was in a position where he couldn't write. He might have been hiding somewhere. He told someone what he wanted to say to you and that someone typed out the note and took it to Mr. Alburg to sign.''

''Or perhaps scrawled her own version of Alburg's signature on it,'' Mason said.

''Oh, you lawyers, with your everlasting suspicions! You make me sick.''

''I'm sorry. I can't successfully represent Morris Alburg until I know a lot more about you than I do now. Do you happen to have a driver's license with you?''

''No. Mr. Alburg specifically identifies me in this letter.''

''But there's no one to identify the letter.''

''Oh, nuts! I told Morris I'd bet you'd be like that. So I suppose you've got to see Morris face to face and have him tell you I'm Dixie Dayton and that you're to represent me, and show you the birthmark on my left hip and then give you a banker's guarantee. . . . Oh, all right, I'll go get Mr. Alburg and bring him here—and it's going to be dangerous.

''If he doesn't get Fayette first, George Fayette is going to kill him. And a fat lot *you* care! You with your lawyer's skepticism. If your client gets killed trying to come here to identify me, you'll know who's to blame.

''All right, wait right here.''

''And if you should see Morris Alburg,'' Mason said, ''tell him to come to me at once before he tries to deal with Fayette or with anyone else. Tell him I'll be waiting here and that I'll tell him how to handle the situation.''

She was standing at the door, one hand on the knob, looking at him over her shoulder, her eyes dark with emotion.

''So that's what you want,'' she said scornfully. ''Darned if I'm not sorry I opened up and talked to you the way I did. I thought you were a shrewd criminal lawyer who knew his way around. You talk like a reformer. I might as well write to Prudence Penny and say, 'My dear Miss Penny: What shall I do? There is a gunman who wants to kill me. He's almost succeeded twice in the last twenty-four hours, and now I know where I can put my finger on him. What should I do?'

"And instead of saying 'rub the guy out,' Prudence Penny would say, 'My dear Miss Whosis: You must remember that we have laws to take care of people of that sort. You should consult the authorities at once and tell them about your danger. They'll know what to do.'

"Perry Mason," she went on scornfully, "the great lawyer—Prudence Penny. Why the hell don't you get one of those encyclopedias on etiquette and a Gideon Bible, and throw your law books out the window?"

She slammed the door behind her so hard that the mirror which was hanging over the washbowl jumped and started to vibrate.

Perry Mason sat perfectly still, his eyes on his wrist watch, wondering if Paul Drake had had time to get his operatives placed, and whether they would be successful in following the girl.

Chapter 7

Mason once more paced the floor of the hotel bedroom, plainly showing impatience.

He had only a few minutes to wait.

Exactly seven minutes and five seconds from the time the door had closed on the departing figure of the young woman, fingertips tapped gently on the panel of the door, an all but inaudible knock.

Mason detoured in his floor-pacing to twist the knob and pull the door open.

Paul Drake, somewhat disheveled, in need of a shave, grinned at Mason and said in a low voice, "Okay, Perry."

Mason said, "Did you get . . . ?" He ceased talking as Drake placed a warning finger to his lips and pushed his way into the room.

"What gives?" Mason asked in a low voice.

"She's still here in the hotel," Drake said.

"You got on the job yourself?"

"I had to, Perry, I couldn't get the people here in time, and I jumped into my clothes and beat it up here as fast as I could. At that, I didn't do you any good."

"How come?"

"The girl who handles my switchboard was planted in the corridor. She had to register and get a room in order to do the job we wanted. She put on a maid's cap and an apron and was out in the corridor when your girl came out. In place of taking the elevator down to the lobby, however, the way we had expected, this jane took the elevator *up*."

"Oh-oh," Mason said.

"Now there is only one floor above this," Drake said,

"so my operative felt she could take the stairs and not be too far behind. Of course, she'd figured the lay of the land the first thing she did and before the action started, so she knew her way around."

Mason nodded.

"She sprinted up the stairs, opened the door and was only a second or two behind the elevator. Your girl was walking down the corridor. She stopped in front of 815, took a key from her purse, opened the door and walked in. My operative ran on tiptoe down the corridor and was in time to hear the door being locked from the inside."

"So then what?"

"So then she listened at the door long enough to hear low voices, one of them a man's voice. Evidently that jane is registered there in room 815. We had no signals to cover that emergency, so my operative had to dash down to where I was sitting in my car to tell me what had happened and ask for instructions. I felt the hotel room was all the address you needed and I couldn't leave my office switchboard shut off any longer, so I sent my girl back to the office and I came up to report. I stopped by the desk long enough to find out that room 815 is rented to a Mrs. Madison Kerby."

"The clerk suspicious of you?" Mason asked.

"The hell with him," Drake said. "This is one of those dumps. If he'd said anything I'd have told him where he got off at. I presume they're more or less accustomed to having private detectives crawling over the place."

"You mean he knows you're a private detective?"

"Hell, no. I let him think I was on the make. I slipped him a couple of bucks. Frankly, Perry, I don't think he gave a damn."

"So she's here in the hotel," Mason said.

Drake nodded. "It both complicates and simplifies things, Perry. As I tried to point out to you, we're short-handed. I'd instructed my operative to put the finger on the jane who came out of this room and to signal me so I could . . ."

"How was she going to do that, Paul?"

"Simple enough. My operative registered and insisted on getting a room at the front of the building. As soon as your party took the elevator down my operative was going to run into her room, open the window and shine the beam of a flashlight down on my car. I had my rear-view side mirror so adjusted that as soon as the beam of the flashlight hit that it would be reflected in my eyes."

"Nice going," Mason said.

"Just routine," Drake told him, and yawned.

"Well, we've run our quarry to earth," Mason said.

"She's Dixie . . ."

Mason grinned. "She *said* she was Dixie."

"Well?" Drake asked.

Mason shook his head.

"What are you getting at?"

Mason pulled a handkerchief from his pocket, said "Here are three stains of lipstick marked numbers one, two and three. What do you make of them, Paul?"

"You must have had a busy night," Drake said.

"Never mind the wisecracks. What do you make of this lipstick? It is all the same?"

"Two of them are the same. One might be just a little lighter than the other. I'd say—no, wait a minute—they're all the same. I'd say they were all the same shade."

"So would I," Mason said.

"You mean you've been necking with three different gals?" Drake asked.

Mason pulled the lipstick from his pocket, said, "Smear number one was removed from the lips of the girl who claims to be Dixie Dayton. Smear number two was taken from the writing on the bottom of the table here, and smear number three was taken from this lipstick."

"Writing on the bottom of the table?" Drake said.

"Uh-huh."

Mason picked the table up, gently turned it over, and Paul Drake looked at the writing on the bottom of the table and

93

whistled, then said, "How the devil did you happen to find it there, Perry?"

" 'Elementary, my dear Watson,' " Mason said, grinning. "This lipstick was lying on the floor. You notice it's a gold-plated tube of lipstick. It caught and reflected the light. Only a blind man could have missed it."

"All right," Drake said, "I still don't see how it happened that you looked at the bottom of the table."

"Take a look at this lipstick," Mason said. "A woman's lips are smooth. This lipstick was drawn across something rough which grooved deep lines in it and made it overlap the edges.

"So naturally I started looking around to see what the lipstick had been used on besides a person's lips."

"And you found this table," Drake said.

Mason nodded.

"Now wait a minute," Drake said, "this may be on the level, Perry. You were supposed to meet Morris Alburg here?"

"That's right."

"And—What the hell, Alburg and some woman, perhaps Dixie Dayton, were here in this room. Somebody slipped in and had a gun trained on them, and . . ."

"You'll notice the imprint of the gun on the bedspread," Mason said. "It's quite plain."

Drake followed the direction of Mason's finger and said, "Damned if it isn't, Perry. . . . My gosh, that does it! That really ties the thing up! They sat here. They knew they were going to be taken for a ride. They wanted to leave you some message. They had no chance to do it, but the girl acted as if she wanted to look her best when she was bumped off, so she opened her bag, took out her lipstick and started messing around with it. It was all very natural and no one noticed her when she surreptitiously scribbled this message. She was afraid you'd never find it in time to do any good, so she dropped her lipstick on the floor, feeling certain you'd see

94

that. Then they prodded her with the gun, and told her it was time to go.''

"Sounds logical all right," Mason said without enthusiasm.

"Gosh," Drake told him, "I can't understand why you're so calm about it, Perry. Jeepers, let's go to work on this thing. Let's start figuring this message. Let's— What do you think? Think we'd better get the police?''

"I think so."

Drake looked at him and said, "You're the damnedest guy I ever saw. At times you get all worked up over something and want me up out of bed at three o'clock in the morning, then you fool around and take something like this in your stride and don't seem to be in a hurry about it. Those folks are in danger. Whether we find them alive or dead depends on how long it takes us to decipher that message and bring help to them.''

"Could be," Mason said.

"What the hell's wrong?" Drake asked.

"This message," Mason said, "is supposed to have been written surreptitiously on the underside of the table by some woman who was playing around with her lipstick, and managing, whenever the attention of her captors was distracted, to write something on the bottom of the table. Is that the idea?''

"Well, that certainly is the way it looks to me," Drake said.

Mason took a notebook from his pocket, put it on his knee and said, "Now, this represents the top of a table. Take a pencil and write the word 'help' on there.''

"Okay," Drake said, "what does that prove?''

"Now then," Mason said, "turn the notebook upside down. Pretend that's the bottom of the table. Now you're sitting at the table. Here, if it'll help you any, hold this notebook against the bottom side of the table. Now, take the pencil and write the word 'help' on the bottom side of the table.''

"All right," Drake said sarcastically, "anything to accommodate. But it seems to me a hell of a way to waste time."

He seated himself in the chair. Perry Mason held the notebook firmly against the bottom of the table. Drake wrote the word "help."

Mason brought the notebook back to the top of the table.

"Well, I'll be damned," Drake said. And then suddenly said, "Let's do that again, Perry."

Mason held the notebook against the bottom of the table, and again Drake wrote the word "help." Again he turned the notebook face up on the table and shook his head dubiously. "It's a new one on me," he said. "Of course, it's logical enough, when you come to think of it. It just never occurred to me, that's all."

"Every time you write something on the undersurface of a table, you *have* to write it that way," Mason said. "Hold this notebook up in front of a mirror now and it spells 'help' perfectly, but when you look at it like this it's a good example of what is known among kids as 'looking-glass writing.' "

"Therefore," Drake said, "you feel that this message was not written by someone who was seated at the table."

"That message," Mason said positively, "was written by someone who had no need whatever to hide what she was doing. She simply turned the table upside down and wrote the word 'help' and then that string of figures."

Drake nodded.

"The message," Mason said, "could be a trap."

"In what way?"

Mason ignored the question and continued to think out loud. "We feel certain that the message is a fake because it couldn't have been written in the manner in which it's supposed to have been written. Therefore there must be some reason why that message was written."

Drake watched him silently.

Mason held up two fingers. "First," he said, touching his

thumb to the index finger, "the message is a trap. Second, the message is a blind."

"What do you mean, a blind?"

Mason said impatiently, "We know that Morris Alburg was in this room. At least he said he was."

"It was his voice all right?"

Mason nodded. "I recognized his voice. The man was terribly excited. He was in this room, or at least that's where he said he was, and there was no reason why he should lie."

"Then what happened to him?"

"Then," Mason said, "someone held a gun on him, and Morris left a message. Perhaps there was a girl with him and she left a message in lipstick."

"But I thought you just said she couldn't have done that, that it would be . . ."

Mason motioned him to silence. "The parties who took Morris Alburg out of this room discovered that a message had been left. Perhaps they didn't have time to find the real message so they left an obvious blind alley for me. . . . Now let's take another look at that table, Paul."

Together the two men studied the bottom of the table.

"It doesn't look to me as though there had been any other message here," Drake said.

"Apparently not. Let's look around. Perhaps the message was in some other place and they couldn't find it, and wanted to fix it so I couldn't. The people who took Alburg out of the room must have been in a hurry."

"Aren't you getting rather farfetched with this thing?" Drake asked.

Mason said impatiently, "There's a reason for everything. There's a message on the bottom of that table. There's a reason for it. I want to find out what the reason is."

"But why should somebody leave one message in order to destroy another if he didn't know about the other message?"

"They must have had a suspicion there was another message, but didn't know where it was. So they decided they'd

97

leave a message that would be a blind. . . . Start looking around, Paul. Let's see what *we* can find.''

Mason opened the closet door, looked on the inside of the doorjamb, looked on the space at the back of the door which was disclosed when the door swung outward on the hinges.

He searched the inside of the closet, the inside of the bathroom.

"Finding anything?" Drake asked.

Mason came to the bathroom door and shook his head.

Drake, who had been making a rather desultory search, said, "Suppose we explore the idea that it's a trap, Perry. What would it be?"

Mason said, "It could be a trap laid for us. It could be something to make us waste a lot of valuable time. Since I'm convinced the whole thing is phony I don't want to waste time on it."

"But it means *something*, Perry."

"Sure it does," Mason said, "probably a book. Take the words '262 V 3.' That probably means page two-sixty-two of volume three."

"That's it," Drake exclaimed, "and the 'L 15 left' would mean line fifteen in the left-hand column."

"Obviously," Mason said, "it's a book in a series of three volumes, then, that are divided into columns. What would that mean, Paul?"

Drake frowned thoughtfully. "Could it be a set of law books, Perry?"

Mason said, "More apt to be the volumes you're looking at right now."

"I don't get it. . . . Oh, you mean the telephone directory. But they don't come in marked volumes."

"These do. See that paper pasted on the back?"

Paul Drake picked up one of the books and turned it over. "Keymont Hotel Telephone Directory No. 1, Room 721," he read. "Obviously the type of joint where the tenants steal anything that isn't nailed down. . . . Gosh, Perry, let's look!"

Drake grabbed volume three of the telephone directory, turned the pages, counted down the lines, then read off, "Herbert Sidney Granton, 1024 Colinda Avenue."

"Mean anything?" Mason asked.

"Hell, yes." Drake said excitedly. "It's a name I've heard. It— Wait a minute, Perry."

He whipped out a notebook, thumbed the pages, said, "Sure. It's one of the aliases of George Fayette who was arrested for bookmaking, and whose case seems simply to have evaporated into thin air. . . . Gosh, Perry, let's go and . . ."

Mason shook his head.

"You mean we don't follow up this lead?" Drake demanded.

"Not yet," Mason said, "we finish looking."

Mason looked on the undersides of the chairs, crawled under the bed, and said, "Paul, that's a movable mirror over the washstand. Take a look on the back of it, will you?"

Mason was still under the bed when Drake called out excitedly, "Something here, Perry."

Mason hastily crawled out, dusted off his clothes, and walked over to where Drake had swung the mirror out from the wall.

In lipstick on the back of the mirror were the figures 5N20862.

"Now that," Mason said, "is probably the license number of an automobile."

The two men stood studying the string of figures which had been written in lipstick on the back of the mirror.

"I don't get it," Drake said.

"I do," Mason said. "Morris Alburg and some woman were in this room. Someone got the drop on them, or for some reason they had to leave. They wanted to leave a message for me. The girl used lipstick and wrote the message on the back of the mirror while she was standing up in front of it apparently making up her face. No one caught her at that time. But as they left the room something caused them to realize she'd left a message in lipstick. They were afraid I'd find it. So they went back and baited a trap, leaving such an obvious message that even a blind man couldn't fail to see it."

"Then you think this one is the original message, and that it's genuine?" Drake asked, indicating the lipstick on the back of the mirror.

Mason nodded. "And that the one on the bottom of the table is a trap."

Drake said, "It looks very much like the license number of an automobile, all right."

"How long will it take you to trace that license number?" Mason asked.

"Let me get to the phone," Drake told him. "It shouldn't take more than a few minutes."

"Wait a minute," Mason said, "not from here, Paul."

"No?"

"No. The only person on duty downstairs is that night clerk. I have an idea that he's pretty much interested about what's going on. If he listens in while you're tracing that car he might get a good idea of where we're going after we leave here. And no one is keeping an eye on the girl who was in here. . . . How long will it take to round up some men and put a tail on that girl in 815, Paul?"

"Not *too* long."

Mason said, "Hang it, Paul, I think this is a case for the police. I think we're getting beyond our depth."

"Do you want to give the police a ring?"

"Not right like that," Mason said, "but I would like to have a little police action if we can figure out just the right way to get it—and how to control it once we got it. . . . And there's still something screwy about this thing."

"How do you mean?"

"That license number on the back of the mirror," Mason said.

"What about it?"

"Who left it there?"

"Probably the real Dixie Dayton," Drake said. "She was

100

here with Morris Alburg. They were waiting for you. Somebody had them spotted. They left the door unlocked so you could walk in without making any commotion.''

"That part of it checks," Mason said. "I'll ride along with you that far, but keep talking, Paul. What happened after that?"

"Someone who knew where they were, someone who didn't want them to get in touch with you just opened the door and walked in. And when he walked in he had a gun in his hand.''

"So then what?"

"So then he told them they were going to have to take a ride, and probably Dixie Dayton said, 'All right, boys, let me make up my face first,' and walked over to the mirror and took her lipstick and started putting on a little lipstick and smearing it around with the tip of her little finger. While she was doing that she kept watch in the mirror to see what was going on.

"Alburg may have acted a little rusty, or perhaps they thought he was going to act rusty, so they moved in on him, and Dixie immediately stepped up to the mirror, moved it out an inch from the wall and marked down the license number of the automobile.''

"What automobile?" Mason asked.

"One that would give us a clue as to where they were being taken.''

"You mean she'd know the license number of the car that was waiting?''

Drake frowned. "No, I guess that's out.''

"And then they were forced to accompany the people who had entered the room?'' Mason asked.

"Sure.''

"Down the elevator, across the lobby, out into the night?''

Drake suddenly became thoughtful.

"Sounds like one of those things they do in motion pictures,'' Mason said.

"Well, it *could* have been done," Drake said. "Damn it, Perry, it *has* been done."

"And this car number?" Mason asked.

"That stumps me," Drake admitted.

Suddenly Mason snapped his fingers.

"What?" Drake asked.

"We're looking for an automobile," Mason said. "This may be the license number of the automobile that was driven by the potential kidnapper, the automobile that has the bullet hole in the right front door."

"Could be," Drake said, frowning in thoughtful concentration.

Mason said, "This gives us two messages, Paul. One of them could be a genuine message left by Morris Alburg's woman companion, whoever she was, and the other one a fake message left by other persons. Now the fake message points directly to George Fayette. What would that indicate?"

Drake said, "I'm inclined to play along with this Herbert Sidney Granton from the telephone directory. It won't do any harm to go out there."

"I'm afraid it will, Paul."

"Why?"

Mason said, "We're working against time. Someone wants to send us on a wild-goose chase. The thing I can't understand is why the wild-goose chase should lead to Fayette, who is one of the conspirators, unless for some reason they have decided that they don't want Fayette any more. Perhaps they're going to sacrifice Fayette. But if so . . . Hang it, it doesn't make sense, Paul."

"They're not going to sacrifice him because in that event Fayette would talk," Drake said.

"Unless," Mason said suddenly, "he'd be in a position where he couldn't talk. . . . Paul, let's find out more about what's in room 815. Let's . . ."

The door of the room opened abruptly. Lieutenant Tragg of Homicide Squad, accompanied by another officer whom

Mason didn't know, stood on the threshold and said, "What the hell do *you* know about room 815?"

"Well," Mason said, "we're honored by unexpected visitors, Paul. What brings you here at this hour in the morning, Lieutenant?"

"Line of duty," Lieutenant Tragg said. "What about 815?"

"Oh," Mason said, "we were talking about getting a little sleep and leaving a call for eight-fifteen."

Tragg's face darkened. "Mason, you keep on with this kind of stuff and you'll be where you won't need to leave a call. You'll get up at six-thirty in the morning, have coffee and mush pushed through the bars and like it. Have you ever met Sergeant Jaffrey?"

Mason acknowledged the introduction. "I thought I knew most of the boys on Homicide," he said.

"He isn't on Homicide," Drake said in a low voice. "I know him, Perry. He's on the Vice Squad."

Jaffrey nodded curtly to Drake.

Lieutenant Tragg said, "Sergeant Jaffrey is in charge of the Vice Detail. Bob Claremont was working under him when he was killed and this whole damn thing is tied in with Claremont's murder. Mason, you're in bad. Now what the hell did you have to do with room 815? Let's have a straight answer, because this time the chips are on our side of the board."

"Frankly," Mason said, "I wanted Paul Drake to shadow the occupant of room 815 because I wanted some more information about her."

"About *her*?"

Mason nodded.

Tragg said, "What are you doing here?"

"I came to meet a client."

"Listen, Mason, I'm going to lay it on the line with you. We know all about . . ."

"I wouldn't do that, Lieutenant," Sergeant Jaffrey interrupted. "Let *him* answer questions."

103

Tragg brushed the interruption to one side, said, "I'm going to give you a fair deal, Mason, with the cards on the table and not try to trap you. This hotel is a dump. Usually anything that goes on here doesn't attract any attention, but the occupant of 813 heard the sound of an argument, and what he thought was a muffled shot. He called the police."

"How long ago?" Mason asked.

"Not very long ago," Tragg said. "We just got here. A radio car showed up within two minutes of the time the telephone call came in. They found the door of 815 unlocked, a body on the bed, and notified Homicide Squad. I happened to be working with Sergeant Jaffrey on another angle of the case and we made time getting here.

"The dead man on the bed in room 815 is a rather chunky chap, with dark complexion and exceedingly bushy black eyebrows that almost meet at the bridge of the nose. The driving license in his pocket says his name is Herbert Sidney Granton, and he resides at 1024 Colinda Avenue. I put my men in charge and started giving the clerk the works. He's one of these fellows with a photographic memory for faces. I asked him if anything unusual was going on in the hotel, and he said that Perry Mason was here, that he thought Mason had gone to room 721, that he'd been joined by a private detective, and that a woman had registered whom he took to be an operative of some sort. Now then, what the hell's going on here?"

Mason glanced at Paul Drake. "Our investigations lead us to believe that Sidney Granton is an alias of George Fayette, and that George Fayette may have had something to do with the attempt to kidnap and kill Dixie Dayton. Aside from that, I can't tell you a thing."

"Aside from that," Tragg said grimly, "you don't have to. If you want to play it the hard way, that's the way we'll play. You'll not be permitted to leave the hotel. Go on down in the lobby and wait until I get ready to question you."

"You mean you're holding us as material witnesses?" Mason asked.

104

Sergeant Jaffrey, a heavy-shouldered individual, moved a belligerent step forward. "Not as witnesses, but as suspects in the murder of Herbert Sidney Granton," he said. "Now get the hell out of here."

Chapter 8

The lobby of the Keymont Hotel was a scene of activity. Newspaper reporters and photographers came in and snapped flashlight photographs, entered the elevator and rattled up to the upper floors.

A uniformed police officer sat behind the desk. By police orders, no unusual number of automobiles were permitted on the outside. From the street, the Keymont Hotel seemed to present the perfectly normal appearance of a second-rate hotel. It was that dead hour of the night which occurs well before the first streaks of daylight silhouette the city's buildings against a pale skyline. It was too early for the morning traffic, too late for even the last of the revelers. A few venturesome cab drivers, cruising dispiritedly because there was nothing else to do, would occasionally crawl along the all but deserted street. The city-wise eyes of the drivers noticed an unusual bustle about the lobby of the hotel. There would be a brief slackening of pace, then the cab would cruise on. The Keymont Hotel was the Keymont Hotel—just one of those things.

The elaborate police trap had so far been unproductive. No one except police and the newspapermen had entered the hotel. No one had tried to leave.

The night clerk, held in police custody, seated across the lobby from Mason and Paul Drake, glanced from time to time across at the lawyer and private detective. His face held no more expression than a good poker player shows when he picks up his hand.

Newspaper reporters, trying to interview Mason, received merely a shake of the head.

106

"Why not?" one of them asked.

"I'm co-operating with the police," Mason said. "They want me to tell my story to them and to no one else."

"That's okay. We'll get it from the police."

"That's the way to get it."

"You talked with them already?"

"Some."

"That isn't the way they feel about it."

"I can't help how the police feel."

"Suppose you tell us just what you've told them, and . . ."

Mason smiled, shook his head.

The newspaperman pointed his finger at Paul Drake.

"No comment," Drake said.

"Hell, you're co-operative."

"I have to be," Drake said.

The switchboard buzzed into noise.

The uniformed officer behind the desk plugged a line in, said, "Hello. . . . Okay, Lieutenant."

He pulled the line out of the plug, nodded to one of the plain-clothes men in the lobby and exchanged a few words of low-voiced conversation.

The plain-clothes man came over to where Mason and Drake were seated, said, "Okay, boys. The lieutenant will see you now. This way."

He led the way past the elevator to the stairs, up a flight of stairs, down a corridor, past a uniformed officer on guard, and opened the door to what was evidently the most pretentious suite of rooms in the house.

Lieutenant Tragg, smoking a cigar, lounged in a comfortable chair at the far end of the room. Slightly to one side, Sergeant Jaffrey was seated in an overstuffed chair smoking a cigarette. On the other side of Lieutenant Tragg, at a table on which a piano light shed illumination, a police shorthand reporter had his notebook in front of him and held a fountain pen poised over the pages.

Mason gave the book a quick glance as he entered the

room, and noticed that perhaps twelve or fifteen pages had already been covered with shorthand notes.

"Come on in and sit down," Tragg invited. "Sorry I had to keep you boys tied up, but that's the way things are."

Drake and Mason found chairs.

"Now then," Tragg said, "let's have the story."

Mason said, "A client telephoned me and asked me to meet him in 721. He told me to walk in without knocking. I went up to 721 and entered the room."

"Anybody there?" Tragg asked.

"No one."

Tragg said, "Shortly afterwards you telephoned Paul Drake. The switchboard records show that a call was put through from room 721 to Drake's office."

"That's right."

Tragg turned to Drake. "And what did *you* do, Drake?"

"I followed Mason's instructions."

Tragg said evenly and suavely, "Mason cuts a lot of corners, Paul. He's very skillful, very adroit, and he knows every comma and semicolon in the law. He hasn't been disbarred.

"He drags you along with him. You don't know periods and semicolons in the law. You have a license as a private detective. You can lose that license pretty damned easy. Now then, let's hear you talk."

Drake glanced apprehensively at Mason, looking for some sign. Mason's face was completely devoid of expression.

Sergeant Jaffrey said, "Now, I'm going to tell you guys something. This case is tied up with the killing of Bob Claremont. Bob was one nice boy. However, that's neither here not there. Bob Claremont was a cop. He was killed by a bunch of penny-ante slickers who thought they had the town sewed up, and Bob was on the trail of something big. You can't tell me that he just got bumped off because he was going to pinch some guy for being a bookie. Now, you guys may think you draw a lot of water, but that isn't going to cut any ice with me. I don't give a damn who you are. I'll take you

108

down to headquarters and work you over if I have to. I want to hear some conversation out of you birds, and I want the answers to be the right answers.''

Lieutenant Tragg, with a warning motion to Jaffrey and a glance at the shorthand reporter, said hastily, ''Understand, we aren't making any threats, but we feel that you gentlemen owe us a voluntary statement. We want it to be truthful. We want it to be accurate. We want it to be complete. And I warn you that if you start holding out on us we are in a position to crack down on you. Now tell us what happened.''

Mason said, ''A client telephoned me to come to that room.''

''Who was the client?''

''I can't tell you.''

''What happened?''

''Someone came to the room.''

''The client?''

''Not the one who telephoned me, no.''

''And then what happened?''

''The person who was in the room left for a few minutes. I wanted Paul Drake to get on the job and shadow this woman. I telephoned him. That's just about all I know.''

Sergeant Jaffrey got up out of his chair.

''Just a minute, Sergeant,'' Tragg said hastily, and this time unmistakably motioned toward the shorthand reporter. ''Let's interview Paul Drake. He doesn't have the professional immunity and privileges that a lawyer does, and I think under the circumstances he's going to be more co-operative—a lot more co-operative.''

Lieutenant Tragg turned to Paul Drake. ''All right, Drake, this is a murder case. We have every reason to believe that you have evidence dealing with the homicide. I'm not trying to pry into your private relationship with Perry Mason, but I want your story of everything that happened that can have any possible bearing on that homicide. Now get started.''

Drake coughed nervously, shifted his position.

''And we don't want any run-around,'' Sergeant Jaffrey

said. "Not from you. This is a show-down. Whether you go on making a living out of running a detective agency, or whether you're all done and buttoned up, is going to be determined within the next few minutes right here in this room, so start talking."

"Perry," Paul Drake said in an agonized voice, "I've got to tell what I know that's evidence."

Mason said absolutely nothing.

"And we don't have all night," Sergeant Jaffrey said.

"You kept us waiting more than an hour," Mason reminded them.

"That'll be all out of you," Sergeant Jaffrey said. "We kept you waiting because we were getting some evidence, and don't kid yourself we haven't got it. We can check up on you boys. This is one chance we have to find out which side of the fence you're on. Start talking, Drake."

Drake said, "I was at home asleep. The telephone rang. Mason wanted me to find out who was in room 721 with him."

"Man or woman?"

"A woman."

"Did he mention a name?"

"If he did, I can't remember. I was rather sleepy at the time. He said this woman had been in the room and had gone out and was going to come back. He wanted me to tail her and find out who she was."

"All right, you're doing better," Jaffrey said, assuming an attitude that was slightly less belligerent. "Let's hear the rest of it."

"I only had a few minutes in which to work," Drake said. "I knew that I would have to have someone on the outside of the hotel and also someone who could put a finger on this woman when she came out of 721. I felt certain that it would be impossible to have one person do both jobs. She'd be suspicious of anyone she happened to meet in the corridor when she emerged from 721, doubly suspicious of anyone

110

who might happen to ride down in the elevator with her at that hour in the morning.''

Tragg nodded.

Drake said, "It was an emergency. You may know how Perry Mason is when he's working on a case. He wants everything, and he wants it fast. He's an important client. He accounts for a good percentage of my business. I cater to him.''

"Never mind that. What did you *do*?'' Tragg asked.

"I telephoned my office to find out if anyone was immediately available. No one was. I have a switchboard operator who seems to be very competent.''

"Her name?'' Sergeant Jaffrey asked.

"Minerva Hamlin.''

"Go ahead.''

"I telephoned Minerva to close up the office temporarily, to look in the lockers where we keep occupational disguises, to take a maid's cap and apron, put them in a suitcase, dash to the Keymont Hotel, register and tell the clerk she had to have a room that was on the front of the hotel.''

"Why the front of the hotel?'' Tragg asked.

"So she could signal me,'' Drake said. "She was to put on the maid's uniform and hang around in the corridor so she could see who came out of 721. When the girl started down in the elevator Minerva was to run to her room and signal me with a flashlight. I was parked in front with a car. At that hour of the night there wouldn't be much chance of slipping up. If I knew when the woman was taking the elevator down, I'd be in a position to watch her as she crossed the lobby and follow her as she went out. . . . I parked my car where I could see into the lobby and see the elevator. I had my outside rear-view mirror adjusted so that I could pick up a signal made with a flashlight from a front room.''

"Damn good work,'' Jaffrey admitted grudgingly.

"What happened?'' Tragg asked.

"I stopped by the office and picked up Minerva Hamlin. We made it up here in record time. I parked my car, adjusted

111

the rear-view mirror so I could pick up any flashlight signals, sat and waited. Minerva went into the hotel, told the clerk she needed a front room, registered, and was shown to her room. Of course, she immediately put on the maid's disguise and walked over to where she could see 721."

"Then what?"

"Then nothing happened," Drake said, "until I saw Minerva herself emerging from the elevator. She seemed rather upset about something."

"Go ahead," Tragg said.

"She crossed the lobby and came out to report directly to me. That was something she shouldn't have done. However, we'd been in pretty much of a hurry and we hadn't had a chance to agree on signals that would cover unexpected developments. She thought I should know what had happened, and she had to tell me. There was no other way to relay the information."

"All right, what had happened?"

Drake related Minerva's actions up to the point where the girl she was shadowing went into room 815.

"Then what?" Tragg asked.

"Then Minerva waited awhile, realized that Mason would be getting nervous, that I might want to change my entire plan of operations, so she dashed down and across the lobby, and out to where I had parked my car."

"What did you do?"

"I went up and reported to Perry Mason."

"What did Minerva do?"

"She went back to the office," Drake said.

"She didn't shadow room 815?"

Drake shook his head. "Remember, I had parked my car where I could see the elevator. That meant the night clerk saw the whole business. When Minerva came running out to report to me he knew that I was waiting there to shadow somebody. I felt that Minerva's usefulness was finished. She couldn't drive the car and shadow the girl. That was in my department. I felt pretty certain the woman would stay in room 815, at least until I had time to get some instructions from Mason. . . . In the meantime, we'd called a couple of operatives, who were presumably on their way to the office. I told Minerva to send them down and have them report to me as soon as they arrived. . . . Now then, gentlemen, that's my story."

"That's a hell of a story," Jaffrey said.

"It's the truth," Drake told him hotly.

"Is it the *whole* truth?" Tragg asked.

"It's the truth so far as it relates to room 815."

"We're interested in finding out something about this woman."

"Of course, I never did see her," Drake said.

Jaffrey got up from his chair, looked meaningly at Tragg and left the room.

Tragg said, "Well, when you joined Perry Mason in room 721 did you find anything that was significant?"

Drake glanced once more at Mason. There was an agonized question in his eyes.

Mason said suavely, "I assume that you have made a thorough search of the room, Lieutenant?"

"I'm asking questions of Paul Drake," Tragg said.

Mason shrugged his shoulders. "Tell him anything that he wants to know, Paul. That is," he added hastily, "anything that you found or discovered."

"You mean anything that I found?" Drake asked.

Tragg nodded.

"That's one thing," Drake said, "but how about conversations?"

"We want all conversations," Tragg said.

"No conversations," Mason supplemented.

"I think we're entitled to them," Tragg said.

"Why?"

"We want to check on whether Drake is telling the truth."

Mason's eyes narrowed thoughtfully for a moment, then he said suddenly, "When I entered that room, Lieutenant, I noticed an imprint on the bed which looked as though some-

113

one had been sitting there. There was another imprint on the bed. It looked as though a gun had been put down on the bedspread.''

"I know," Tragg said.

"And," Mason said, watching him shrewdly, "I found something else. A tube of lipstick."

"Where is it?"

Mason reached in his pocket, took out the lipstick and handed it over to Lieutenant Tragg.

"You've messed this all up now," Tragg said, "so there aren't any fingerprints on it."

Mason said, "That certainly was careless of me."

"Damned if it wasn't!" Tragg flared angrily.

"Of course," Mason went on, "if the Homicide Department had telephoned me and said, 'Look here, Mason, we're not ready to announce it right at the moment, but in about fifteen minutes there'll be a murder committed in room 815, and the young woman who's talking with you at the moment is going to room 815'—then, of course, I would have taken steps to preserve fingerprints. . . .''

"We don't want any sarcasm," Tragg said, "we want facts."

"That's what you're getting."

"What about the lipstick?" Tragg asked.

Mason, watching Tragg's face for expression as a hawk might watch the entrance to a rabbit warren, said, "You'll notice the end of that lipstick looks as though it had been rubbed across some relatively rough surface, rather than merely used to decorate some woman's mouth."

"And what do you deduce from that?"

Mason, his eyes gimlets of watchful inquiry, said, "I thought someone might have used the lipstick to write a message."

"And what did you find?"

"We found a message," Mason said.

"Where was the message?"

"It was on the underside of the table."

114

"That was all?" Tragg asked.

"What do you mean, that was all?"

"You only found one message?"

Mason said, "I was trying merely to explain things to save Paul Drake embarrassment."

"Don't save anybody embarrassment," Tragg said. "Did you find more than one message?"

Mason remained silent.

Tragg whirled to Drake. "Did you find more than one message?"

Drake glanced at Mason.

The lawyer nodded.

"Yes," Drake said.

"Where was the other one?" Tragg asked.

"On the back of the mirror."

"What were those messages?"

"I can't remember them verbatim," Drake said. "They're still there."

"Did you try to decipher them? The one on the underside of the table, did you feel that it was a code, and did you crack the code?"

"Sure," Mason said. "It wasn't much of a code. It related to the room's telephone directory, volume three, page two-sixty-two, line fifteen of the left-hand column. That was the listing of Herbert Sidney Granton."

The door of the room opened. Sergeant Jaffrey returned, nodded to Lieutenant Tragg.

"And the other message?" Tragg asked.

"On the back of the mirror," Drake said. "We didn't decipher it. We thought it might be the license number of an automobile. We were about to look it up when you gentlemen came in."

"Now was there something that made you feel one of those messages was a decoy?" Tragg asked Paul Drake.

Drake said, "I think Mason and I had some discussion about the messages, and whether they were both—well, what—well, how they happened to be written."

"What was the discussion?"

"Gosh, I can't remember all of it."

"Remember some of it then."

"I'll interpose a question," Sergeant Jaffrey said. "Did Mason tell you the name of the client who telephoned him and told him to be there in that room?"

Drake shifted his position.

"I want an answer, yes or no," Jaffrey said.

Drake hesitated, then said, "I believe he did."

"Who was it?"

"I don't think I have to tell that," Drake said.

Jaffrey glanced at Tragg. "Yes or no?"

"Yes."

"Who was it?"

"I don't think I have to tell you."

Tragg's face held no expression, but there was a swift glitter of triumph on the face of Sergeant Jaffrey.

Abruptly Mason said, "Go ahead and tell him, Paul. Give him the names of the clients, tell him everything that happened in that room."

Drake looked at him in surprise.

"Don't you get it?" Mason said. "They're trying to trap you so they can take your license away from you. They were outside of that door during all of our conversation, or else there was a bug in the room, and they have the whole damn thing. All they're trying to do now is lay a trap so that they can get your license."

Sergeant Jaffrey came up out of the chair with a bound. He walked over to Mason and grabbed hold of the lapels of his coat, jerking the lawyer up out of the chair. His beefy shoulders were packed with power. One big, hamlike hand locked itself in the folded layers of the lawyer's coat and the other was drawn back for a punch.

Tragg came up out of his chair hastily. "Hold it, Sergeant, hold it," he said sharply, and then added, "A shorthand reporter is taking down all of this conversation." Then he went on smoothly, "The shorthand reporter, of course, is not trying to take down the motions of everyone in this room or describe what is happening every time anyone gets up out of a chair."

He glanced quickly at the shorthand reporter to see that the man appreciated the hint he was dropping.

Slowly Sergeant Jaffrey released his grip on Mason's coat.

Mason straightened out the lapels of his coat and said, "I think Sergeant Jaffrey lost his temper, Paul. You can see that he grabbed me and messed up my coat and necktie and was on the point of hitting me when . . ."

"That's merely Mr. Mason's conclusion," Jaffrey said smugly. "I did no such thing. I merely put my hand on his shoulder."

Lieutenant Tragg said wearily, "I told you, Sergeant, that we'd do better if we interrogated these men separately. I think we'd better do it now."

"All right, wise guy," Sergeant Jaffrey said to Mason, "now go on back down to the lobby and wait."

"And I take it," Mason said, "that while Sergeant Jaffrey was gone from the room, he sent an officer up to Drake's office to bring Minerva Hamlin up here."

"Out, wise guy," Jaffrey said, holding the door open, "and if you don't get out fast this once I really can *'lay my hand on your shoulder'* and the shorthand record will show I was amply justified."

"I'm leaving at once, Sergeant," Mason said, smiling, "and I'd advise you to answer all questions about everything that took place in that room, Paul."

With which Mason bowed himself out of the room.

He had barely crossed the threshold when the door slammed with such force that it threatened to dislodge the plaster.

The uniformed officer waiting outside the door said to Mason, "Back to the lobby, Mr. Mason."

Chapter 9

Mason took the elevator to the lobby and started for the street door.

A uniformed officer barred his way.

"I've been interrogated and discharged," Mason said.

"No one's told *me* you're discharged," the officer said.

"I've told them all I know. I've been interrogated by both Lieutenant Tragg and Sergeant Jaffrey. What more do you want? I have work to do."

"Perhaps they'll want to interrogate you again."

"They didn't say so."

"They didn't say anything about letting you go. Not to me."

"They kicked me out."

"Then wait in the lobby."

Mason went back to the desk. The clerk had been displaced by a plain-clothes man who seemed affable but who evidenced no desire to assist Mason in his predicament. "Plenty of chairs over there, Counselor," he said. "The morning newspaper has come in, in case you care to read."

"Thank you," Mason said. "Any restrictions on telephoning?"

"Not so far as I know."

Mason located a lone telephone booth, crossed over to it, dropped a coin and dialed the number of Della Street's apartment.

He could hear the phone ringing repeatedly, and then Della Street's voice, thick with sleep, saying, "Hello, yes— Who is it, please?"

"Wake up, Della," Mason told her. "The fat's in the fire."

118

"Oh, it's you, Chief!"

"That's right. Is the phone by the side of your bed?"

"Yes."

"Then jump out of bed," Mason told her. "Go splash cold water on your face, then get back to the telephone. I want you wide-awake for this and can't take chances on you going back to sleep. They may cut me off any minute."

"Just a second," she said.

Over the telephone Mason could hear the thud of her feet on the floor. A moment later she was back, saying, "Wide-awake, Chief. What is it?"

Mason said, "I'm at the Keymont Hotel. Morris Alburg called me and asked me to join him in room 721. He failed to meet me there. Someone else did."

"Man or woman?" she asked.

"Woman."

"Was it . . ."

"Careful," Mason warned. "No names. Just keep listening, Della."

"All right, go ahead."

Mason said, "You remember that first night we were talking with Morris Alburg he mentioned that he had at one time employed a detective agency instead of a lawyer."

"Yes, it seems to me— Yes, I remember. Why, is that important?"

Mason said, "We have the residence number of the cashier at Alburg's restaurant. Evidently she knows something about his business affairs, and he trusts her.

"Get your clothes on, Della, call a taxi, start working the telephone. Get Morris Alburg's cashier to tell you the name of the detective agency Morris employed. In case she doesn't know it, get her to meet you in Alburg's restaurant. Have her open the office safe, get at his books. Then take the classified telephone directory and get the names of all the licensed private detectives in the city. Then start checking back on Alburg's books. You'll probably find a check record listed alphabetically, or else you may find it listed some other way—

I don't know just how he keeps his books. . . . Are you following me?"

"Right abreast with you."

"Get his books," Mason said, "and start checking any remittances which he may have made against the list of the private detectives."

"Okay. Suppose we find one. Then what do we do?"

"Wait for me," Mason said. "I'll be there as soon as I can get there."

"You just want that information. You don't want us to get in touch with the agency?"

"It isn't a woman's job," Mason said. "It's going to be a tough, hard-boiled, dog-eat-dog proposition. . . . In case the phone rings at Alburg's place, answer it. I may call you."

"I'm getting started right now," she said, her voice crisp and alert.

"Good girl," Mason told her.

He hung up the telephone, went back to a chair in the lobby, read the newspaper for a while, then strolled over to chat with the plain-clothes man at the desk.

"I guess it's all right to let you send out uncensored telephone calls," the man said, his voice showing anxious speculation. "Nobody told me it wasn't all right, and nobody told me it was."

"Oh, sure," Mason said, "no one would want to interfere with my business. After all, a citizen has *some* rights."

The plain-clothes man grinned, then suddenly looked up at the door.

Mason followed the direction of his eyes and saw an efficient, trim-looking young woman, clad in a somewhat mannishly tailored outfit, leaving an automobile and being escorted into the hotel by a uniformed officer.

Mason waited until they were halfway across the lobby, then stepped forward with a smile, said, "Minerva Hamlin, I believe."

Her eyes lit up. "Oh, yes," she said. "You must be Mr. Mason. I'm . . ."

The uniformed officer stepped in between them and said, "Nix on it. No talking. No conversation."

"Good Lord," Mason protested, "what kind of an inquisition is this?"

"You heard me," the officer said. "No conversation."

He took Minerva Hamlin's arm and hurried her toward the elevator.

The plain-clothes man behind the desk stepped out into the lobby and said, "Sorry, Mr. Mason, but you aren't supposed to talk with witnesses yet."

"Good Lord," Mason said, "she's one of Paul Drake's assistants. I employed her. I'm paying the bill for her time right now."

"I know, but orders are orders. We're working on a murder case."

"Can you tell me why all this air of mystery? What all this elaborate trap is about? Why people are being held here and not permitted to leave the hotel?" Mason demanded indignantly.

The plain-clothes officer grinned a slow, friendly grin, and said, "Hell, no," and then added, "and you're a good enough lawyer to know that, too. Go on back and sit down."

Mason watched the elevator indicator swing slowly around until it came to the second floor and then stop.

"The officers must have taken over the bridal suite for their interrogations," Mason said.

The plain-clothes man laughed. "A bridal suite in a dump like this," he said.

"Isn't that what it is?" Mason asked.

"Hell, they're *all* bridal suites."

"Had much trouble with the place?"

"Ask Sergeant Jaffrey the next time you see him. He's on the Vice Squad. He knows the place like a book."

"Any homicides?" Mason asked.

"It isn't that kind of a joint. Just a dump. It . . ."

A light flashed on on the switchboard, and the plain-clothes man put the headset over his head, said, "Yes, what is it? . . . Right now? . . . Okay, I'll send him up."

He turned to Mason and said, "They want you upstairs, same room. You know, the 'bridal suite.' "

"Okay," Mason said.

"Can I trust you to go up by yourself without doing any exploring, or shall I delegate an officer to . . ."

"I'll go right up," Mason said.

"All right, you know where it is."

"Sure," Mason said.

"On your way. They're waiting."

Mason pressed the button on the elevator. When the cage came back to the ground floor, he got in, closed the door, pressed the button for the second floor, stepped out of the elevator, and the uniformed office in the corridor jerked his thumb toward the suite. "They're waiting for you, Mr. Mason."

Mason nodded, entered the suite, noticing as he did so that the notebook of the shorthand reporter had now been half-filled with notes, indicating that the somewhat dejected-looking Paul Drake, who seemed as wilted as a warm lettuce leaf, had been submitted to a searching interrogation.

Drake gestured toward the young woman, said, "This is my night switchboard operator, Perry, Minerva Hamlin."

"How do you do, Mr. Mason," she said, with the close-clipped accents of a young woman who prides herself on her business efficiency.

Mason said, "Tragg, I've told you that I was responsible for Miss Hamlin being sent down here. I wanted to find out the identity of the person who was in room 721 with me."

"We know all about that," Sergeant Jaffrey said.

Lieutenant Tragg produced a photograph. "Now, Miss Hamlin," he said, "we're going to ask you a question. It's a very important question both to you and to your employer. I want you to be very careful how you answer it."

"Why, yes, of course," she said. "I'm always careful."

"I may as well tell you," Lieutenant Tragg said, "that a

122

murder has been committed in this hotel. We are investigating that murder and certain things indicate that we're working against time. I don't want to threaten you, but I do want to warn you that any attempt to stall us or to delay matters may make quite a difference. I think you are aware of the penalties for suppressing evidence."

She nodded, a swift decisive nod of affirmation.

"Now wait a minute," Sergeant Jaffrey said, "let's do this thing right, Tragg."

"How do you mean?"

"We're going to have an identification of a photograph. This girl may be all right. She may not. I can tell you a lot of things about this dump. I've been in it a hundred times. They've pulled everything here from call girls on up, or down, whichever way you want to look at it. Now, Frank Hoxie, the night clerk, has one gift. He never forgets a face. You can show him a photograph and if he's ever seen the face he'll remember it—even if it's after weeks, and even if it's someone who just casually walked across the hotel lobby."

"Okay," Tragg said, "let's get him in, but we can ask Miss Hamlin . . ."

Jaffrey said with a significant jerk of his head, "Let's get Hoxie up here *first*. Show him the picture. Let's find out definitely who this dame really is."

Lieutenant Tragg hesitated a moment, then picked up the telephone and said to the plain-clothes man who was at the switchboard, "Send up Frank Hoxie, the night clerk. . . . That's right. Send him up here right away."

He hung up.

Jaffrey said, to no one in particular, "Of course, in a way you can't blame the place. It's a run-down dump and no one is going to put up money to bring it back into shape, not with this location, not with the reputation the place has, and not with the price that hotel furnishings are selling for these days. They tell me they try to do the best they can, and I'm inclined to believe them, but once a place gets this reputation, a certain class of trade gravitates toward it and there's nothing much you can do about it."

Tragg nodded.

Mason said casually, "That picture, is it anyone I know?"

"We don't know," Jaffrey said.

"Perhaps I could tell you."

"You haven't told us who the woman was who was in the room with you yet," Jaffrey said.

"I don't know," Mason said.

"She told you she was Dixie Dayton, didn't she?"

Mason started to say something, then changed his mind and remained silent.

"We'll get around to you in a minute," Jaffrey said. "We have an ace or two up our sleeve on this deal. . . . Don't think this is just an ordinary murder case, Mason. This is going back to a cop killing. This Dixie Dayton is hot as a firecracker. She's tied up with Tom Sedgwick, who, from all we can tell, fired the shots that killed Claremont. Of course, we don't have anything to say about what cases a lawyer takes, but we sure as hell can put the heat on a private detective if we have to—and we had to."

"I think Lieutenant Tragg knows how I feel about this," Mason said. "I'm not sticking up for any cop killers."

"The hell you're not," Jaffrey grunted.

"But," Mason went on, "how do *you* know who's guilty? You haven't a confession, have you?"

"I know," Jaffrey said, "it's the old line of hooey. You lawyers always pull it. A person is presumed to be innocent until he's convicted. Every citizen is entitled to a jury trial and counsel to defend him. You wouldn't represent a guilty person. Oh, no, not you! The law presumes your clients innocent until you get done defending them, or until . . ."

There was a trace of irritation in Lieutenant Tragg's voice as he interrupted. "Let's try as far as possible to confine our conversation to the investigation, if you don't mind, Sergeant. You see, I want the shorthand reporter to be able to

124

state that he took down every word that was uttered in this room and I don't want to have too big a transcript."

"And don't want to have Sergeant Jaffrey cast as the villain of the piece," Mason said, grinning.

"Well," Tragg told him, "you know as well as I do, that if you can bait him into saying something he shouldn't, you'll subpoena the records and have a field day kicking him around the courtroom."

"You misjudge me," Mason said with elaborate politeness.

"Yeah!" Sergeant Jaffrey said sarcastically.

The uniformed officer opened the door. The slender, pale-faced night clerk, whom Mason had seen at the desk when he had first entered the hotel, came into the room and stood somewhat ill at ease in the presence of the officers.

Sergeant Jaffrey said, "Now, Frank, there's nothing to be afraid of here. This is something you personally aren't mixed up in. It isn't like a raid by the Vice Squad. This is Homicide, and we want your co-operation."

The clerk nodded.

"I want you to know you're going to get a square shake here," Jaffrey said. "I'm going to see that you do. No one's going to push you around. This is Lieutenant Tragg of Homicide, and he wants to ask you to identify a photograph. I told him that you had a photographic memory, that you never forgot a face, and darn seldom forgot a name."

There was a slight smile around Hoxie's lips. "I try to be efficient," he said, "and I think it's part of the duties of a hotel clerk to be able to call guests by their name—when they want to be called by name."

"I know," Jaffrey said, grinning. "All you have to do is remember the name of John Smith and you can greet nine people out of ten who register at this place . . ."

"You'll pardon me, Sergeant, but we're trying to run a clean place. Ever since that last time when—and that really wasn't our fault."

"Oh, I know, I was kidding," Sergeant Jaffrey said. "Let it go. Take a look at that picture, will you, Frank?"

Lieutenant Tragg extended the picture.

Hoxie took the photograph, studied it for a moment, then nodded his head.

"You've seen her?"

"She's the one who was registered in 815."

"Did you register her?" Tragg asked.

"No, a man registered her in. He said she was his sister-in-law who had come for a visit. Mrs. Madison Kerby was the name."

"But she's the one who was in 815?"

"She's the one. I remember giving her the key."

"There's no question?"

"None whatever."

Lieutenant Tragg's nod was suddenly triumphant. "Will you take a look at that photograph, Miss Hamlin," he said. "We think that's the woman all right, but we want your identification."

"Of course," Mason pointed out, "there are a lot of different ways of making an identification. This cumulative . . ."

"That'll do," Tragg said. "We don't want any comments from the audience, Mason. . . . Miss Hamlin, just look at that picture. I don't want you to be influenced one way or another by what anyone has said. I want you simply to tell us whether that's the woman you saw leave room 721, take a room key from her purse, and enter room 815."

Minerva Hamlin took the picture, studied it carefully, then frowned. "Of course," she said, "I . . ."

"Now, remember," Sergeant Jaffrey interposed, "that lots of times a photograph doesn't look too much like person until you study it carefully. Take a good long look at it. This is important. This is important to everybody. Don't say yes, right off the bat, and don't say no. We don't want you to say it's the woman unless it was, but we sure don't want you to boot the identification and do something you'll be sorry for."

"I think—I—I think it is."

"Take a good long look at it," Sergeant Jaffrey said. "Study that picture carefully."

"I have done so. I think this is the woman."

"That isn't the strongest way to make an identification," Lieutenant Tragg said. "Can't you do better than that?"

"I've told you that I thought it was the woman."

"You don't ordinarily make mistakes, do you? You look to me like a rather efficient young woman."

"I try not to make mistakes."

"And you're not vague in your thinking, are you?"

"I hope not."

"All right," Sergeant Jaffrey said, "never mind the thinking then. Is this the woman or isn't it?"

"I think—" She paused as she saw the grin on Sergeant Jaffrey's face.

"Go ahead," Lieutenant Tragg said.

"It's the woman," she said.

"Now, then," Mason said, "may I see that photograph? You know I had a better opportunity to look at the woman who was in room 721 than anyone else. Miss Hamlin, of necessity, had only a quick glimpse of her when she . . ."

"Who was the woman who was in 721 with you?" Lieutenant Tragg asked.

"I don't know," Mason said.

Sergeant Jaffrey said to Minerva Hamlin, "Write your name on the back of that photograph."

"And the date," Lieutenant Tragg said.

Minerva Hamlin did so, then Tragg passed the photograph over to Frank Hoxie. "Write your name on it."

Hoxie complied.

"And the date," Sergeant Jaffrey said.

Mason said, "If you'll let me look at it, Lieutenant, I'll . . ."

Sergeant Jaffrey stood up. "Look, Mason," he said, "you have a certain immunity as a lawyer. The law gives you a loophole. You can squirm out of giving us information. You can claim that things that were said to you were privileged communications from a client. We can't put pressure on you. Now, I'm going to ask you straight from the shoulder whether the woman who was in that room with you was Dixie Dayton, and whether she didn't tell you that Morris Alburg was going to kill George Fayette.''

Mason said, ''Permit me to point out two things, Sergeant. If the woman in that room was *not* Dixie Dayton, then anything she said wouldn't have the slightest evidentiary value against anyone. If she *was* Dixie Dayton, but wasn't acting in concert with Morris Alburg, nothing she said could be used against Morris Alburg. And if this person *was* Dixie Dayton and *was* my client, anything that she said to me concerning her case would be a confidential communication.''

''That's just what I thought,'' Jaffrey said. ''Let me see the picture, Lieutenant.''

Lieutenant Tragg handed him the picture.

Sergeant Jaffrey promptly thrust it into the inside pocket of his coat.

''I think that's all, Mason,'' he said. ''Drake, you've been yelling about having to go back to run your business. Go ahead. Mason, I guess we can dispense with any more assistance from you.''

''And do I get to see the photograph?'' Mason asked.

Jaffrey merely grinned.

''I'll tell you this much, Mason,'' Lieutenant Tragg said, ''this is an authentic photograph of Dixie Dayton, the girl who left town at the same time as Thomas E. Sedgwick, on the night that Bob Claremont was murdered.''

''Why give him information when he won't give us any?'' Jaffrey asked.

''I want to be fair with him,'' Lieutenant Tragg said.

Jaffrey snorted. ''Let him be fair with us first.''

Tragg turned to the shorthand reporter. ''You have my statement that this is an authenticated photograph of Dixie Dayton?''

The shorthand reporter nodded.

"I think that's all," Tragg said. "This time, Mason, you can leave the hotel."

"Can I take one more look in room 721?" Mason asked.

Lieutenant Tragg merely smiled.

Sergeant Jaffrey gave a verbal answer. "Hell, no," he said.

Tragg said, "Come to think of it, Sergeant, it might be better to hold Mason and Paul Drake here until we've located that—that thing we were looking for."

Jaffrey nodded emphatically.

"You may go, Miss Hamlin," Lieutenant Tragg said. "Drake, you and Mason can wait in the lobby."

Sergeant Jaffrey flung the door open. "This way out," he said.

Mason waited in the hallway for Minerva Hamlin.

Abruptly Jaffrey stepped out and said to the uniformed officer who was guarding the corridor, "Here, take this girl down and put her in a taxicab. Send her back to her office. Don't let anyone talk with her."

"Look here," Drake said, "this is my employee. I have to give her some instructions about how to run the office until I can get back and . . ."

"Give them to me," Jaffrey said, "and I'll pass them on to her."

Chapter 10

Drake and Mason sat in the lobby, impatiently watching the hands of the clock. Daylight had started to filter through the big plate-glass windows of the lobby. A few early trucks rumbled past. A milk wagon went by.

"What the devil are they looking for?" Drake asked Mason.

Mason shrugged his shoulders. "I suppose they gave you the works, Paul."

"They gave me the works," Drake said, and then added fervently, "and how!"

"What did you tell them?"

"I followed your instructions. I didn't hold out on them."

"It's a cinch," Mason said, "that that room was wired for sound. As nearly as I can figure it out, Morris Alburg expected to get some witness in there. He wanted me to interrogate that witness and he wanted to have a record of what was said. I'm willing to bet money that the adjoining room, or some room nearby, had a complete recording outfit."

"I gathered that was what you had in mind," Drake said.

"Their questions were too apropos to be just groping in the dark," Mason told him. "Having a shorthand reporter there and asking us those specific questions, particularly bearing down on you the way they did, meant that they were loaded for bear and were trying to get your license. That's why I told you to tell them the whole thing.

"Well, they sure knew everything that went on in that room," Drake sad. "I'm satisfied you're right, Perry. I wasn't too certain at first, but after they asked me questions about the messages written in lipstick I knew that you were on the right track."

"The question is," Mason said, "how far back those records go, how much they know."

"I think there's a gap of some sort," Drake said. "They sure want to know what happened when you entered the room, just what was said. They kept trying to find out from me what I knew about that."

"What did you tell them?"

"All I knew, which wasn't much."

Mason said, "Look, Paul, there aren't too many authorized private detective agencies here in the city. Now, then, suppose you had a job and you wanted to have a tape or disc recording made, just whom would you get?"

Drake said, "We all of us have sound equipment, Perry. We have to be a little careful about how we use it, but we have tape recorders, microphones, and the best of the agencies have all the latest gadgets."

"What do you mean by that?"

"These machines that you can leave on a plant," Drake said, "without necessarily having to monitor them. The feed is automatic. There's a relay of acetate discs so that a fresh one comes on as soon as one has been filled up. There's a clockwork mechanism by which the machine automatically shuts itself off it there's silence in the room for a period of around ten seconds. Then as soon as any sound comes over the wires, the machine cuts in again. . . . Or, of course, you can set them for continuous recording. Often when we want to know what's going on in a room over a twenty-four-hour period we put the machine on its automatic adjustment. In that way the disc revolves only when people are talking."

"They work pretty well?"

"Pretty well," Drake said. "Of course, those are the latest gadgets, and conversations of that sort aren't much good as evidence because there's no way of telling how much time elapses between conversations, and there's no one to testify to the fact that conversation took place in the room where

131

the microphone was placed. Theoretically it would be possible for someone to get into the room where the recording mechanism was housed and fake the thing."

"I know," Mason said, "but it's a good way to check on . . . Oh-oh, here's Tragg. He looks tickled to death."

Lieutenant Tragg left the elevator, walked over toward Mason and Drake, said, "I'm sorry we had to inconvenience you fellows, but you know how it is. This is a murder case. . . . Everything's okay. You can go now."

"Thanks," Drake said and started for the door.

Mason held back. "Your friend Sergeant Jaffrey seems to be of the old school."

"If you had to contend with the things he has to fight, you'd be hard-boiled, too," Tragg said.

"Got the case all solved, Lieutenant?"

Tragg hesitated a moment, then said, "I'll tell you one thing, Mason—you'll read it in the papers anyway, so you may as well know it."

"Shoot."

"That number that was penciled in lipstick on the back of the mirror was the license number of George Fayette's automobile. It was registered under the name of Herbert Sidney Granton. That was his latest alias. And when we found that automobile, which we finally did, we found a nice bullet hole through the right front door. A bullet that had been fired from the inside. Seems safe to assume that was the car that was used in the attempted kidnaping and murder of Dixie Dayton."

"But Fayette wasn't driving it," Mason said.

"Fayette wasn't driving it," Tragg said. "We're having the car processed for fingerprints and before too very long we may know who *was* driving it."

Mason frowned thoughtfully.

"And personally I wouldn't blame Morris Alburg for beating George Fayette to the punch," Tragg said. "Actually it would have been self-defense. Fayette was dynamite. But Alburg is a red-hot target not because of Fayette, but because he's teamed up with Dixie Dayton, and until Dixie Dayton produces Tom Sedgwick we're going to raise merry hell with your clients, Mason. I thought you might as well know it.''

''You didn't think that was any secret, did you?'' Mason said, and headed toward the exit.

supposed to be playing ball with them, but even if she couldn't, she never ran to Jones-to do the statement that Alburg was going to the police, however.

"That ...... Oh ...... Oh ...... Oh ...... Oh, she ...... Oh ...... wouldn't ...... be ...... long ...... too ....

Chapter 11

Mason said to Drake, "Go on up to your office, Paul. Talk with that girl of yours and find out if she's really positive about her identification of that photograph."

Drake paused with one foot on the running board of his car. "You think she's made a wrong identification?"

"I'm damn near certain of it."

"She's pretty efficient, Perry."

"Look at it this way," Mason said. "That room was wired. There was a bug in it some place that we didn't find. That means it was done cleverly and was a professional job."

"Well?" Drake asked.

"Now, then, Morris Alburg wanted me to meet him in that room. . . . Either Morris wired the room or he didn't."

"Well, let's suppose he didn't," Drake said.

Mason shook his head. "Somehow that idea doesn't appeal to me, Paul. The facts are against that supposition."

"Why?"

"Morris wanted me to meet him in that room. He had something he wanted, some witness he wanted to interrogate, something that he wanted recorded. He wanted me to do the questioning. He was all hooked up for a big killing. Something happened to him."

"Well?"

"Figure it out," Mason told him. "Morris Alburg apparently is playing hand in glove with this Dixie Dayton. Now *if* that had been the real Dixie Dayton who was talking with me she would have been in touch with Morris Alburg and therefore would have known the room was wired.

"In that event she'd probably have told me, because I'm

134

supposed to be playing ball with them, but even if she hadn't, she never would have made the statement that Alburg was going to kill George Fayette."

"That sounds logical," Drake admitted.

"On the other hand," Mason said, "if something had happened to the real Dixie Dayton, if Morris Alburg was being detained somewhere against his will, and this woman was sent to stall me along, knowing that I had never met Dixie Dayton, and if she knew that George Fayette had been killed, or was about to be killed, and wanted to lay a perfect trap for my clients, she'd have said exactly what this woman said."

"Then you don't think the woman was Dixie Dayton?"

Mason shook his head.

"Sounds reasonable," Drake said. "I wish you could have got a look at that picture."

Mason said, "I can't help but feel that we're playing for big stakes, Paul. Fayette was just a tool. When Fayette bungled the job of getting Dixie Dayton rounded up he didn't do himself any good, and then when he made the mistake of coming to my office and trying to get information under the guise of being an insurance agent, and when he realized that the woman who had been trying to follow him the night before was my secretary, he put himself on a spot.

"In addition to that, the automobile that had been used in the kidnaping attempt was his own automobile, registered in his name. Someone had the license number. That made Fayette a cinch for police interrogation."

"You mean members of his own mob killed him?"

Mason said, "I can't picture Morris Alburg as getting in that hotel room and killing Fayette in cold blood."

"You never know what these chaps will do when they get crowded into a corner," Drake pointed out.

"I know," Mason told him, "but let's look at it this way, Paul. Suppose the thing was a beautiful trap. Suppose Alburg and Dixie Dayton were there in room 721 waiting for me,

135

and suppose someone came in and got the drop on them and took them out of the hotel."

"Sounds rather melodramatic," Drake said. "I told you before, it sounds like the movies."

"Well, there may have been more than one man," Mason said. "There may have been a couple, and you don't know that they walked across the lobby of the hotel."

"That's true, of course."

"But," Mason told him, "let's look at it from the standpoint of a case in court. Suppose some phony is in that room with me and tells me that Morris Alburg, who is working with her in a common cause, is out killing George Fayette so that Fayette won't kill him. She makes it sound rather reasonable. An attempted self-defense by first launching a counteroffensive."

"Well?" Drake asked.

"And," Mason said, "that conversation is recorded on acetate discs, and the police have those discs. Then your secretary and the hotel clerk identify the woman who was talking with me as Dixie Dayton. The corpse is found in her room. How much of a chance would that leave a defense attorney?"

Drake gave a low whistle. "I hadn't thought of it that way. You'd have about the same chance as the proverbial snowball."

"That's exactly it," Mason said. "Now, I don't believe that woman *was* Dixie Dayton, and I sure don't want to have your girl get off on the wrong track. Get up and talk with her, and then I'm coming up."

"You're not driving up with me?"

"You take your car and I'll take mine. I've got places to go and things to do. I want to locate the person who put in that sound equipment. I want to find out how much stuff the police have, and how much they don't have."

"The police will beat you to it," Drake said. "If that room was wired they'll find out who . . . ."

"They may and they may not," Mason told him. "We're

working against time and so are the police. Get up to your office, Paul, and I'll join you in a few minutes."

Drake nodded, jumped in his car and stepped on the starter.

Mason found his own car, drove down the street until he came to an all-night restaurant with a telephone booth, and stopped to call Morris Alburg's restaurant.

Della Street answered the phone.

"You on the job, Della?"

"Just got here," she said. "I have the cashier—it was a job getting her up out of bed and down here and . . ."

"You have the safe open?"

"Yes. She has no recollection of any detective agency, and Alburg didn't keep a check register. But we've found a mass of check stubs, and we're going through them, comparing them with names of the private detectives in the classified directory. It's a terrific job. Where can I reach you if we strike pay dirt?"

"Sit right there until I get there," Mason said, "unless, of course, you should get anything within the next few minutes. In that case call me at Paul Drake's office. I'll be there for a while, then I'll join you within fifteen or twenty minutes."

"All right. We'll keep plugging, Chief, but it's a terrific job. He paid for meats and groceries, paid help and personal bills, all from one checking account, and we have stacks of check stubs here."

"Stay with it," Mason said. "I'll be there to help as soon as I can tie up some loose ends. Be good."

" 'Bye now," she said, and hung up.

Mason drove to his office building, swung his car into the all but vacant parking lot and rang the bell for the elevator.

The night janitor said, "Good morning, Mr. Mason. You're certainly an early bird this morning."

"Not early, late. Has Paul Drake gone up?"

"About five or ten minutes ago."

"That's fine," Mason said. "Take me up."

"You must be working on something big," the janitor said hopefully.

"Could be," Mason told him, signing the register in the elevator.

When the elevator came to a stop, Mason stopped at the door of the Drake Detective Agency, pushed open the door of the reception room and saw Paul Drake standing, with a rather puzzled expression, looking down at Minerva Hamlin, who was sitting rigidly, her mouth an angry straight line.

Drake looked up and said, "Hello, Perry. I'm not doing so good."

"Is the purpose of your visit," Minerva Hamlin asked acidly, "to influence me in my testimony? Am I supposed to commit perjury as part of the routine duties of this office?"

"Wait a minute," Mason said. "Take it easy. No one wants you to commit perjury."

"Well, Mr. Drake seems to challenge my identification."

"Now, wait a minute," Mason said, "let's not get off on the wrong track. The identification of the woman who came out of room 721 may be a matter of the greatest importance."

"I'm not entirely dumb, Mr. Mason. I think I understand that."

Mason said, "That woman told me that she was Dixie Dayton."

"Well, she certainly should know who she is."

"But," Mason went on, "there were reasons why it might have been to the advantage of certain people to run in a ringer."

Minerva Hamlin sat in front of the switchboard, coldly erect and determinedly silent.

"Now, then," Mason went on, "you did a very good job. You stepped in on an emergency in a marvelous manner, and . . ."

"You may spare the flattery, Mr. Mason."

"I'm not flattering you. I'm telling you that you got on the job, and did a swell job, but the fact remains that you had to be masquerading as a maid in order to pick up the trail of the woman who came from room 721. You didn't dare to do anything that would make you look too conspicuous. Your whole plan of operation was to try to look inconspicuous."

"I will agree with you that far."

"So," Mason said, "you weren't in a position to stare at the woman who came out of the room."

"I didn't have to stare."

"You followed her down the corridor."

"That's right."

"You must have had only a momentary glimpse of her face."

"I saw her face."

"But it was necessarily a momentary glimpse."

"Mr. Mason, are you trying to make me out a fool or a liar, or both?"

"I'm simply pointing out certain obvious facts," Mason said. "Therefore it's difficult for you to make an identification of that face from a photograph. If you saw the person herself it might be different, but . . ."

"I am quite certain that the woman whose photograph I saw was the woman who left room 721. Moreover, she went directly to room 815 and took a key from her purse. You have heard the testimony of the night clerk, who is very positive that the woman is the one who rented room 815."

"That's just the point," Mason said. "They had you in a position where they brought a lot of subtle influence to bear on you. They had the clerk identify the photograph as being that of the woman who rented room 815. Therefore it was only natural that you'd assume . . ."

"I am not that easily influenced, Mr. Mason. I think I able to do my own thinking, and I think I am rather efficient in that thinking. May I say that I don't like this attempt to make me change my testimony?"

"Good Lord," Mason said with exasperation, "I'm not trying to make you change your testimony. I'm only trying to point out to you the importance of being certain, and the fact that it was exceedingly difficult for you to have had a good enough look at the face of that woman to make a positive identification."

"I am quite capable of making my own decisions, Mr. Mason. I am a very determined person, Mr. Mason."

"Damned if you aren't!" Mason said, and turned on his heel. "Come on, Paul, we're going places."

"Where?"

"I'll tell you when we get started."

Drake said, "I have some long-distance calls coming in from the East . . ."

"Forget them."

"I gather," Minerva Hamlin said icily, "that you don't care to tell me where Mr. Drake can be reached in case those calls come through."

"I don't know where he can be reached," Mason said.

She turned back to the switchboard with an aggressive shrug of her shoulders.

Drake followed Mason out into the corridor.

"Good Lord, what a girl," Mason said. "Where the hell did you get her, Paul?"

"Through an employment agent. She's certainly efficient, Perry."

"She thinks she's efficient," Mason said. "She's a woman who wants to do her own thinking for herself, and then wants to do your thinking for you. . . . Come on, Paul, we're going down to Morris Alburg's."

"There won't be anyone there this early in the morning."

"Forget it," Mason said. "Della Street is down there checking over the books. If Alburg was responsible for having room 721 wired I think we can find something. I'd like to beat the police to it for once in this case."

"Of course," Drake said, "so far you don't have any positive evidence that the room was wired, and . . ."

"That's evidence I'm going after," Mason said. "Come on, you can ride with me."

"Why don't you ride with me, Perry?"

"I can't take that long. Come on, we're going places."

140

Drake groaned. "At least, Perry, have some decent regard for safety even if you don't for the speed laws. At this hour of the morning traffic is beginning to pick up and—well, it's dangerous."

"I know," Mason said. "Get in."

Mason whipped his car out of the parking lot, swung it down the street and gathered speed. Paul Drake, rigidly bracing himself, glanced apprehensively at each intersection as Mason snaked the car through the early morning traffic, and finally braked it to a stop in front of Alburg's restaurant.

He banged on the door and Della Street opened it.

"Getting anywhere, Della?" he asked.

"We've just struck pay dirt, Chief," she said. "A check for a hundred and twenty-five dollars was made a year and a half ago to an Arthur Leroy Fulda, who is listed as a private detec . . ."

"Know him?" Mason asked, turning to Paul Drake.

"Sure, I know him," Drake said.

"What sort of a fellow is he?"

"All right. I think he's on the square. He's— Gosh, Perry, I bet that's it, all right."

"What is?"

"Fulda just recently put in a line of ultramodern sound equipment. He was telling me about it. Some of this latest automatic stuff, too."

"Where does he live?" Mason asked.

Drake said, "His office is . . ."

"Where does he live?"

"I've checked the telephone directory," Della Street said, "and he has an address on East Colter Avenue—1325. I don't know whether it's an apartment house or . . ."

"East Colter," Mason said musingly. "That probably will be a residence. . . . Telephone his office, Della, just to make certain he isn't there and— No, he won't be. He'll be at home *if* the police haven't picked him up as a witness, and, of course, we have no way of knowing that until we can get out there. Come on, Paul, let's go."

"Do you want me to wait here?" Della Street asked.

Mason shook his head. "That's the information we want. Close up the place, send the cashier home, turn out the lights, and forget about the whole thing, Della. Take the cashier out for a cup of coffee and some ham and eggs if she wants them. Get her to keep her mouth shut."

"She's a good girl. I think she will. She . . ."

"Okay," Mason said, "we're going out to round up Fulda. Thanks a lot, Della."

"I hope he's the one you want, Chief."

"He has to be," Mason said. "The whole thing checks in. Get the books back in the safe and close the place up, Della. The police may be around here before too very long. Come on, Paul, let's go."

Chapter 12

Traffic signals on the through boulevard changed from the static amber warning signals to synchronized stop-and-go lights when they were half a mile from East Colter Avenue. Mason slowed down in order to ease his way through the signals, then turned on East Colter Avenue and found the number.

"Doesn't look as though anyone's up," Drake said.

Mason parked the car at the curb, ran up the steps to press the front doorbell.

After he had rung for the third time, slippered feet sounded in the corridor, and a sleepy-eyed man in dressing gown, pajamas and slippers, opened the door and blinked at his visitors.

"What's the trouble?" he asked.

Paul Drake said, "You know me. Fulda. I've met you a couple of times and . . ."

"Oh, yes, Mr. Drake. How are you?"

"This is Perry Mason," Drake introduced.

"I'm very glad to know you, Mr. Mason. You'll pardon my appearance. . . . What seems to be the matter? Is there something I can do for you?"

"We want to talk," Mason told him.

"Now?" he asked.

"Now's the best we can do," Mason said. "I'd have preferred an hour ago."

Fulda raised inquiring eyebrows, started to say something, checked himself, and said, "Come in."

A woman's voice called anxiously from a bedroom, "What is it, Arthur?"

"It's all right, honey," Fulda said, his voice edged with impatience. "Go back to sleep. Just a couple of men to . . ."

"What are they?"

"A detective I know and . . ."

Bare feet hit the floor. There was a shuffling sound, then a moment later a woman, in housecoat and mules, stood in the doorway.

Fulda's voice held savage rebuke. "I'm sorry it bothered you, honey. *Go back to bed.*"

She continued to stand there in the doorway.

"My wife," Fulda said. "This is Mr. Mason and Paul Drake, honey. Paul Drake's a detective who has an office . . ."

"Oh, a *private* detective."

"Yes," Fulda said. "Don't worry. Just go back to bed."

She hesitated a moment, then smiled, and said, "Make yourself at home. Can I fix you some coffee?"

"You don't need to get up, honey."

"No, it's all right. I'll fix some coffee. Just a few minutes. Do sit down."

Fulda pressed a button which turned on a gas furnace, said, "Sit down, gentlemen. I take it this is something urgent?"

"That's right," Mason said. "We haven't got a lot of time."

"How much time?"

"I don't know. Tell me all you know about that job at the Keymont Hotel."

Fulda, who had been lighting a cigarette, paused, and held the match near the end of the cigarette. "The Keymont Hotel?" he asked.

"Room 721," Mason said. "Come on, make it snappy."

"I don't know what the devil you're talking about, Mr. Mason."

Mrs. Fulda, who had started for the kitchen, stopped at the swinging door, holding it partially open, waiting and listening.

Mason said, "Don't be a sap, Fulda. You were in on that
144

job. You wired the rooms. Now I want to know how long you stayed there. I want to know whether you were there personally, or whether you had somebody on the job, or . . ."

"Good Lord," Fulda said. "Do you mean to say you two have come barging out here and pulled me out of bed in order to ask me a fool question like this?"

"Exactly."

Fulda made a show of anger. "Well, I resent that! I have absolutely nothing to say to you gentlemen. If you want to ask me questions about routine business, you can come to the office after nine o'clock. Furthermore, I see no reason for being questioned. Now, since you gentlemen seem to be in a hurry and working on an urgent matter, I'm not going to detain you any further."

Mason said, "That's your position?"

"That's my position."

"Want to change it?"

"No."

Mason said, "I think you're covering up, Fulda. I have an idea you were in on that job. If you were, it's pretty important that we find out just what . . ."

"I know you, Mr. Mason, and I know your reputation, and I don't intend to be browbeaten in my own home. I've given you my answer and that's final. Now, do you gentlemen want to come to my office at nine o'clock?"

"No," Mason said.

"All right, you don't have to."

"We're going to talk right here."

"We've already talked."

"Sure we have," Mason said. "We've said about one-half of what we're going to say."

"It seems to me I have already expressed myself clearly. I've said everything I care to say."

Mason said, "All right, now *I'll* tell *you* something."

"You don't need to tell me a thing, Mr. Mason."

"I know," Mason said. "You're one of these smart fellows, you know it all."

"Mr. Mason, I resent that."

"Go right ahead," Mason said, "resent it. If you were really smart you'd at least listen until you knew what the score was."

"I know what the score is right now."

"Like hell you do," Mason said. "There was a murder committed in the Keymont Hotel."

Fulda made an elaborate gesture of shrugging his shoulders. "I guess those things happen even in the best of hotels."

"And the Keymont isn't the best," Mason reminded him.

Fulda said nothing.

"The Homicide Squad went into action," Mason went on. "They found that room 721 had been wired. The wires ran into another room. Presumably there was a lot of high-priced equipment in use; equipment that recorded conversations, automatic stuff that would switch on and off . . ."

"And simply on the strength of that you come to see me?"

"And," Mason continued, without apparently noticing the interruption, "Lieutenant Tragg of Homicide is very anxious to find out who had done the wiring."

· "Naturally he would be."

"Now, Lieutenant Tragg didn't say anything to me," Mason said, "but my best guess is that he's starting to trace this equipment, and that shouldn't be too hard. I would gather that it's very modern, very recent, very expensive, and right up to the minute. Whoever bought that equipment probably didn't pay all cash for it. It's probably being purchased under contract. There are serial numbers on the machines. Lieutenant Tragg will get those serial numbers. He'll call up the manufacturers. They'll refer him to their local agency. The local agency will get out its contract and . . .

"Oh, my God!" Fulda said, and sat down in the chair as though somebody had knocked the props out from under him.

Mason nodded to Mrs. Fulda. "I think," he said, "your husband is going to want some of that coffee."

146

She continued to stand in the doorway for a moment, then silently glided into the kitchen. The swinging door closed, then, after a moment, was pulled open and left open.

"I'd never thought of the serial numbers," Fulda said.

"You should have," Mason told him. "You should have thought of that the first thing."

"I felt—felt I could— Well, I didn't realize they'd trace me that ay or that soon."

"What's your story?"

"I want time to think."

"I know," Mason said, "you came home, got out of your clothes, mussed up your hair a little bit and decided you'd bluff it out. You scared your wife half to death, and you're pretty badly frightened yourself now. What happened to frighten you?"

"I—I don't know."

"All right, let's find out. Tell us your story and tell it fast. There's just a chance we can help you."

"I—I don't know what to do."

"Start talking."

"I specialize in sound equipment—"

"Yes, I know."

"In recording conversations—blackmail and things of that sort in the criminal field, and recording speeches and depositions, courtroom proceedings and so forth in the non-criminal field."

"Tell us about the Keymont Hotel," Mason said.

"Not so long ago," Fulda said, "I did a job for Morris Alburg. It was—well, it was confidential."

"It won't be," Mason said.

"Well, it is now."

"By the time the district attorney starts asking questions—"

"That's different."

"I'll read about it in the papers then."

"All right," Fulda said, "you'll read about it in the papers, but until you do, it's confidential. All I can say is it was

147

a blackmailing job, and it was carried through very successfully.''

"How long ago?"

"A little over a year ago."

"Then what?"

"So yesterday afternoon Morris Alburg came to me. He
wanted me to fix a setup in the Keymont Hotel, and—well,
of course, it had to be very confidential and . . ."

"Go on," Mason said, "that isn't what's worrying you.
Tell us what's worrying you."

"Well," Fulda said, "the damn fool told me that he was
wanted by the police and that put me in a spot."

"Did he say what he was wanted for?"

"He said they were looking for him and he was keeping
under cover."

"And you took the job on that basis?"

Fulda nodded morosely.

"All right," Mason said, "you don't need to tell the police *all* the conversation you had with your client. So far as
you were concerned it was a routine job. What did you do?"

"I got my sound equipment together, went up to the hotel,
told the clerk my sister was coming on an evening plane and
I wanted two rooms, preferably adjoining."

"And he wouldn't give them to you?"

"He said he didn't have two adjoining rooms, but he did
have two rooms on the same floor. I asked him where they
were located and he said they were 721 and 725, so I told
him I'd take a look at them."

"You went up and looked them over?"

Fulda nodded.

"Then what?"

"They were ideally suited. I told him that I was going to
move in, that I'd sleep for a while before dinner and didn't
want to be disturbed because I was going to meet my sister
on the night plane."

"How did that register?"

"He gave me a knowing leer and let it go at that."

"So what did you do?"

"All of this modern sound equipment is fixed so it resembles hatboxes, suitcases and that stuff."

"I know," Mason said.

"The bellboy got a hand truck and we moved the stuff up. We distributed it. Some in 721, some of it in 725."

"Then what?"

"Then after the boy left, I moved it all down to 725, all the recording machinery and all that stuff, and left nothing in 721 but a microphone. I did a good job concealing that."

"How? In the wall?"

"No. These new jobs are slick. The bug was in a reading lamp I clamped to the head of the bed. Aside from the fact it looked too classy for the dump it was in, it was perfect. I ran the wires along the picture molding, then out through the transom and down the corridor and into 725. I had to work fast, but I was all prepared to work fast, and I did a good job of it."

"Then what?"

"Then I tested the equipment to see that it was working, and then left word for Morris Alburg to come to room 721, that everything was all right."

"How did you leave word?"

"I called the number he had given me and said that if Morris came in to say that Art had told him everything was okay."

"That's all?"

"That's all."

"Then what?"

"Then I holed up in 725."

"Wasn't the equipment automatic?"

"That's right, but I wanted to make certain that it was working. And I thought Alburg would want a witness. It was new equipment and I wanted to monitor the conversations myself. You should always do that if you're going to testify. You can't introduce evidence if you simply show that you

149

went away and left a room, and when you came back you found certain acetate discs on the machine, you . . ."

"Don't bother trying to educate me on the law of evidence," Mason said. "Tell me what you did."

"Well, I lay down in 725 and went to sleep."

"When did you wake up?"

"I woke up about eight-thirty or nine o'clock, I guess. I went out and had something to eat and called that number again and asked if Morris Alburg had been in. They said he had and that he'd received my message."

"You didn't tell them who you were?"

"Just Art."

"All right, then what?"

"I filled up on a good dinner. I got some sandwiches and a thermos bottle of hot coffee, and went back to the hotel."

"Then what?"

"I read for a while, then dozed off, and was suddenly awakened by the sound of my equipment being turned on."

"What happened?"

"Well, that stuff is equipped so that when there are voices in the room that's wired the machines turn on automatically and start recording. I heard the click of the switch, and there's a green light that comes on on the recording machine when everything is working all right. I jumped up off the bed, went over and saw that everything was coming in all right. I plugged in earphones and could hear the conversation."

"What was the conversation?"

"Morris Alburg and some woman were talking and—well, I couldn't get it."

"What couldn't you get? You mean the recording didn't come in clearly or what?"

"Oh, the equipment was working fine. It was the conversation that I couldn't follow. It was a peculiar conversation."

"What was peculiar about it?"

"Well, evidently Morris and a woman were in there and they were expecting you to come, and Alburg said, 'He'll be here any minute. I phoned him and he said he'd come right

150

up,' and the woman said something about him being late, and then all of a sudden the conversation seemed to veer off on a peculiar tangent."

"What sort of a tangent?"

"Well, for a while there they had talked—oh, just casually. Alburg said, 'I want you to tell him just what you told me. I want you to be frank with him. He's my lawyer and everything is going to be all right. Now I'm telling you everything is going to be all right. You'll be taken care of and all that.' "

"And then what?"

"Then Alburg began to worry and said that you might have gone back to sleep, so he told the girl to call you, and there was silence for a moment, and then the girl said in a low voice, 'Call the police.'

"A second later the phone rang and the girl laughed and said, apparently into the telephone, 'Of course not—just a gag. Forget it,' and hung up.

"After that I heard sounds of motion. Someone would start to say something and stop suddenly in mid-sentence."

"What sort of sounds of motion?" Mason asked.

"I can't very well describe it."

"Struggle?"

"I wouldn't go so far as to say that—peculiar sounds."

"Then what?"

"I heard the woman say, 'Just lipstick. You ruined my mouth,' and then a little while later a door opened and closed."

"Then what?"

"Then nothing else. There was five seconds of silence and then everything clicked off."

"Then what?"

"Then after ten or fifteen minutes there were more voices, and these were different people. There was a man and woman, and the woman said, 'I tell you she left a message somewhere,' and the man said, 'We haven't time to look for it. How did she leave it?' and the woman said, 'Probably written in lipstick,' and the man said, 'Give me your lipstick and I'll fix that.' ''

"Then what?"

"Then more sounds and again the equipment went silent."

"And after that?"

"After that you came, Mr. Mason, and I guess you know as much about what happened then as anyone. When I heard you telephone for Paul Drake and tell him to get someone on the job, I decided it was time for me to get out. Things were getting a little bit too hot. It certainly wasn't the ordinary kind of assignment I was called in on, and I heard you mention things that disturbed me a lot. I—well, I felt that if I got out no one would know I'd been in there. They would feel that the equipment was registering all by itself."

Mason nodded.

"It wasn't until after I got home," Fulda said, "that I realized what an utterly asinine thing I'd done. I'd taken the recorded discs with me."

"You mean you'd filled up more than one record?"

"No, but, without thinking, I slipped in a fresh disc when I left so the machine would be loaded with a fresh one. We get to do that so it's almost second nature. You want to have it so the machine is fully loaded at all times. There's enough on there to cover a two-hour-and-thirty-minute recording when it's full, and—well, I didn't want to have any slip-ups.

"That's one thing about the machine that they haven't been able to lick as yet. Suppose it's on automatic, and you come in and have a talk with someone at ten o'clock at night. You go out and close the door. Five seconds later the equipment clicks off. Then at three o'clock in the morning someone comes in and opens the door and starts talking. The sound even of people moving around in the room immediately actuates the relay switch and turns the machinery on and it starts recording. . . . Now, when I play that disc back to a client, it will sound as though there was a continuing conversation except for a five-second pause. There'll be nothing to show that one conversation took place at ten o'clock in the evening, and the next conversation, which apparently follows right along with it, took place at three o'clock in the morning. That's one of the reasons why you should monitor the equipment. . . . Well, that's the story."

"And what are you so frightened about?"

"I felt that if no one found out the room was wired I could go back and get my equipment out, but that if it should be discovered the room was wired—well, Morris had told me he was keeping under cover and—well, there were complications. Sometimes the police don't like to have us move in and wire a hotel that way. It's always advisable, wherever possible, to use a private office somewhere rather than a public hotel. . . . And if it became a police case they'd know I had been there because they could listen back on the discs and find out when the conversation started.

"I assumed the police would know, for instance, that you entered that room, and about what time—and the night clerk saw me go out. If it became a police case I'd be in a mess."

"All right," Mason told him. "It's a police case. You're in a mess."

The aroma of freshly made coffee came from the kitchen and penetrated to the living room.

Mason motioned to the telephone. "Call Police Headquarters."

Fulda hesitated. "I'm in so deep now, I . . ."

"Call Police Headquarters. Ask for Homicide Squad. See if Lieutenant Tragg is still on the job. Tell him your story."

"How should I explain the fact that I'm calling Homicide?"

"Tell them I told you to," Mason said.

Fulda hesitated.

From the door between the kitchen and the dining room his wife's voice said sharply, "You heard what Mr. Mason said, Arthur. He knows best."

Fulda glanced at Paul Drake. Drake's countenance was completely wooden.

"Well—" Fulda said reluctantly, and walked over to the telephone.

He called Police Headquarters, asked for Lieutenant Tragg, learned that Tragg was not in and left his name and telephone number. "Tell Lieutenant Tragg to call me as soon as he comes in," he said. "He— Well, I prefer to talk with Lieutenant Tragg. It's about some sound equipment and . . . That's right, that's the place. The Keymont Hotel. . . . That's right, I'll be right here. Tell him to call me. I'll be waiting right by the phone."

He hung up, and said to Mason, "I hope that was the right thing to do."

Mason, who had been standing at the front window, turned and said over his shoulder, "I've just saved your license for you, you damned fool. Lieutenant Tragg is just parking his police car at the curb. That call will save your life."

"Lieutenant Tragg!" Fulda exclaimed. "How in the world did he get here this soon?"

"He probably located you the way I told you he would," Mason said.

Steps pounded on the porch. The chimes sounded on the door. Mason turned the knob and pulled the door open. "Walk right in, Lieutenant," he said. "You're just in time for coffee."

Tragg's face darkened. "What the hell are you doing here, Mason?"

"Asking questions."

"All right," Tragg said, "you've asked the questions. I'll get the answers. . . . Your name Fulda?" he asked the man back of Mason.

"That's right," Fulda said.

"You wired 721 and 725 in the Keymont Hotel?"

Fulda nodded. "I've been trying to get in touch with you, Lieutenant. I called Homicide Squad and left a message."

Tragg's mouth was grim. "Let's hope," he said, "for your sake, that you did, because it's going to mean all the difference in the world in the way you get treated."

"You can ring up and find out that I did," Fulda said.

"In that case, that's the one only *really* smart move you've made so far," Tragg said.

Mrs. Fulda appeared from the kitchen, smiling somewhat nervously. "Good morning, Lieutenant. I'm Mrs. Fulda. I'm just making some coffee for the gentlemen and perhaps if you'd . . ."

"I'll drink all of it," Tragg said. "The gentlemen are leaving. They can get their coffee at a restaurant."

She smiled rather vaguely as though at a joke.

"I mean it," Tragg said. "What were they doing out here, Fulda?"

"Why, just asking me a few questions."

"That's fine," Tragg said. "Now I'll get the answers, and I'll also ask you a couple of questions that they didn't know about, and, believe me, *those* are the questions that are going to count."

Chapter 13

The morning mail brought the letter from Morris Alburg. A check for $1,000 was enclosed.

The letter, however, as a rather harassed, nervous Mason pointed out to his secretary, was something less than a masterpiece of clarity. It said simply:

DEAR MR. MASON:

You will remember the fur coat matter. I want you to represent me and the girl in that thing. I am enclosing a thousand dollars as a retainer, and there's more where that came from if you need it.

Hastily,

MORRIS ALBURG

Mason angrily tapped the letter with his forefinger. "Represent him in 'that thing.' . . . That's broad enough to include every crime in the Penal Code."

"And probably does," Della Street said.

At three-thirty that afternoon, Paul Drake, looking worn and haggard, tapped his code knock on the door of Mason's private office.

Della Street admitted him. Drake dropped into the big overstuffed chair, stretched, yawned, shook his head, and said, "I can't take it any more, Perry."

Mason grinned. "You're just out of practice, Paul. You haven't been working for me enough lately. What you need is a few more sleepless nights to keep in training."

Drake said, "For a fact, Perry, I used to be able to keep

156

going all night and through the next day and keep alert. Now I have spells of being groggy.''

Mason merely grinned.

''How about the Chief?'' Della Street asked. ''He had a million problems confronting him this morning and . . .''

''Oh, him,'' Drake said. ''You never need to worry about him. He's the old human dynamo. He manufactures energy faster than any human being can use it up. If we only had some way of soldering wires on him we could get rich selling surplus energy to run-down millionaires.''

''What's on your mind beside all that stuff?'' Mason asked.

''That girl,'' Drake said. ''Minerva Hamlin.''

''What about her?''

''I rang her house fifteen minutes ago and told her mother I wanted to speak with Minerva as soon as she wakened. I wanted her to call me.''

''Well?''

''She wasn't home.''

''Go ahead.''

''She was down at Police Headquarters. The mother—now get this, Perry—the mother said she had been called down about half an hour ago to make an identification.''

Mason whistled.

''Does that mean they have Dixie Dayton?'' Della Street asked.

''It could mean a lot of things,'' Mason said, pushing back his desk chair and getting to his feet. ''Hang it, I don't like that, Paul.''

Mason started pacing the office.

''I don't like it either.''

''Under ordinary circumstances, wouldn't she have called and reported to you, at least told you what they said they wanted her for?''

''That depends on what you mean by 'ordinary circumstances,' Perry. She's one of these self-sufficient women who wants it definitely understood she isn't going to stand for any

157

foolishness. She's been so satisfied with herself that she had me feeling the same way."

"I doubt if she's really efficient," Mason said. "She's simply cultivated an efficient manner. She's acting a part, the part of extreme competence, probably aping a secretary she saw in a show someplace, and that was merely an actress portraying a part the way she thought it should be portrayed."

Drake said, "I've been checking up on her a little bit, Perry—"

"Go ahead," Mason said, as Drake hesitated.

"Well, I always felt she was thoroughly competent, but I find that the other help doesn't think very much of her. She always *seems* to have the situation well in hand, but, damn it, she *does* make mistakes. I found that out. The girl who comes on in the morning and takes over the switchboard after she leaves has been covering up a few of her boners."

"What were they?"

"Minor matters. A couple of the operatives who have been in on night stuff have tried to kid her along a little bit and she's frozen them in their tracks."

"Making passes?" Mason asked.

"Hell, no," Drake said, "just the ordinary stuff that happens around an office—or should happen around an office where people are supposed to be working together with some degree of co-operation.

"You know how it is, Perry, in a business like mine where things are more or less informal, you get a sort of family relationship. Of course, the girl who comes on during the night shift always is a more or less queer fish. She starts in at midnight and quits work at eight in the morning. For the most part the switchboard and office end doesn't amount to anything, so in order to keep her busy we usually have her do the typing work on most of the cases. She files letters that have been written during the day, and types out the operatives' reports.

"For instance, a man will come in at five or six o'clock
158

in the evening. He's been working on a case all day. Most of those fellows can bang out a report with two fingers on a typewriter if they have to, but it'll be a pretty botchy job of typing and a pretty sketchy job of reporting, so I encourage them to sit down at a dictating machine and tell the story—not in too great detail, but enough of a picture so the client will really know what's going on, and in that way we keep better records.''

Mason nodded.

''The girl who comes on at four o'clock and works until midnight transcribes part of them, and the girl who comes on at midnight and works until eight transcribes the rest of them, does the filing and does the odd jobs.

''Now, Minerva has been working on that stuff, and apparently she's made some bad boners. For instance, there has been trouble with the files, and probably it goes back to mistakes Minerva made. Then, again, some of those reports are pretty juicy, you know, Perry, and sometimes the fellows, when they happen to be working nights and come in to make a report before they go off duty, will kid along about the cases. The girls usually hand it right back—just the usual good-natured stuff that goes on around an office. . . . Well, Minerva doesn't stand for any of that. She's Madam Queen as far as the operatives are concerned. She's all efficiency and ice water.''

Mason said, ''I suppose in the long run a girl gets so damn tired of hearing some of those near-smutty stories over and over and over again. . . .''

''Oh, I know,'' Drake said, ''but a girl who's really human will manage to laugh as though it's a new joke—just so things don't go too far. . . . What the heck, Perry, you know what I'm trying to tell you. We may have some trouble with this girl. It bothers me that she didn't call me to tip me off.''

''What did you ring her up for?'' Mason asked.

''I made up my mind I was going to fire her,'' Drake said.

''For heaven's sake, don't do that. Not right now, anyway.''

"Why not?"

"It will look as though we're taking it out on her because she made that identification of the photograph. That would antagonize a jury."

"Of course," Paul Drake pointed out, "the girl could really have been Dixie."

"Yes," Mason admitted dubiously. "She could have been."

The telephone rang sharply.

"See who it is," Mason said.

Della Street picked up the telephone, answered, said "Yes, Gertie. . . . Why, what . . . Just a moment."

She motioned to Perry Mason with excitement. "Morris Alburg on the line."

"Well, thank heavens," Mason said. "It's about time that boy made a report."

Mason picked up the telephone, said, "Hello, Morris. What the devil is all this about and where are you?"

"I'm in jail," Morris Alburg said.

"What?"

"In jail."

"The devil you are! How long have you been there?"

"Since nine o'clock this morning."

"Oh-oh," Mason said, and then added, "Why didn't you telephone me?"

"They wouldn't let me."

"Did you tell them you wanted to talk with your lawyer?"

"I told them everything. I haven't been in this jail very long. They've been shunting me around, keeping me traveling in an automobile, taking me from one precinct to another . . ."

"You're down at—?"

"That's right. I'm at the Central Precinct now."

"I'll be there," Mason said.

Mason hung up the telephone, dashed over to the closet and grabbed his hat.

"What is it?" Drake asked, as Mason made for the door.

"Same old run-around," Mason said. "They've had Morris Alburg since nine o'clock this morning and they've been keeping him buried. Just now they're letting him call his attorney. That means they've squeezed everything out of him they can possibly get. . . . Stick around, Paul, so I can get you if I need you. I'll be wanting you, and don't fire Minerva—not yet."

Chapter 14

"All right," Mason said, as he settled himself in the straight-backed chair in the visitors' room, "tell me what happened."

Alburg put his head in his hands. "Honestly, Mr. Mason, I'm in a mess, one hell of a mess. . . . You got my letter with the check?"

"Yes, I got your letter with the check," Mason said, "and I knew just as much when I finished reading it as I knew before. How did you get picked up?"

"I was on my way up to your office."

"*My* office?"

"That's right."

"What happened?"

"I get to the entrance of your building. A plain-clothes man jumps out of the crowd. He grabs me. They shove me into an automobile. I'm away from there before I even have a chance to know what's going on."

Mason said angrily, "Why didn't you stop someplace and telephone me? I'd have told you to keep away from the office. You might have known they'd have a man planted there. That and your restaurant were the first places they'd look. . . . Now, what happened? Go on, tell me the story."

"The worst part you haven't even heard yet."

"All right," Mason said, "give me the worst part."

"I had the gun."

"*The* gun?"

"That's right."

"What gun?"

"The gun the police say killed Fayette."

162

Mason regarded him with frowning disapproval.

"It's not what you think, Mr. Mason. It's a long story and . . ."

"Well, tell it and make it short," Mason said. "What's Dixie Dayton to you?"

"She's sort of related by marriage."

"How come?"

"Thomas E. Sedgwick is my half-brother. Does that mean anything to you?"

"That means a lot," Mason said.

"Sedgwick was making book. He was one of these smart boys. I warned him. He was in love with Dixie Dayton. She warned him. We kept trying to straighten that boy out. It's no use.

"He thought he was smart. Sure, there was a payoff. So what? He thought he had a license. You don't get a license from a payoff. You get trouble. You get money for a while, sure. Then you get trouble.

"All right. Tom gets trouble. He won't listen. A new cop gets on the job. He gets a tip on Tom. He don't make a pinch. Tom could square a pinch. He wants to get Tom so he can maybe prove a payoff. That's hell."

"Claremont had the goods?"

"On Tom I guess, yes."

"On the payoff, I mean."

"On the payoff he has suspicion only. That's why he wants Tom. He wants it Tom should squeal, should sing to a grand jury. What a mess! Tom don't get it at first. This cop gets the goods. He has Tom dead to rights. And he don't do a thing. Tom thought he wanted a cut. He don't want no cut. He wants Tom should squeal.

"Tom is dumb. Like I tell you, Mr. Mason, that boy thinks a payoff is a license. But the payoff ain't dumb. He gets the tip. He tells Tom to sell out, to get out until things blow over. This cop is smart. He's traced the payoff."

"Who was the payoff?"

"Fayette. He's the first step."

"What happened?"

"Tom, he can't stand any subpoena. You know what happens if he gets a subpoena to the grand jury. Tom sells out. He takes it on the lam."

"Then what?"

"They say this cop was smart. He was watching for Tom to do that. Once Tom pulled that sell-out-and-run stuff, the cop had him. They say Tom bumped him off. I don't know. Tom swears he didn't. Dixie believes in him."

"Oh, yes?" Mason said. "And how did Dixie explain to you the fact that Tom had Claremont's service revolver among his cherished possessions?"

Alburg jumped up as though his chair had been wired. *"Had what?"* he shouted.

"Pipe down," Mason said. "She had Claremont's gun."

Alburg put his head in his hands. "That does it! Now we're in a jam right. Then Tom *did* kill him."

"It sure looks like it," Mason said.

"Oh, what a mess! And what the hell, I'm in it right with Tom and Dixie."

"Damned if you aren't," Mason said. "And you might as well include me while you're taking inventory."

"Oh, what a mess!" Morris said.

"Never mind feeling sorry for yourself now, Morris. There isn't time for that. How about Fayette? Did you kill him?"

"No, no, of course not. Me, I don't kill anyone!"

"You say the police found the gun on you?"

"Yes."

"How do you know that was the gun that killed Fayette?"

"The police said so."

"When?"

"About fifteen minutes ago. That's why I'm here. They wanted a ballistics test. When they got it, they booked me and then let me call you."

"How long have you had that gun?"

"That's just it. I only had it—since the shooting."

"Tell me the whole story."

"Where do I start?" Alburg asked.

"Start at the beginning, and be sure it *is* the beginning."

"I've already told you about Tom Sedgwick . . ."

"Never mind him. Tell me about Dixie, *all* about her."

"Tom and Dixie . . ."

"Are they married?"

"That's one of those things, Mr. Mason. Tom had been married. There was difficulty over the divorce. You can't blame him and Dixie . . ."

Mason said, "Don't be a fool. The last thing I'm interested in right now is their morals. If they're married they can't testify one against the other. If they're not—"

"They're not."

"All right then, tell me about Dixie; about when she came back."

"Well, I haven't heard anything from Tom or Dixie. I'm scared stiff I will! A cop killing, Mr. Mason! You know what that is. Then all of a sudden Dixie walks into the place. I have to grab a table. My knees go no good. She gives me a cold eye as a tip-off that I am to treat her as a stranger. Then she says she wants a job."

"What did you do?"

"I gave her a job. I had to. Tom was broke and sick. He's hot. The police didn't know about Dixie."

"Dixie Dayton's not her real name?"

"Dixie, yes, her first name. The other, no, of course not."

"And her Social Security number was faked?"

"Yes."

"What about the fur coat?"

"I am terribly sorry about that. She leaves that with me, and I wrap it up and store it in a closet. I don't think about moths. I think about me. She is hot and I am scared. I keep it back out of the way where no one can see it. She comes back. She wants her coat. I bring it out. . . . Well. You saw it."

"What did she say?"

"She says nothing. She starts wearing it. She cries like hell when she thinks I don't see her."

"Why did she come back here?"

"I tell you, Tom has the T.B. They are up in Seattle. In the winter it rains and it's cold. Tom could take it no more. Dixie says they had to come back. They might beat the rap here, but he'd have died sure like hell if he'd stayed up there. Dixie has ideas. When she gets one you can't talk her out of it. My doctor tells me Seattle is damp in winter but people up there live long as hell. Dixie thinks Tom dies if he stays another winter. Maybe she's right. Maybe she's wrong. She think she's right. I don't know.

"Dixie thinks everything is fixed, she can come back, no one knows. Tom she has hid—but good. Dixie's smart as hell, one smart woman—the best!"

"She wasn't clever enough to keep from having . . ."

"Oh, sure, Fayette. He knew about Dixie. The police didn't. Fayette must have kept a watch on my place—the police, no—Fayette, yes."

"Just who is Fayette?" Mason asked.

"Fayette," Alburg said, "handled the payoff. I don't know him from a lamp post. The name I know, nothing else. Dixie comes out to wait on customers. She sees him sitting there at a table by himself. She damn near falls over. . . . Fayette would kill. He'd told Tom if Tom ever come back, or ever got a subpoena for a grand jury, it's curtains, and . . ."

"So Dixie ran out the back."

Alburg nodded. "Sure. She thought they'd torture her to make her tell where Tom was."

"I'm damned if I get it," Mason said. "If there was a payoff there must have been hundreds of bookies paying off, and . . ."

"But there's only one cop murder, Mr. Mason. I can't prove nothing. Dixie can't prove nothing. But we both think Fayette kills that cop. If Tom comes back and maybe gets a good lawyer. . . . What the hell?"

166

"All right," Mason said, "go on and tell me what happened."

"What happened?" Alburg exclaimed. "Everything happened. First, I am sitting pretty, then the roof caves in. Dixie says no one knows Tom is back. No one is ever going to find where he is. Then they walk in on her. She runs out; she almost gets killed. The cops come in. The cops don't know Tom is my half-brother, but they know there is something. They don't know who Dixie is, but they're going to find out. I start getting under cover. There's a bar where I have a friend. He'd protect me every time. Dixie knows that place. She calls me up. I tell her to stay under cover. I'm under cover. It's hell."

"Go on," Mason said.

"Then some woman calls the place. She tells the cashier, who I can trust, that she has to get a message to me. The cashier is smart. She says give her the message. So the girl tells her to have me call a certain number and ask for Mildred."

"You did?"

"Sure. I go to a pay station. I call the number. I say, 'Who the hell's Mildred?' "

"And what happened?"

"I'm thinking it's a trap. Maybe cops are coming in the door. I am at a pay station where I can get out quick."

"Go ahead."

"This girl Mildred, she wants to talk. I tell her forget it. I've got no time to talk. Quick, what do we do?

"She says, 'Don't be a dumbbell. You're hot. Dixie's hot. I know who killed the cop.'

"I think it's a trap. I say, 'Yes. You are smart. Who killed the cop?' She says, 'George Fayette.' I ask her how she knows. What's it to her? She says Fayette sold her out. He two-times with another woman. She won't stand for it. To hell with Fayette. If I meet her at the Keymont Hotel she tells me the story. She gives me the evidence. What the hell would you do?"

"What would I have done?" Mason said. "I'd have telephoned my lawyer quick."

"Not that quick," Alburg said. "I have been at the phone long enough. I don't want them to trace the call. I say, 'All right. You stay at that number. I'll call you back.' So what do I do? A while ago a waitress tries to blackmail me. I get a smart detective. He gets the whole proposition on tape recording. That waitress she is out of luck quick, like that. So I say to myself, 'I will be smart. I will get a sound recording. I will get Mr. Mason.' "

Mason frowned. "Suppose it had been a police trap?"

"What the hell? I have to take a chance. I'm hot. I can't go back to my restaurant. The restaurant is my business. If I don't go back I lose my business. I have to do something. One thing else you don't know. That Dixie can take a look at a number and flash, like that, it's in her mind. When Dixie works for me I never need a telephone book. I show her a number once. She remembers it. Always for numbers that girl is smart. Anything with figures."

"Go ahead," Mason said.

"When she runs out the back door of the restaurant, running from Fayette, she sees the car come. It's coming toward her. She looks at the car. She sees the number on the front license plate. Then there is a man with a gun. She runs and he shoots, but she remembers the license number."

"Go ahead," Mason said.

"She tells it to me. I am smart; I have connections. I look it up. It is a car registered to Herbert Granton. Dixie remembers Granton is a name Fayette uses sometimes when he is being respectable. All right, we have an ace in the hole. Maybe a smart lawyer can do us some good if he finds that automobile and it has a bullet hole."

"Go ahead," Mason said.

"So I get the detective to go first to the Keymont Hotel. He sizes the place up. He gets the room all wired. He says he will be where he can listen. Everything is fixed. I wait
168

until after midnight, then I ring this girl. I tell her, 'All right, Mildred, you come to the Keymont. Room 721.' ''

"The girl had first told you about the Keymont Hotel?''

"That's right.''

"Weren't you suspicious about going there?''

"Sure, I'm suspicious, but what are you going to do? I told her, 'Not the Keymont. Someplace else.' She said, 'No, I am hot. Fayette will kill me. If he thinks I would give him a double-cross we would be rubbed out. I am at the Keymont and I don't dare to go out. You get a room in the Keymont. You tell me where that room is. I will come to you. I will give you evidence.' So I get this room 815. I get it for Dixie. I register her as Mrs. Madison Kerby and I pay in cash.''

"Now I begin to get the picture," Mason said, "but why . . . Well, never mind. Tell me what happened.''

"So, I call you. I get you. I have the room wired. I make a date with the girl. We go to the room.''

"Did you have a gun?" Mason asked.

"Sure I had a gun. What the hell?''

"All right, go ahead.''

"I want you there all the time. If it is the police, you can be the smart lawyer. If it is a witness and she really has evidence, you can sew the thing up.''

"What happened?" Mason asked.

"I am worried. All the time I worry. The older I get the more I worry. I think about this; I think about that. Always I am worried. Too many taxes. Too many responsibilities. Too much labor trouble. Costs of running the business too high. Worry, worry, worry. All the time worry.''

"Go ahead.''

"So I am worried you get my call and go back to sleep. That would be the bad thing. After we are in the Keymont, I tell Dixie to call that number where we get you. Be sure Mr. Mason don't go to sleep.''

"You gave Dixie the number?''

"Sure Dixie has the number. She was with me. I tell you she remembers numbers like a flash.''

"Go ahead."

"So Dixie is at the telephone. She just gets the night clerk. She is ready to give the number when the door opens. Two men and a woman walk in and I know the minute I look I am licked. I reach for my gun. Dixie is smart. She says on the telephone, 'Call the police.' That's to the clerk."

"What happened?" Mason asked.

"Somebody clips Dixie. They put a hand over her mouth."

"What about your gun?"

"My gun!" Alburg said, and laughed sarcastically. "My gun is on the bed. Two men have guns in their hands. A gun on the bed is no good against a gun in the hand."

"Why didn't you give the detective who was listening in the other room some sort of a signal?"

"Because they are too damn smart. They know that room is wired as well as I do. Every time I try to say something a man puts his finger to his lips and jabs the gun in my guts. Then I try to get smart and say something anyway, and a blackjack hits me on the side of the head. I am sick to my stomach with pain. My knees are hinges that don't work. That's the story."

"That isn't the story," Mason said. "Go on. Tell me what happened."

"What the hell? We go to a freight elevator. They take us down the freight elevator. There is a car in the alley. I am put in the back seat and then down on the floor. They hold their feet on me. That is the way the cop got killed. They put him in a car and hold their feet down and they blow his brains out."

"Go ahead," Mason said.

"We go to an apartment hotel. We go up a back elevator, but I am smart. I have to go to the bathroom. In the bathroom there is a towel. The name of the apartment hotel is on it."

"Do you remember it?"

"Of course I remember it. It is the Bonsal. *B-o-n-s-a-l.* I am in apartment 609-B."

"Then what?"

"Then, after a long while, I go down the back way again. They are taking me for a ride. We go up a side road out of the city. I am still down on the floor. A man takes out a gun and puts it at my head. I am ready to grab and just then the driver tells, 'Look out!' He throws on the brakes."

"What had happened?"

"I don't know what had happened. I know what did happen. I am on the floor. The man holding the gun on me is thrown forward against the back of the front seat. I grab the gun. The car comes to a stop. I have that door open so fast you think I am greased, like lightning. I hold the gun. I say, 'Stick 'em up, you guys,' and then I am in the brush like a deer."

"It was brushy?"

"We stop on a steep hill in a park. There is thick brush and the car is right by the edge of the steep bank. I go like a deer, I tell you. How I run!"

"Then what?"

"Then I walk and walk and walk and walk. I get a bus. I wait for a while to make sure you are in your office. I want to call you on the phone, but I am not like Dixie. I don't remember the number you gave me to call. So I sit in a little greasy spoon restaurant. I wait. Then I get a taxi. I go to the office and they grab me."

Mason thought the situation over. "Did you talk to the police?"

"Sure I talked to the police. I take them to the very place where I jump from the car. I show them my tracks."

"Did they see the tracks?"

"Sure they saw the tracks. They see where I am jumping down the hill like a deer, forty feet at a jump. They laugh. They tell me I can leave tracks anywhere."

"So then what?"

"Then we go to the Bonsal Hotel Apartments."

"And what happens?"

"I don't know. The police go up to apartment 609-B. They

171

don't tell me. I think something is haywire. They act like they have me hooked.''

''And you told this story to the police, just as you are telling it to me now?''

''That's right. That's my story.''

''Did the police take down what you said in shorthand?''

''Yes.''

''Then,'' Mason said, ''it's not only your story, but you're stuck with it.''

Chapter 15

Mason was checking out of the jail when the man at the desk said, "There's a telephone call for you, Mr. Mason. Do you want to take it?"

"Probably not," Mason said.

"It's from someone here in the jail."

Mason said, "You have a couple of thousand people here. I suppose about fifteen hundred of them want to see me, hoping that I'll find some way of getting them out. Can't you get a name for that call?"

"It's a woman," the man said. "She's over in the women's ward. She says her name is Dayton."

Mason frowned for a moment, then said, "Give me that phone."

"Hello," Mason said into the phone. "Who is it?"

"Dixie Dayton."

"Which one?"

"What do you mean?"

"I've already talked with one young woman who said she was Dixie Dayton and who . . ."

"Oh, Mr. Mason! That was a trap that had been laid for you, after they kidnaped me. I've seen you at Morris's restaurant and you've seen me—not to notice me, perhaps, but you'll remember me when you see me. You and Miss Street walked right past me when—when I tried to run away and got hit by . . ."

"Where are you now?"

"In the women's detention ward."

"How long have you been there?"

"Since about nine o'clock this morning."

173

"What do you want?"

"I want to talk with you about—about what happened."

"Why didn't you call me earlier?"

"They wouldn't let me. They were taking me around different places and putting me in a police show box with other prisoners for someone to identify."

"I'll be over," Mason said.

He hung up the telephone, said, "Thank you," to the man on duty at the desk, took the elevator, walked across to the women's detention ward, and said, "You know me. I'm an attorney. I want to see Dixie Dayton. Do I need a pass?"

The matron smiled and said, "It's all fixed up for you, Mr. Mason. I knew she wanted to see you, and when I heard you were in the building I had them send up a pass. It's all here. You may go right in."

"My, but you folks are co-operative," Mason said.

"We try to be."

Mason started to say something, then changed his mind, and went on in to where a woman, who had been waiting impatiently, jumped up with eager anticipation.

"Oh, Mr. Mason, I'm so glad to see you! So glad!"

Mason sized her up. "It took you long enough to get in touch with me."

"I did it just as soon as they'd let me."

"I'm not talking about after you were picked up. What were you doing all last night?"

"Oh, Mr. Mason, it was terrible. Morris and I were kidnaped at the point of a gun there in the Keymont Hotel."

"Who did it?"

"I don't know who they were, but George Fayette was back of it."

"And Fayette is dead," Mason said, "so he can't deny it."

"Don't you believe me?" she asked, suddenly piqued at his manner.

Mason said, "I never disbelieve a client, but whenever I'm listening to a client's story, I'm constantly wondering

174

how a jury is going to react to that same story. . . . I just finished talking with Morris Alburg. No one's going to believe his story.''

''What's wrong with it?''

''Everything.''

She said, ''Well, you won't believe mine, either. Your own witness identified me.''

''What witness?'' Mason asked sharply.

''The one who works for the Drake Detective Agency, the one you hired to shadow the woman who was in the room with you.''

''She identified you?''

''That's right.''

''Now, get this,'' Mason said, ''because it's important. Was she brought to your cell to make the identification, or did she pick you out of a line-up, or—?''

''She picked me out of a line-up.''

Mason frowned, said, ''I've talked with Morris Alburg. He's given me the overall picture. Tell me what happened after you and Morris were separated.''

''I was taken to an apartment in . . .''

''I know, the Bonsal Apartments.''

''Well, that's what I *thought* it was. That was the name on the towels, but I don't think it was the Bonsal Apartments.''

''Why?''

''Because—well, when I was taken to the Bonsal Apartments by the police . . . it wasn't the same.''

''Then what?'' Mason said.

''They treated me rather well. They had some coffee and ham and eggs sent up, and they gave me freedom to move around the apartment, except that the drapes were all drawn across the windows and I was told not to touch them unless I wanted to get hurt.''

''I know,'' Mason said. ''They left you alone. You went to the bathroom. You found towels. They had the name 'Bonsal Hotel Apartments' on them. You took one to use as evidence.''

"No, I didn't take one. I was afraid they'd count the towels and find one missing, but I did remember the name."

"Go on," Mason said, "then what?"

"Then along about daylight this morning they took me out the back entrance, down a freight elevator, and into an alley. They made me get down on the floorboards of a car, and . . ."

"I know," Mason said, "you had a chance to escape. They were going to take you for a ride and kill you, but they got careless—"

She started shaking her head.

"No?" Mason asked.

"No."

"Well, suppose you tell me what did happen."

She said, "They drove me to the airport. They told me that they were sorry, that they'd made a terrible mistake in my case, that they had found out I was all right and on the up-and-up, that I had better leave town, however, because the police were looking for me."

"Who was doing all this?" Mason asked.

"Two people whom I had never seen before."

"Men?"

"Yes."

"Did they try to molest you in any way?"

"No, they were perfect gentlemen."

"You were held prisoner in the apartment?"

"That's right."

"Then they took you out and told you there'd been a mistake made?"

"Well, something of that sort. They said that I was all right, and they were going to let me go, and . . ."

"And what's the rest of it?" Mason asked.

"They gave me a ticket to Mexico City, told me there was a plane leaving in fifteen minutes, and I'd better get aboard."

"What did you do?"

"It sounded like a perfectly swell idea to me. I wanted to

176

get just as far away as I could, and Mexico City seemed like a wonderful place to go."

"Did they say anything about Morris, or did you ask them anything about Morris?"

"They told me they'd let Morris go, too, and he was going to join me in Mexico City. They told me to go to the Hotel Reforma and that Morris would either be there when I arrived, or would be on the next plane, or that he might possibly make this plane."

"Did you ask for any explanations?"

"Mr. Mason," she said, "I'd been held a prisoner. I didn't think I was ever going to come out of it alive. The plane was leaving in fifteen minutes. I had a chance to get away from those people. I thought they might change their minds. Five minutes earlier I had been satisfied I wouldn't be alive for more than a matter of hours. . . . What would *you* have done?"

Mason said, "I'd have gone into the air terminal and climbed aboard the plane to Mexico City."

"That's exactly what I tried to do."

"What stopped you?"

"A plain-clothes man."

"Where was he?"

"Waiting by the gate."

"And what did he do?"

"Took me into custody. Took me down to the jail. They asked a lot of questions."

"What did you tell them?"

"Not too much. I was trying to protect—well, you know who." She hesitated.

Mason started to say something.

"No names, please," she said.

"Someone you're fond of?"

"Yes."

"All right," Mason said. "What did you tell the police?"

"I told them about what had happened."

"All about the Bonsal Hotel Apartments?"

177

"Yes."

"They took you there?"

"Yes."

"Did you know the number of the apartment you were in?"

"Not the number, but I could pick out the location. I knew that we got off at the fourteenth floor, and we were in the first apartment on the right."

"Go on, what happened?"

"The elevator didn't seem to be exactly the same, and—well, the first apartment on the right was occupied by an elderly couple who had been there for ten years. They seemed to be people who are entirely trustworthy and they swore they hadn't been out all evening, that they had watched the television, then gone to bed about ten o'clock."

"The officers ask you about that gun?"

"What one?"

"The one in Seattle."

She hastily put her fingers to her lips, her eyes filled with panic. She said, "A gun in Seattle? Really, Mr. Mason, I don't know what you're talking about. I haven't the faintest idea."

"What are you charged with?" Mason asked.

She said, "I think it's—well, I'm not exactly charged yet, but I think I'm being held on suspicion of murder of George Fayette, being an accessory or something. They think that Morris and I did the job together."

"Did they tell you anything about what evidence they had against you, try to break down your story, tell you that you had been seen here, there or some other different place?"

She shook her head. "Not a bit of that, no."

"And they haven't asked you about that . . ."

Her finger once more came to her lips. She looked apprehensively around the walls of the room and said, "Mr. Mason, *please*!"

"All right," Mason said.

"Mr. Mason, are you going to represent me?"

"Probably."

"And you think everything will be all right?"

"That," Mason told her, "will depend on whether or not the jury believes your story."

"Well," she said, "won't the jury believe me?"

"Hell, no," Mason said. "Not *that* story."

Chapter 16

Mason, pacing the floor of his office, said, "It's a lawyer's nightmare."

Della Street nodded sympathetically.

"Put them on the stand and let them tell their stories," Mason said, "and my clients will go to the death cell and I'll be the laughingstock of the town."

"Well," Della Street said defiantly, "how do you know the story isn't the truth?"

"I don't. It may be true. The trouble is it doesn't *sound* like the truth. It sounds exactly like a story a lawyer would have cooked up. It's one of those stories that accounts for everything, yet everything about it is improbable."

Paul Drake said, "Suppose you don't let them tell that story, Perry . . ."

"Hell," Mason said disgustedly, "they've told it. The newspapers are full of it."

"I know, but I mean on the witness stand."

Mason said, "The public knows generally what the story is. If I keep my clients off the witness stand and state that it's up to the prosecution to prove its case beyond all reasonable doubt, you know what people will think. They'll think that their story was so terrible their own lawyer was afraid to let them stand cross-examination."

"So what *do* you do?" Drake asked.

"I'm damned if I know," Mason said. "You know the story *could* be the truth. Some super-slick murderer could have carefully planned it so that these people would both be picked up by the police, so that they'd tell a story that would be just good enough to sound like the fabrication of a half-

180

smart lawyer, but just bad enough to get them stuck in front of a jury with a first-degree murder rap.''

"Couldn't you convince a jury that that actually was what happened?'' Della Street asked.

"I don't know,'' Mason said. "I doubt if I'm *that* good.''

He turned to Paul Drake. "Paul, we stand one chance, one mighty slim chance, and that is to find that girl who was in the room with me, the girl who claimed she was Dixie Dayton.''

"Well,'' Drake said, "where do I start looking?''

"You start combing the past life of George Fayette. You find out everything about him. You look up every woman who was ever connected with him—and then you won't find anything.''

"Why not?'' Della Street asked. "It sounds logical.''

"If the story that we're getting is true,'' Mason said, "the people who are back of it would be too smart to use any girl who could ever have been tied up with George Fayette. She'll be an absolute stranger. Someone whom no one would have thought of. Probably someone from another city.''

"And what do we do if we find her?'' Drake asked. "You go on the stand and swear you had a conversation with her, she swears that you didn't, and then Minerva Hamlin says you're mistaken.''

"I don't want to get on the stand, Paul.''

"Why not?''

"It puts me in the position of being both a lawyer and a witness, which is unethical.''

"Why is it unethical?''

"The American Bar Association frowns on it.''

"Let 'em frown,'' Drake said. "Frowns don't hurt. Do they slap?''

"They don't like it.''

"Is it illegal?''

"No.''

"I think we're doing Minerva Hamlin an injustice,'' Drake

said. "She'll probably come around all right. It was just an ordinary mistake she made, and . . ."

"She spoke up too fast," Mason said. "You can see what happened. They showed her the photograph and she made one of those snap judgments saying that she thought it was the girl. Then they told her to study the photograph, and she kept looking at it and looking at it. By the time she saw Dixie Dayton in the line-up, she had become so familiar with her face from looking at the photograph that she just knew the girl was familiar and so went ahead and identified her."

"That stuff happens a lot of times, all right," Drake said. "I know that it bothers the police. They get a lot of false identifications that the public never hears about. People study a photograph of a suspect so much that the features become familiar.

"A couple of weeks ago the police had a case where three people, who had been studying the photograph of a suspect, picked him out of a line-up and made a positive identification. Then it turned out he was in jail in San Francisco at the time the crime was committed. Just one of those cases of photographic identification."

Mason nodded and started to say something but stopped when the telephone rang.

Della Street picked the receiver off the hook, turned to Drake and said, "It's for you, Paul."

Drake took the telephone, said, "Hello. . . . Yes, this is he. . . . What is it? . . . Oh, now wait a minute. Don't get any false ideas. . . . Now, is that final? You're absolutely certain? . . . You've misunderstood him. . . . Here, wait a minute, who's this? . . . What? . . . No, I haven't anything to say other than that the girl's mistaken. We have positive evidence of it. . . . No. Absolutely positive evidence. . . . I'm not disclosing what it is. You can call Mr. Mason if you want details."

Drake slammed up the phone, turned to Perry Mason, said, "That damned, double-crossing, grandstanding district attorney!"

"What's he done now?" Mason asked.

"You just wait until you hear what he's done," Drake said indignantly.

"I'm waiting."

"He's got Minerva Hamlin up in his office. That was her on the phone. She was calling from the D.A.'s office."

"Okay, so what?"

"She told me, in the manner of one reading from a prepared statement which had been carefully written out and which she was holding in front of her on the desk, that she was leaving my employ because she felt that undue pressure was being brought to bear on her to make her tell a falsehood in connection with the identification of Dixie Dayton."

"A beautiful grandstand," Mason said.

"Wait a minute. You haven't heard the half of it yet," Drake said. "I started to argue with her but she said, 'That's final, Mr. Drake. The resignation takes effect immediately, and I have accepted a position in one of the county offices at a larger salary. And here's someone who wants to talk with you.' . . . And this fellow came on the line—a newspaper reporter. He wanted some comment. You heard what I said."

"I heard what you *said*," Della Street remarked.

"You should have heard what I was thinking," Drake said, then added hurriedly, "No, you shouldn't either."

Mason said, "Well, there's only one thing to do now. I'll have to sit in on the preliminary and try every trick of cross-examination to look for a weak spot in the prosecution's case. It's a cinch the defendants' case won't stand up."

Chapter 17

Hamilton Burger, the big, barrel-chested district attorney, who managed to clothe himself with an air of unctuous dignity in keeping with his concept of the office he held, arose as soon as the case had been called, and said, "I wish to make a few preliminary remarks, Your Honor."

"Very well," Judge Lennox said.

"I wish to object to Perry Mason as attorney for the defendants in this case. I believe the Court should disqualify him from appearing as such attorney."

"On what grounds?"

"Mr. Mason is a witness for the prosecution. He has been subpoenaed by the People as a witness. I expect to call him and examine him as such."

"Mr. Mason is a witness for the *prosecution*?" Judge Lennox asked incredulously.

"Yes, Your Honor."

"That's rather unheard of, for an attorney for the defense—"

"Nevertheless, Your Honor, I have carefully gone over the legal grounds," Hamilton Burger said, "and Mr. Mason is fully competent as a witness. He is the main witness on whom I must rely to prove a very important link in the chain of evidence. I expect to call him as my witness. He is under subpoena and he is, therefore, a necessary witness in the case. I can assure the Court and Counsel that I consider him a most important witness."

"Have you been subpoenaed, Mr. Mason?" Judge Lennox asked.

"Yes, Your Honor. A subpoena was served on me."

"And you are appearing as attorney for both defendants?"

"That's right."

"Your Honor," Hamilton Burger said, "I am proceeding jointly against both Morris Alburg and Dixie Dayton on a charge of first-degree murder, and I expect to be able to prove that they not only conspired to bring about the death of George Fayette, but they committed an overt act in furtherance of that conspiracy, and thereafter they did actually murder George Fayette.

"I hold no particular brief for the decedent. His record, as the defendants will probably attempt to show, is not that of an estimable citizen, but rather is interspersed with occasional tangles with the law. There are also intervals during which we are unable to account for where he was, or what he was doing. It is quite possible that the defendants thought Fayette might be endeavoring to blackmail them in connection with another crime which, of course, Your Honor, is entirely separate and apart from this present case, except that evidence will be introduced for the purpose of showing motivation."

"You are, of course, aware of the fact that there can be no evidence of another crime, Mr. District Attorney. The defendants are called upon to meet one accusation and . . ."

"And that rule, Your Honor," Hamilton Burger interrupted firmly and positively, "is subject to the well-recognized exception that when evidence of motive has to do with another crime, that evidence is perfectly admissible."

Judge Lennox said, "I have always enforced the rule rather strictly in this court. I think there is a tendency at times to relax this rule far too much. Quite often under the guise of proving motivation or a similar pattern of crimes, an attempt is made to prejudice the defendant."

"I understand, Your Honor, but when you hear the evidence in this case I think you will realize that it falls well within the exception, and that the prosecution is amply justified in introducing evidence of another crime, the murder of a policeman who . . ."

"Another murder?" Judge Lennox interjected.

"Yes, Your Honor."

"By both defendants?"

"No, Your Honor. By the defendant Dayton. That is, she was involved in the murder of a young police officer, and it was because of an attempt to cover up her connection with that crime that this murder took place. . . . It may well be that the decedent, George Fayette, was blackmailing her in connection with that other murder."

"Well," Judge Lennox said, "this presents an interesting situation. You object to Perry Mason appearing as attorney for the defendants?"

"Yes, Your Honor."

"What do you have to say with reference to that, Mr. Mason?"

"I say it's none of his business," Mason said curtly.

Judge Lennox flushed.

"Without meaning any disrespect to the Court," Mason added. "I'll handle my own business, and the district attorney can handle his."

"It's unethical," Burger said.

"You watch your ethics, and I'll take care of mine," Mason snapped.

"Come, come, gentlemen," Judge Lennox said. "Let's not have personalities interjected in this case. Do you think Mr. Mason is disqualified, Mr. District Attorney?"

"I think he should disqualify himself."

"There is no specific statute against it?"

"It is a matter of good taste and good ethics."

"We'll discuss ethics at the proper time and the proper place," Mason said. "As far as good taste is concerned, I now have a matter of my own to present. I submit to Your Honor that when a district attorney influences a young woman, who is one of my witnesses, to resign her position, hurl an accusation at her employer that he is trying to get her to perjure herself, and arranges to have the press present while she is so accusing her employer in a telephone conversation—that when he bribes the young woman to take such a step by seeing that she is offered a position in one of the county offices at a greater salary . . ."

"I object to the use of the word 'bribe,' " Hamilton Burger said.

"Pardon me," Mason said with elaborate sarcasm. "Perhaps I should have said that you *influenced* her to take such a step."

"I didn't do any such thing," Hamilton Burger said. "She did whatever she did of her own free will and accord."

"You'd arranged for the job in the county office before she picked up the telephone to submit her resignation," Mason said.

Hamilton Burger said, "Nonsense."

"Deny it," Mason challenged.

"I don't have to."

"You don't dare to."

Judge Lennox banged his gavel. "Now, gentlemen, I don't know what this is all about. I haven't read the papers in connection with this case, but obviously there is acrimonious feeling between Counsel. I want it controlled. I want Counsel to confine themselves to the trial of the case. You go ahead, Mr. District Attorney, and put on your first witness, and the Court will rule on matters as they come up."

"Specifically, I object to Mr. Mason appearing as attorney in the case."

"Is there any law that disqualifies me?" Perry Mason asked.

"As I have previously pointed out to the Court, it's a matter of ethics."

Mason said to Judge Lennox, "If the district attorney wishes to set himself up as an arbiter of good taste and good ethics, I submit that using an offer of county employment to get a young woman to quit her position and make a public accusation . . ."

"We won't go into that, Mr. Mason," Judge Lennox said, "and as far as this Court is concerned, Mr. District Attorney,

Mr. Mason is not actually disqualified. If you have subpoenaed him as a witness, and if he is called as a witness, he'll have to take the stand. If he takes the stand he'll be subject to the same rules of examination as any other witness. Now proceed with your case."

"Very well, Your Honor," Hamilton Burger said. "My first witness will be the autopsy surgeon."

In swift, kaleidoscopic sequence of routine witnesses, Hamilton Burger laid the foundation for the murder charge: the discovery of the body of George Fayette, the nature of the bullet wound, the recovery of the bullet, the microscopic characteristics of the bullet for the sake of subsequent firearms identification.

"I'll now call Carlyle E. Mott."

Mott took the witness stand and the district attorney qualified him as an expert on firearms and ballistic evidence.

"Mr. Mott, I call your attention to the bullet, People's Exhibit A, which has been identified as the fatal bullet which brought about the death of George Fayette. I will ask you if you have examined that bullet."

"I have."

"Through a microscope?"

"Yes, sir."

"You have made photographs of that bullet?"

"Yes, sir."

"Have you been able to determine the type of weapon from which the bullet was discharged?"

"I have."

"What weapon was that?"

"The weapon which I have here in my hand. A Smith and Wesson police special, thirty-eight caliber, with a three-inch barrel."

"We ask that that be introduced in evidence as People's Exhibit B," Hamilton Burger said.

"No objection," Mason said.

"Cross-examine," Burger snapped.

"No questions," Mason said.

Hamilton Burger, caught completely by surprise, blurted, "You mean you aren't going to ask him about—" He stopped abruptly, catching himself as he realized what he was saying.

"Call your next witness," the judge said.

A distinctly annoyed Hamilton Burger called as his next witness the officer who had arrested Morris Alburg as he stepped from a taxicab in front of Mason's office.

The officer testified to making the arrest and to finding the revolver in Morris Alburg's possession, the revolver from which the bullet had been fired which had killed George Fayette.

"Cross-examine," Burger said.

"How do you know this is the same gun?" Mason asked the officer.

"Because I took the number of the weapon, sir."

"Did you make a note of that number in writing?"

"Certainly."

"Where?"

"In my notebook, a notebook I always carry with me."

"You know what that number is?"

"Certainly."

"You can give us that number?"

"Yes, sir. It is S64805."

"You've remembered it all this time?"

"Yes, sir."

"Then you didn't need to write it down, did you?"

"I wrote it down in order to be safe."

"And this is the same number you've written down?"

"Yes, sir."

"You may know it's the same number that's on the weapon, but how do you know it's the same number you wrote in your notebook?"

"Because I looked at the notebook just before I came to Court to make sure."

"Oh, then you weren't sure?"

"Well, I was just guarding against the possibility of any mistake."

"And you arrested Morris Alburg on the morning of the third?"

"At about nine o'clock. Yes, sir."

"And took the gun from him at that time?"

"Yes, sir."

"When did you write the number in your notebook?"

"I've already told you. That's the number of the gun. I wrote it down so there'd be no mistake."

"When you arrested Morris Alburg?"

"Approximately, yes."

"What do you mean by approximately?"

"At almost the same time."

"Within five seconds of the time you made the arrest?"

"Certainly not."

"How many seconds?"

"I can't answer that. I don't compute time that way. That's the number of the gun I took from the defendant, Morris Alburg."

"What did you do with that gun?"

"I put it in my pocket as evidence."

"Then what?"

"I gave it to the district attorney, who in turn gave it to the ballistics expert, Carlyle E. Mott."

"And it was at Mott's suggestion that you wrote the numbers in the notebook?" Mason asked, his manner casually matter-of-fact.

"That's right."

"At the time the gun was given to him?"

"No, when he returned it to the district attorney with his report. He said that it would be necessary to identify this gun at all stages of the proceedings."

"So then you wrote down the numbers on a gun which Mott handed you?"

"Well, it was the same gun."

"How do you know?"

"I could tell by looking at it."

"What distinctive markings were on this particular gun

which enabled you to distinguish it from any other Smith and Wesson gun of similar caliber and design?''

The witness was silent.

"Don't you know?"

"If I could look at the gun," he said, "I think I could tell you."

"Certainly," Mason said sarcastically. "You'd pick up the gun and turn it over and over, hoping you could find some scratch or some identifying mark, but tell us *now* what identifying mark was on the gun."

The officer looked bewildered for a minute before answering, "I can't recall."

The judge turned to the discomfited witness. "You took a revolver from the defendant Alburg, is that right?"

"Yes, sir."

"And you turned that over to the district attorney?"

"Yes, sir."

"Who, in turn, turned it over to the ballistics expert?"

"Yes, sir."

"And sometime later, when the ballistics expert returned that weapon to the district attorney, with a report that it was the weapon which had fired the fatal bullet, it was suggested by the ballistics expert that it would be necessary to have an absolute identification of this weapon in order to enable it to be introduced in evidence?"

"Yes, sir."

"And you were then asked how you could identify this gun. Is that right?"

"Well, generally."

"Is that right, or isn't it?"

"Mr. Mott suggested that I should write the number in my notebook."

"So you took out your notebook and wrote it down at that time?"

"Yes, sir."

"And was there then some discussion about what your testimony would be?"

"Well, not at the time. That was later."

"Call your next witness," Judge Lennox said to Hamilton Burger, and his manner was distinctly frigid. "This witness is excused."

Burger braced himself for a new attack and said, "My next witness will be Arthur Leroy Fulda."

Fulda took the stand, was sworn and testified to his conversation with Morris Alburg, to his installation of the sound equipment in the Keymont Hotel, to the conversations that he heard and the recordings that were made.

The witness identified half a dozen plastic discs, explained how they were fed into a machine in relays so that there was a continuous transcription of conversation.

"Now then, Your Honor, I move to introduce these discs in evidence," Hamilton Burger said.

"I'd like to examine the witness briefly on this particular point," Mason said.

"Very well," Judge Lennox said. "Go right ahead."

"How do you know these are the same records that were left in the hotel room?"

"Actually, Mr. Mason, I can only testify as to the first one. As to the others, all I can say is that they look like records which I left on the machine. I have been informed that they were taken from the hotel room in which I had left my equipment."

"That's all," Mason said. "No objection to the introduction of the records."

"I assume you mean Record Number One?" Judge Lennox said.

"No, the whole batch," Mason said. "A witness who is as truthful as this witness is quite likely to have an opinion I can trust. If he thinks these are the same records I'm willing to let them go in, subject to my right to object to any conversation that may be on those records as incompetent, irrelevant and immaterial, but the records themselves may be received in evidence."

Judge Lennox smiled and said, "Well, that's refreshing

candor on the part of Counsel—and on the part of the witness. Very well, the records will be received as evidence."

"Now, then, in regard to these records," Hamilton Burger said, "there is a conversation in which the defendant, Dixie Dayton, states in so many words to Perry Mason that her codefendant, Morris Alburg, is out murdering George Fayette. I want the Court to listen to that conversation. I want the Court to note that Mr. Mason accepted this information and did absolutely nothing about it. He did not communicate with the police. He did not . . ."

"Are you now trying to show that *I* am a conspirator?" Mason asked.

"You've criticized my methods of preparing a case," Burger said. "I want the Court to realize exactly what happened."

Mason said, "Then you'd better show it by evidence, not by a statement."

"You don't deny that this conversation is on this record, do you?"

"I deny that Dixie Dayton at any time told me her codefendant, Morris Alburg, was planning to murder George Fayette."

"But the record is right here. You can hear her voice."

"How do you know it's *her* voice?" Mason asked.

"I'm sure it is."

"Then get on the stand and testify it is, and I'll cross-examine you, and the judge can reach an opinion as to your assumption that it's the same person."

"I don't have to do that," Burger said. "I can do it another way."

"Go ahead and do it, then."

Burger said, "Miss Minerva Hamlin will be my next witness. . . . Miss Hamlin, come forward and be sworn, please."

Minerva Hamilton marched to the witness stand, her manner that of a young woman who is intent upon creating an impression of brisk competence.

Under Burger's questioning, she testified with close-clipped, precise, well-articulated words, telling her story in a manner which unquestionably impressed Judge Lennox.

She described the emergency, the fact that she was called on to leave the switchboard and go at once to the Keymont Hotel, the arrangements that she made with Paul Drake by which she would flash an identification signal when the young woman in question started to leave the hotel, her acting the part of a maid in the hotel, and the time she spent watching room 721 in order to see who emerged from it.

"And finally," Hamilton Burger asked, "someone did emerge from it?"

"Yes, sir."

"A man or woman?"

"A woman."

"Did you have an opportunity to look at this woman?"

"That was what I was there for."

"That is not exactly an answer to the question," Hamilton Burger pointed out. "Did you . . ."

"Yes, I did."

"You noticed her particularly?"

"Yes, sir."

"And you saw this woman emerge from room 721?"

"I did. Yes, sir."

"Who was that woman?"

"Miss Dixie Dayton, one of the defendants in this case."

"Will you please designate the woman."

"The one I am pointing at."

"The record doesn't show the one that you're pointing at. May I ask Miss Dayton, the defendant, to stand up?"

"Stand up," Mason said.

Dixie Dayton stood up.

"Is that the woman?"

"That is the woman."

"Let the record show," Hamilton Burger said, "that the identification is that of the woman who stood up, and the woman who stood up is Dixie Dayton, one of the defendants in this case.

"What did you do when this woman left the room?" Burger asked.

"I followed her."

"Where?"

"She took the elevator. The elevator went up. I ran up one flight of stairs. I was on the seventh floor, and there were only eight floors in the hotel. I therefore knew she couldn't go up more than one floor. I felt that I could get up there almost as soon as the elevator."

"And you did so?"

"Yes."

"And where did this woman go?"

"She went to room 815, the room where the body of George Fayette was subsequently discovered by the police."

"This same woman?" Burger asked.

"This same woman."

"You're positive?"

"Positive."

"And who was that woman?"

"I have already told you."

"I mean, who was the woman who went to this room 815?"

"The defendant, Dixie Dayton."

"The same person who stood up? The same person you have previously identified?"

"Yes, sir."

"Cross-examine," Burger said to Perry Mason.

Minerva Hamlin turned to face Perry Mason with eyes that flashed antagonism, a manner that plainly showed she intended to give tit for tat, and that no adroit cross-examination was going to confuse *her*.

Mason's attitude was that of an older brother asking an impulsive younger sister to confide in him.

"Miss Hamlin," he said, "you didn't know Dixie Dayton, did you?"

"I had never seen her until she stepped out of that room."

"You didn't know who she was at the time?"

"I saw her, I didn't know her name, no."

"And the police showed you a photograph of Dixie Dayton and asked you if that was the same woman, didn't they?"

"Yes."

"What did you tell them?"

"I told them it was."

"Didn't you tell them that you *thought* it looked like the same woman?"

"Well, if it was the same woman it would look like her, wouldn't it?"

There was a ripple of merriment in the courtroom at her tart rejoinder.

"That," Mason said, "is quite true. Since you ask me the question I'll be only too glad to answer it, Miss Hamlin. You might pardon me also if I point out that if it had not been a photograph of Miss Dayton, that it still might have looked like her. Photographs are frequently confusing."

"They don't confuse me. I have a very keen eye."

"And yet you couldn't make an absolutely positive identification the first time you saw that photograph, could you?"

"Well, I told them—well, it depends on what you mean by 'positive.' "

"Well," Mason said smiling, "what do *you* mean by it?"

"When I'm positive, I'm positive."

"So one would gather," Mason said. "You weren't quite as positive then as you are now."

"Well, I've had a chance to see the woman herself since then. The photograph didn't—well, it . . ."

"Do you mean it didn't look like her?"

"No, it looked like her."

"But you were still a little doubtful?"

"I wanted to be perfectly fair, Mr. Mason."

"And you still do, don't you?"

"Yes, sir."

"Now," Mason said, "when you first saw that photograph

196

you couldn't be absolutely positive. You weren't positive. You said you thought it might be the same woman, but you couldn't be certain."

"That was when I first glanced at it."

"So you studied the photograph, didn't you?"

"Yes, sir."

"And did you become more positive as you studied the photograph?"

"Yes, sir."

"However, you weren't completely convinced from just looking at the photograph, were you?"

"No, sir. What completely convinced me was when I saw the defendant in a police show-up, or shadow box, or whatever it is they call them."

"And then you were certain?"

"I picked her out of a line of five women who were standing in the box. I picked her out unhesitatingly."

"And that was after you had been studying her photograph?"

"Yes, sir."

"Now, let's be frank, Miss Hamlin, isn't there at least a distinct possibility that you had studied that photograph so carefully in making a conscientious attempt to determine whether it was or was not a photograph of the person you saw leaving the room, that when you saw the defendant your mind almost subconsciously identified her with the photograph, and therefore you made the identification?"

"When I saw that woman in the line-up I was absolutely positive she was the woman who had been leaving the room in the hotel."

"Now, would you be good enough to explain to the Court just where you were when the woman left the room in the hotel."

"You mean room 721?"

"Yes."

"I was down at the end of the corridor by the fire escape, pretending to go about my duties as maid."

"And what particular duties were you doing at the time?"

"I pretended to be knocking on a door, as though I were checking towels."

"I assume from your manner that you're a rather remarkably efficient young woman, are you not, Miss Hamlin?"

"I try to be."

"And in acting the part of the maid you did your conscientious best to act just as a maid would do under similar circumstances?"

"Mr. Mason, I am interested in amateur theatricals. I have studied acting. I think I have the ability to be a very good actress. I try to be efficient in everything I do. I realize that in order to portray a persona and act a part successfully, you have to visualize that you actually are that person."

"So you visualized that you were the maid?"

"Yes, sir."

"And went about doing things just as a maid would do?"

"Yes, sir."

"And a maid wouldn't take too keen an interest in a woman who stepped out of a room and walked down the corridor, would she?"

"Just a glance, that's all."

"So you, making a good job of acting the part of the maid, gave just a glance?"

"Yes, sir."

"Now, why had you gone to the end of the corridor by the fire escape?"

"I think that is quite obvious, Mr. Mason. I didn't want to have the person who emerged from that room inspect me too closely. Therefore I went to the far end of the corridor. I knew that when she emerged from the room, no matter where she was going, whether she went to the elevator or the stairs, she would have to walk along the corridor. Under those circumstances, she couldn't meet me face to face."

"In other words, she turned her back to you?"

"Yes. But not before I had seen her face when she emerged from the room."

"How far was the door of that room from where you were standing at the end of the corridor?"

"I don't know. Twenty or thirty feet perhaps."

"How was the corridor illuminated? What kind of lights?"

"It was a dim illumination, but I saw her all right, Mr. Mason. I looked at her. I made up my mind I'd take a good look at her, and I did."

"You gave her just a glance, just as a maid might have looked up casually from her work?"

"Well, I—I took a good look."

"A few moments ago," Mason said, "you testified that you gave her a casual glance."

"Well, with me, a casual glance is a good look."

"I see. But it wasn't good enough so you could *positively* identify her when you first saw that photograph?"

"A person hesitates to make a *positive* identification from a photograph."

"That's all," Mason said.

"And now," Hamilton Burger said, "I'll call my main witness. Mr. Perry Mason take the stand, please."

Mason unhesitatingly walked forward, held up his hand, took the oath and seated himself on the witness stand.

"This is, of course, a most unusual procedure," Judge Lennox said.

"It's a situation I tried to avoid," Hamilton Burger pointed out. "I tried to avoid it by every means in my power."

"To ask an attorney for the defendants to give testimony which would help convict the defendants is, of course, an anomalous situation," Judge Lennox observed dubiously.

"That is the reason it is considered unethical for an attorney to act in a dual capacity," Burger said. "I tried to spare Mr. Mason the embarrassment of being placed in such a position."

"He is a necessary witness?" Judge Lennox asked.

"Absolutely, Your Honor. As the Court will realize from a contemplation of the evidence as it now stands in this case, it's necessary for me to prove the identity of the people who were participating in the conversation which took place in that room.''

"Of course, the conversation itself hasn't been admitted yet.''

"That's what I'm laying the foundation for, Your Honor.''

"Of course,'' Judge Lennox pointed out, "the situation would be simplified if the defendants had some other attorney associated with Mr. Mason, who could assume charge of the defendants' case at this point.''

"That would not be satisfactory either to the defendants or to me, Your Honor,'' Mason said. "We've heard a lot of talk about ethics. Perhaps, if the Court please, I should quote from a California decision reported in 187 California 695, where the Court says:

" 'We are of the opinion that too much importance has been given, and too much irritation developed, over the fact that much of the evidence for the plaintiff was given by one of the attorneys in her behalf, as a witness in the case. So far as the court is concerned such testimony is to be received and considered, as that of any other witness, in view of the inherent quality of his testimony, his interest in the case, and his appearance on the witness stand.

" 'The propriety of a lawyer occupying the dual capacity of attorney and witness is purely one of legal ethics largely to be determined by the attorney's own conscience. While it is not a practice to be encouraged, it may often occur that conditions exist in which an attorney cannot justify or fairly withhold from his client either his legal services or his testimony as a witness.' ''

Judge Lennox seemed impressed by the citation. "Very well, Mr. Mason,'' he said, "your position seems to be legally sound. In fact, from time to time you seem to find yourself in predicaments from which you extricate yourself by unusual methods which invariably turn out to be legally sound. The Court feels you are fully capable of looking after your own as well as your clients' interests. We seem to be making judicial history as far as this court is concerned."

"Mr. Mason," Burger said, "I am going to ask you if, on the early morning of the third of this month, you were not present in room 721 at the Keymont Hotel?"

"I was."

"Were you alone?"

"No."

"A young woman was with you?"

"During a part of the time."

"I believe she entered the room after you arrived."

"Yes, sir."

"You went to the hotel?"

"Yes, sir."

"Went to this room?"

"Yes, sir."

"Entered the room?"

"Yes, sir."

"And shortly afterwards this young woman arrived?"

"Yes, sir."

"You went to that room at the request of Morris Alburg, one of the defendants in this case?"

"That question," Mason said, "is improper. It, on its face, calls for a privileged communication between an attorney and client."

"I think the Court will have to sustain that objection," Judge Lennox said.

"I'm not asking him for the conversation. I'm simply asking him if he went there because of such a conversation," Burger said.

"It amounts to the same thing," Judge Lennox said. "You're asking him, in effect, if his client told him to go to this room in the hotel. That, in my opinion, would be a privileged communication. After all, Mr. Burger, you must realize that there are certain peculiar aspects in this situation which are binding on you as well as on Counsel."

"I understand, Your Honor."

"Mr. Mason is occupying the dual role of a witness against his clients, and an attorney representing those clients. The Court will permit the examination of Mr. Mason as a witness, but the Court is certainly going to be very alert to safeguard the interests of the defendants."

"Very well, Your Honor. Now, then, Mr. Mason, I am going to ask you if, while you were present in that room, the young woman who was present in that room did not state to you that Morris Alburg was at that time tracking down George Fayette for the purpose of killing him?"

"Now, to that question," Mason said, "as attorney for the defendant Alburg, I interpose an objection that the question is incompetent, irrelevant and immaterial. As attorney for the defendant Dixie Dayton, I interpose an objection on the ground that if that woman was not Dixie Dayton the statement would be completely irrelevant and hearsay, and if the woman were Dixie Dayton it would be a privileged communication."

"If the Court please, I had anticipated both of those objections," Hamilton Burger said. "The evidence now shows that this woman was Dixie Dayton. Since the conversation related to a crime that had not as yet been committed, but which was about to be committed, the conversation was not a privileged communication. I am, of course, prepared to show the actual conversation. In other words, if Mr. Mason should deny that this statement was made I can impeach him irrefutably by producing the records which have been introduced in evidence, and playing the part of the conversation so that Mason will hear his own voice and the voice of the person who was in the room with him."

"You can't impeach your own witness," Mason said.

"I can on a material point, but not on character," Burger retorted.

"Suppose that person was *not* Dixie Dayton?" Judge Lennox asked the prosecutor.

"Minerva Hamlin has testified positively that it was Dixie Dayton."

"That is the testimony of one witness."

"But that's the only testimony before the Court at this time," Hamilton Burger pointed out.

Judge Lennox ran his hand over his forehead, puckered his lips, swung halfway around in his swivel chair so as to avoid the eyes of Counsel, apparently trying thereby to improve his powers of concentration.

For several moments there was a tense silence in the courtroom.

Judge Lennox finally said, "Ask *him* the question. Put it right up to him. Was that woman Dixie Dayton, or wasn't it?"

"Oh, no," Hamilton Burger said, "that's one question I have no intention of asking."

"Why not?" Judge Lennox asked.

"Because if Mr. Mason should deny that it was Dixie Dayton he would be testifying as my witness. I am only going to ask Mr. Mason questions to which I already have the answers, and the correct answers, so that if Mr. Mason seeks to crucify me by betraying my case in his testimony I have it in my power to send him to prison for perjury."

"I take it," Judge Lennox said, smiling, "I opened the door for that, Mr. District Attorney. I take it you wish to convey that threat to Mr. Mason, and I gave you a good opportunity to do so."

Hamilton Burger was grim. "The fact remains that I have stated my position."

"You have indeed," Judge Lennox said.

There was another period of silence; then Judge Lennox turned to Perry Mason. "I think I'd like to hear your position in this, Counselor."

"As attorney for the defendant Morris Alburg," Mason said, "I would point out that he isn't bound by any statement made by Dixie Dayton."

"As a codefendant and a conspirator, I claim that he is," Burger retorted.

Mason smiled, "Would you contend that any individual

could walk into a hotel room and state that His Honor, for instance, was out committing a murder, and then seek to prove His Honor guilty of the murder by producing the corpse, and a recording of that conversation?''

"That's different," Burger snapped.

"Then would you mind stating exactly how it strikes you as being different?''

"But how about the defendant Dixie Dayton?" Judge Lennox asked.

Mason said, "Your Honor, Dixie Dayton, if she *had* been in that room and if she *had* said that Morris Alburg was out committing a murder, would still not be subject to any prosecution and the evidence could not be introduced in this manner unless she was a party to that murder.''

"But she was," Hamilton Burger said.

"Prove it," Mason snapped.

"That's what I'm trying to do.''

"Then do it in an orderly manner. Get your cart and then your horse, but don't put the cart in front of the horse.''

"Now, just a minute," Judge Lennox said, "there's a peculiar situation here. I can see Mr. Mason's point. It's a carefully thought out point and it seems to be sound.''

"But, Your Honor," Hamilton Burger protested, "can't Your Honor realize the situation? Perry Mason was in that room with Dixie Dayton. Dixie Dayton stated in so many words, and I can assure Your Honor that that is a fact because we have those words recorded, that Morris Alburg was murdering or was going to murder George Fayette. Shortly after that George Fayette was found murdered, and there is ample evidence connecting Morris Alburg with the crime.''

"That's all very nice," Judge Lennox said, "but first you not only have to prove that it was the defendant Dixie Dayton who made the statement, but, as Mr. Mason points out, there must be some privity, some connection, some conspiracy.''

"Of course, as far as the element of conspiracy is concerned, we're going to prove it by circumstantial evidence. We can't introduce a tape recording of the two defendants sitting down and saying in effect, 'Let's go murder George Fayette.' We have to prove that by declarations and conduct of the parties.''

"Of course," Judge Lennox said, "you could simplify the situation by asking Mr. Mason if, at a certain date, Dixie Dayton, the defendant in this case, did not say to him so-and-so and such-and-such.''

"I don't know what Mr. Mason's answer would be to that question. He might deny it and then I would be in a position of trying to impeach my own witness. I don't want to do that. I do want to keep the issues within such narrow limits of proof that Mr. Mason will either answer the questions in accordance with the facts as I understand them, or Mr. Mason will subject himself to a prosecution for perjury.''

"Yes," Judge Lennox said, "I can see your point. I recognize the situation—I may say the dilemma—but the fact remains that it must be solved according to established rules of legal procedure. I think I am going to hold that this witness cannot be forced to answer that question over the objection of Counsel for both defendants. I feel that there must be some further proof of conspiracy before the conversation can be admitted. Are there any further questions of this witness?''

"Not at the moment," Hamilton Burger said.

"Very well, Mr. Mason, you're excused from the witness stand," Judge Lennox said, "and may resume your position as Counsel for the defendants.''

"Subject to being recalled later after more foundation has been laid," Hamilton Burger said.

"That is my understanding of the situation," Judge Lennox ruled. "Go on with your case.''

"I want to call Frank Hoxie as my next witness.''

Frank Hoxie, the night clerk at the Keymont Hotel, was sworn, took the witness stand, and gave his name, address and occupation in a bored tone of voice.

"Are you acquainted with either of the defendants in this case?''

"Yes, sir.''

"With which one?"

"With both."

"What were you doing on the second and third of the present month?"

"Working as a night clerk in the Keymont Hotel."

"What time did you go on duty?"

"At nine o'clock in the evening."

"What time did you go off duty?"

"At eight o'clock in the morning."

"Now when did you first meet the defendant Morris Alburg?"

"A couple of days before . . ."

"Try and make it an exact date."

"On the first of the month."

"Where did you meet him?"

"I was at the hotel."

"At the desk?"

"Yes, sir."

"On duty as a night clerk?"

"Yes, sir."

"And what conversation did you have with Mr. Alburg?"

"He came in and asked for a room. He said his sister-in-law had come to pay him an unexpected visit, and that he wanted to rent a room which she would occupy."

"Under what name did he register?"

"Under the name of Mrs. Madison Kerby."

"You assigned him a room?"

"Yes, sir."

"What room?"

"Room 815."

"That was the room in which the body of George Fayette was subsequently discovered?"

"Yes, sir."

"Did you ever meet the person whom Morris Alburg said was his sister-in-law?"

"Yes, sir."

"When did you meet her?"

"The defendant, Miss Dayton, came to the desk and said she was Mrs. Madison Kerby, and asked for the key to room 815. I gave her the key."

"That was the defendant?"

"Dixie Dayton, one of the defendants, the one who stood up a minute ago."

"When was that room given up?"

"You mean by the defendants?"

"Yes."

"It was never given up. They kept the room until the date of the murder, when they were arrested."

"Did you tell the police who had rented that room?"

"The police were after me pretty hard to find out who had rented it."

"What did you tell them?"

"I told them I'd never seen the people before and didn't know who they were."

"Was that true or false?"

"It was true."

"Perhaps," Burger said, "you can tell us something of what happened on the evening of the second and the morning of the third."

"It was on the morning of the third instant that Perry Mason came to the hotel."

"At about what time in the morning?"

"Sometime around two-thirty in the morning, I think."

"Was the defendant Dixie Dayton in the hotel at that time?"

"Yes, sir."

"How do you know?"

"I had seen her come in and I hadn't seen her leave."

"When did she come in?"

"About half an hour before Mr. Mason did."

"And the defendant Morris Alburg, was he in the hotel?"

"Yes, sir."

"When did *he* come in?"

"About an hour before Mr. Mason arrived."

"You're certain of your identifications?"

"Very certain."

Hamilton Burger turned to Mason and said, "Do you care to cross-examine this witness?"

"I think I do," Mason said.

He pushed back his chair, arose, and faced the young man, whose blue, watery eyes made a valiant attempt to meet his, then shifted away, only to return, and again slither away.

Mason stood holding his eyes steadily on the witness.

Once more the witness made an attempt to meet Mason's eyes, but, after less than a second, he averted his own eyes and shifted his position uneasily on the witness stand.

"How long have you been employed at the Keymont Hotel?"

"Three years."

"Where did you work before that?"

"Various places."

"Can you name them?"

"I sold goods on commission."

"What sort of goods?"

"Novelties."

"Can you remember the name of the firm?"

"No. It was a fly-by-night outfit."

"Did you ever serve in the Armed Forces?"

"No."

"Have you ever held any other salaried position for as long as three years?"

"No."

"You had two weeks' vacation each year as a part of your compensation as night clerk?"

"No."

"No vacations?"

"No vacations."

"You worked there regularly, every night?"

"Well, there was once I was sent to Mexico City on business. It wasn't really a vacation. It was a change."

"What sort of business?"

"To collect a sum of money."

"That was owed to the hotel?"

"Yes."

"You collected the money?"

"I got a promissory note and was advised that would be satisfactory. The management wired me to that effect."

"How long were you gone?"

"Almost a month. It was a difficult piece of work. There were lots of angles."

"For what was the money due?"

"I don't know."

"When was this?"

"About a year ago."

"Exactly what date did you leave? Do you remember?"

"Certainly I remember. I left on a night plane on the seventeenth of— No, if you want to be technical it was on September eighteenth of last year."

"Just how do you fix the date?"

"If you worked in the Keymont Hotel you wouldn't have any trouble remembering when you had a free trip to Mexico City. The manager called me in and told me about this deal and said someone had to be on the ground who could handle the thing. He gave me money, told me to go up to my room, pack a suitcase and get to the airport."

"What time was this?"

"Shortly before midnight, on the seventeenth."

"The plane left at what time?"

"Right around one-thirty in the morning—the eighteenth."

"A through plane?"

"No, I changed in El Paso, and if you want *all* the details, I sat next to a beautiful blonde who gave me the eye and then got sleepy when she found out I was leaving the plane at El Paso. From El Paso down I sat next to a woman who had been eating garlic, who had a kid that was airsick."

The courtroom broke into laughter.

Mason didn't even smile.

"There were some difficulties attendant upon your job in Mexico City?"

"Lots."

"But it was a vacation?"

"It was a change."

"Have you ever tried to leave the Keymont Hotel and secure employment with any other hotel?"

"Oh, Your Honor," Hamilton Burger said. "There's no reason why this witness should be ripped to pieces with *all* the details of his past life. Let Counsel confine his cross-examination to things that have been asked on direct examination."

Judge Lennox said, "It seems to me that there is something unusual about the background here, and I am not going to limit Counsel's cross-examination. The objection is overruled."

"Have you?" Mason asked.

The witness tried to meet Mason's eyes and failed. "No," he said in a low voice.

"Have you," Mason asked, "ever been convicted of a felony?"

The witness started to get up from the witness chair, then stopped and settled back down.

"Oh, Your Honor," Hamilton Burger said, "this is so plainly a shot in the dark. This is an attempt to smear the reputation of a witness whose only fault has been that he has testified against Mr. Mason's clients."

"I think, myself, the question, under the circumstances, is rather brutal," Judge Lennox said. "However, it is a perfectly permissible question. It's one of the grounds of impeaching a witness, and obviously the question has been met with no forthright denial. Therefore I will have to overrule the objection, somewhat against my wishes."

"Have you," Mason asked, "ever been convicted of a felony?"

"Yes."

"What was it? Where did you serve time?"

210

"I served time in San Quentin for armed robbery. Now you know the whole thing. Go ahead and ruin me. Rip me up the back if you want to."

Mason studied the young man for a moment, then moved his chair around the end of the counsel table, sat down, and in a tone of genuine interest said, "I don't think I want to, Mr. Hoxie. I think perhaps we may use this as a point of beginning rather than a point of ending. Did your employers know you had been convicted of a felony?"

"Why do you suppose I was holding down a second-rate job in a third-rate hotel?" Hoxie demanded angrily.

"You're positive of your identifications of the witnesses?" Mason asked.

"Completely positive. I have a knack of never forgetting a face. Once I have seen a person and placed him I never forget him—which is why my services presumably are of some value to the hotel."

"When were you convicted, Frank?"

"Ten years ago."

"And you served how long?"

"Five years."

"And then what?"

"Then I had four or five different jobs, and something was always happening. My record would come up and I'd be thrown out."

"Then what?"

"Then I was picked up on suspicion. Not because of anything I had done but purely because of my record. I was put in a police show-up box and I knew it meant the loss of another job. I was pretty sore about the whole thing."

"Go on," Mason said.

"A police sergeant came to me after one of these show-ups. He sympathized with me and told me he knew how I felt. He said that he had a friend who managed the Keymont Hotel. He said it was a place that had been in trouble with the police and the manager would therefore know just how I felt, and the trouble I was having. This police officer knew I had a great talent for remembering people and he knew the Keymont Hotel was looking for a night clerk because he'd been instrumental in sending the one who had just been employed there to prison.

"He told me he'd had to threaten to close the hotel for good, and this new manager had promised to do his best to keep the place within the law. The police officer advised me to go to this new manager, to tell him all about myself. He said that the only thing for me to do was to get a job where the employer knew all about my past history so I'd have a real chance to make good. He suggested that I go there and tell them frankly my entire history, and he warned me that if I didn't want to try to go straight, I wasn't to apply for the job because the place had a bad reputation and the Vice Squad was watching it."

"You did that?"

"Yes. It was the best advice I ever had."

"And you're well-treated in this job?"

"My hours are twice as long as they should be. I'm paid about half of what I should be getting. I'm treated courteously. I'm told to keep my mouth shut. It's not the best hotel in the city. It's a third-rate hotel and caters to third-rate business with all that it means. I keep my eyes open, my ears open, my mouth shut, and my nose clean, and I'm still there. Now, I take it that answers your question, Mr. Mason, and you've had your fun. Tomorrow regular residents of the hotel will know that the night clerk is an ex-convict."

"For your information," Mason told him, "I think that this is the only time in my courtroom experience I have ever asked a witness if he had ever been convicted of a felony. Personally I believe that when a man has paid his debt to society, the debt should be marked off the books. However . . ."

"Oh, Your Honor, I object to all this self-justification on the part of Counsel," Hamilton Burger said. "He's tipped over the apple cart and ruined this young man's career,

212

and now he's trying to present an alibi in the unctuous manner . . ."

Judge Lennox pounded his gavel. "The district attorney," he said, "will refrain from offensive personalities. Mr. Mason is within his legal rights and the Court thinks it sees the general purpose in the back of Mr. Mason's interrogation. If you have any specific objections to make, make them when Counsel has finished asking his questions. . . . Proceed, Mr. Mason."

Mason said, "Thank you, Your Honor."

He turned to the witness and said, "This police sergeant who befriended you has kept an eye on you?"

"Oh, yes. He's the head of the Vice Squad."

"He checks up on you?"

"Yes."

"Frequently?"

"Sure. They keep an eye on the hotel. Things happen there. We can't help it, but the management doesn't take part in any of that stuff. We don't ask to see the marriage license when a couple registers, but neither do the high-class hotels. We try to keep the bellboys from furnishing call girls, and we don't rent rooms to known dope peddlers.

"That's where my knowledge of faces comes in handy. The hotel was in bad and the D.A. was threatening to close the place up. The owners had to clean up or lose their investment."

And the witness made a little bow to Hamilton Burger, who tried to look virtuously disdainful.

"And because of that the management is anxious to cater to the district attorney?" Mason asked.

"Objected to as calling for a conclusion of the witness," Burger said.

"Sustained."

"How about you yourself?" Mason asked. "Do you wish to cater to the district attorney?"

"I don't want him as an enemy. Any time the authorities

213

turn thumbs down on me, I'm out. But that hasn't made me tell any lies. I'm telling exactly what happened."

"Yet you were glad of a chance to be of assistance to the district attorney?"

"I'm sorry I was ever called as a witness."

"But you welcomed a chance to be of service to the district attorney?"

"I felt it might come in handy sometime, if you want to put it that way."

Mason turned to Hamilton Burger and, "I think it is only fair at this time, Mr. District Attorney, to acquaint the Court with what I understand is the general background of your case."

"I'll handle my case in my own way," Hamilton Burger said.

"However, as I understand it generally," Mason said to the judge, "the police have in their possession a revolver which had been pawned in Seattle. The pawnbroker is here in court and he will presently identify the defendant Dixie Dayton as the person who pawned that weapon. And that weapon was, according to the evidence of the ballistics department, as will be presently brought out by Mr. Mott, the weapon which was used in the murder of one Robert Claremont, a murder which took place something over a year ago here in this city, and, as I understand it, it is the contention of the prosecution that it was because of an attempt to cover up that murder that Morris Alburg and Dixie Dayton planned the murder of George Fayette."

Hamilton Burger's face showed complete, utter surprise.

"Is that generally the background of the prosecution's case?" Mason asked him.

"We'll put on our own case," Hamilton Burger said.

Judge Lennox said, "You may put on your case, Mr. Burger, but the Court is entitled to know generally whether this outline of the background of the case as given by the defendants' Counsel is correct."

"It is substantially correct, Your Honor," Burger said sullenly. "I had assumed Counsel for the defendants would try to keep out this evidence. His statement comes as a surprise."

Judge Lennox frowned. "I can now appreciate the reason for the comments of the District Attorney concerning testimony regarding other crimes which might furnish in some way a motive for the crime charged in this case."

Mason sat in the mahogany counsel chair, his long legs crossed in front of him, his eyes thoughtful, speculative, regarding the young man on the witness stand.

"Now on the night in question you were acting both as night clerk and switchboard operator?"

"Yes."

"And there was a call from room 721—a woman saying, 'Call the police'?"

"Yes."

"Yet you did nothing about that?"

"Certainly I did. The woman hung up. I immediately called back on the phone, and asked what was the trouble. She laughed at me and said to be my age, that it was a gag."

"You did nothing else?"

"Certainly not. I assumed her boy friend had become a little too wolfish and so she decided she'd throw a scare into him. But she obviously wasn't worried."

"Did it occur to you that *another* woman had answered your ring?"

"Not at the time. In the Keymont you don't call the police for anything short of a riot. You handle trouble yourself."

"Yet you did call the police later?"

"When a revolver shot was reported, yes. You can't overlook a revolver shot."

Once more Mason regarded the witness with thoughtful speculation.

"Your employers know about your criminal record, Mr. Hoxie?"

"I've told you they did."

"And it's brought up to you once in a while?"

"What do you mean by that?"

"Whenever you are called upon to do something that might be perhaps a little bit irregular?"

"You have no right to examine me about anything except the facts in this case," the witness retorted.

"Quite right," Mason said, and, without turning his head, said over his shoulder, "Is Lieutenant Tragg in court?"

"Here," Lieutenant Tragg said.

Mason said, "Lieutenant, you have a photograph of Robert Claremont, the rookie cop who was murdered in this city something over a year ago. Would you mind stepping forward and showing that photograph to the witness?"

"What does all this have to do with the present case?" Hamilton Burger asked irritably.

"It may have a great deal to do with it," Mason said, without even turning toward the source of the interruption, but keeping his eyes fixed on the witness. "I take it you gentlemen would really like to solve the Claremont murder?"

"I would," Lieutenant Tragg said, striding toward the witness stand.

Lieutenant Tragg extended a photograph to Perry Mason.

"Show it to the witness," Mason said.

Lieutenant Tragg moved up to stand by the witness, holding out the photograph.

The witness looked at the photograph, started to shake his head, then extended his hand, took the photograph, looked at it and held it for a moment.

It was quite obvious that his hand was shaking.

"You say you never forget a face you have once seen," Mason said, "and therefore you are a valuable asset to the Keymont Hotel. Have you ever seen the face of the man in the photograph?"

"If the Court please," Hamilton Burger said, "this isn't proper cross-examination. If Counsel wants to make this man his own witness he . . ."

"He certainly has a right to test the memory of the witness," Judge Lennox said. "Any witness who makes the unusual statement that he *never* forgets a face he has once seen is testifying that he has a memory which is far better than average. Therefore, under the circumstances, Counsel is entitled to test that memory. The witness will answer the question."

"I can't . . ."

"Careful," Mason cautioned sternly. "Remember you're under oath."

The witness once more held up the photograph. This time the trembling of his hand was so obvious that he lowered the hand hastily to his lap.

"Well?" Mason asked. "What's the answer? Yes or no?"

"Yes," Hoxie said in an all but inaudible voice.

"When did you see him?"

"Oh, Your Honor," Hamilton Burger said, "that is asking too much . . ."

Lieutenant Tragg whirled to glare angrily at the district attorney.

"I'll withdraw the objection," Hamilton Burger said.

"When?" Mason asked.

"If that's really Claremont's picture, I guess it was the night I left for Mexico."

"What time during the night?"

"Early in the evening. There was a little trouble."

"What sort of trouble?"

"He went up to see a tenant. There was a complaint about a quarrel. I phoned up to the tenant in the room. The noise quieted down."

"Then what happened?"

"Nothing."

"Were there telephone calls from that room?"

"I can't remember."

"You have said you never forget a face. Who was the occupant of that room?"

"A regular tenant."

"Who?"

"George Fayette, the man who was murdered on the third of this month."

Perry Mason got up, pushed back his chair, and said, "Thank you, Mr. Hoxie," then to the bewildered court, "Those are all the questions I have."

"You mean you're quitting now?" Judge Lennox demanded incredulously.

"Now," Mason said, and then added with a smile, "and I think if Court will take a thirty-minute adjournment the examination can best be completed by Lieutenant Tragg and in private."

Judge Lennox hesitated, frowned, then reached for his gavel. "I think I get your point, Mr. Mason. Court will take a thirty-minute recess. The defendants are remanded to custody."

And Judge Lennox, with a significant glance at Lieutenant Tragg, promptly left the courtroom for his chambers.

Chapter 18

Mason faced Dixie Dayton and Morris Alburg in a witness room opening off the courtroom.

"All right," he said, "I want some facts. Where can I find Thomas E. Sedgwick?"

Alburg glanced at Dixie Dayton.

She shook her head. "I wouldn't tell anybody—"

"You're going to tell me," Mason said. "We're going to be able to produce him as soon as Lieutenant Tragg finishes with Frank Hoxie."

"Mr. Mason, do you know what you're saying?" Dixie Dayton demanded angrily. "This is a cop murder. The police wouldn't give him a leg to stand on. He wouldn't have a ghost of a chance. They'd railroad him to the death house so fast that he wouldn't know what had happened."

"Why?" Mason asked.

"Why?" Morris Alburg demanded. "What are you talking about? Are you dumb?"

"I'm not dumb and I'm not deaf," Mason said. "Why would they railroad him to the death house?"

"Because that's the way the police are. When you kill a cop the police are all on your neck."

"Why?"

"Because they want revenge, of course, and because I suppose they want to let people know that you can't kill cops and get away with it. That's for their own protection."

"Against whom do they want this revenge?"

"Against anybody that they think is guilty."

"Exactly," Mason said. "They used to think Tom Sedg-

219

wick was guilty. I don't think they'll feel that he's guilty now."

Dixie Dayton said, "He has tuberculosis. He can't do ordinary work. He needs rest. He is having a long, slow fight trying to get better. That's why he did the things he did. That's why he got mixed up in bookmaking. He felt that if he could get funds enough, he could take it easy for a while. He's not bad, Mr. Mason, he—he's human. He did the things that lots of other people were doing, and then—then they framed this cop killing on him just because that rookie cop was concentrating on him, giving him the works."

"You've been protecting him?" Mason said to Dixie Dayton.

She nodded.

"You've been living with him, washing for him, cooking for him, sewing for him, trying to give him a chance?"

She nodded, then said, "I'd give him my life."

"All right," Mason told her. "Give me his address, the place where he can be found right now, and you may save his life and yours, too."

Morris Alburg suddenly turned to face Dixie. "Give it to him, Dixie."

Chapter 19

Mason, Della Street and Paul Drake were in Mason's office when Gertie, the switchboard operator, rang three frantic signals on the telephone.

"That," Mason said, "will be Lieutenant Tragg."

He had no sooner spoken the words than Tragg unceremoniously jerked open the office door, nodded briefly, said, "Hello, folks," and walked over to sit down opposite Mason's desk.

"Well?" Mason asked.

"It's okay," Tragg said.

"Going to tell us about it?"

"I'd rather not."

"We're entitled to it."

"I know. That's why I came here. Give me a little time."

Tragg fished a cigar from his pocket, clipped off the end, lit the cigar, looked at Mason searchingly through the first blue wisps of cigar smoke and said, "What gave you your hunch on this thing, Mason?"

Mason said, "I was faced with clients who had an impossible story. No jury would ever have believed that story. Yet I began to think it might be the truth."

"I don't see how that gives you anything," Tragg said.

"Anyone who can force an attorney to put on evidence that is going to convict his client, yet which he feels is the truth, must be someone who knows something about evidence. The story that each defendant had to tell was so completely phony that if those stories had been told on the witness stand the defendants would have been convicted.

"In one case that might have been an accident. In two cases it showed design. And then I suddenly realized that I was dealing with a pattern. Thomas E. Sedgwick had been placed in such a position. Any story that he could have told would have eternally damned him before a jury. Therefore his only alternative was to take refuge in flight.

"Well, Lieutenant, I simply used an ordinary police method. You catch many of your criminals because of a file you have entitled *Modus Operandi*. It is predicated upon the assumption that a criminal, having once committed a successful crime, will thereafter follow a pattern in everything he does.

"In Sedgwick's case he had an utterly implausible story to tell, and he had possession of a murder weapon. Morris Alburg had an utterly impossible story and a murder weapon.

"It occurred to me that since it was quite apparent Claremont was gunning for the people higher up, he might have made contact.

"There was one feature of the case in my favor. The night clerk never forgot a face. I decided I'd try the case by floundering around with a lot of cross-examination and then slip in a casual question to find out if Hoxie could remember having seen Claremont in the hotel on the night he was murdered.

"When Hoxie told about that sudden trip to Mexico City I understood just what had happened. There was one more question which might have cleared up the case. I thought it would be better for you to ask it privately than for me to ask it in court.

"When I saw Hoxie's hand begin to shake I thought I knew the answer. . . . The question, of course, was whether Fayette had any other visitor in his room when Claremont went up.

"Now, tell me, how far did I miss it?"

"You didn't miss it a damn bit," Tragg said. "I wish you had. The hell of it is that people get a feeling the police are

222

all crooked simply because now and then some big shot starts a shakedown and piles up an individual fortune. That's the way it was in this case. Hell, the guy *owned* the Keymont Hotel. What do you know about that?''

''I was satisfied he did,'' Mason said, ''also the Bonsal Apartments, and probably one other apartment house where the captives were taken and where they saw the towels.''

There was a moment's silence. Tragg puffed on the cigar, then said, ''Bob Claremont wasn't as dumb and as naïve as lots of people thought. He knew that Sedgwick was making book, but he also knew Sedgwick was paying protection. He knew Fayette was the go-between. Claremont was after the sources of protection. He found them, too. The trail led to the Keymont Hotel. And then presumably Bob Claremont got quite a jolt. He found out the real identity of the man he was after. He never left the hotel alive. They took him down in the freight elevator and put him in the car. Then they sent for Sedgwick.''

''Who did?''

''Who do you think? The man who had been taking his protection money. He told Sedgwick he was hotter than a firecracker, that people were wise to the fact that he had been paying for protection. He told Sedgwick he had a twelve-hour head start to get out of town, to sell everything he had for what he could get, and get out.''

''That's the way I had it figured,'' Mason said.

''You know what happened after that. Sedgwick did what he was supposed to do, and by doing it he irrevocably put his neck in the noose.''

''How about the gun?'' Mason asked.

''That was a cinch,'' Tragg said. ''Sedgwick was given to understand that his only chance was to stay out of the state until things cooled off, but to let this one person know where he was all the time. Sedgwick had a gun. It was a Smith and Wesson, but it wasn't the gun Dixie pawned. That was Claremont's gun. Somehow they managed to switch guns on

Sedgwick after the murder. Sedgwick and Dixie must have had a visitor whom they thought was a trusted friend who made the substitution.''

"Why?" Mason asked.

"Because that's the gang's life insurance. They didn't know that Dixie Dayton would ever come back, but they thought she might. I'd a lot rather not talk about it."

"I know," Mason said, "but you have to do it, Tragg. You owe that much to us."

"I know," Tragg said, moodily. "Why the hell do you think I'm here?"

"You got a statement from Hoxie?"

"Of course I got a statement from Hoxie. You did everything except wrap the damn case up in a cellophane envelope and hand it to me on a silver platter. I knew right from the start that there was something fishy about Bob Claremont's murder. I knew that he wouldn't get into a car. I knew that he wouldn't let anybody draw his own gun. The thing was screwy. It had to be. But I couldn't figure out what was wrong with it.

"And then, of course, when you cross-examined Hoxie the thing stuck out like a sore thumb. The Keymont Hotel was in the gambling racket. The D.A. was about to make an investigation. A new manager had been put in. A kid went in as night clerk who had a record. He had a memory for faces. If he'd stayed in town he'd have seen the newspapers the next morning with Bob Claremont's picture. He'd have recognized him as the cop who came to the hotel in plain clothes following a hot lead. Then the tables would have been turned. Hoxie would have been able to control the owners. . . . So they rigged up a deal with the man who was the lead of the dope ring in Mexico. They rushed Hoxie onto a plane, and the Mexican end gave Hoxie a run-around until the Claremont story and picture was out of the papers, and then Hoxie was permitted to come back.

"Things would have stopped there if Dixie hadn't brought

Tom Sedgwick back. Fayette tried to stampede her into an alley where she could be taken for a ride. She didn't react. And Fayette was so confident of success he'd let the muscle man use his car. He thought *he* might be spotted, so he rented a car for the night for his own use.

"Then Dixie ran, there was a bullet hole in Fayette's car, and then the Seattle police discovered Dixie had pawned Claremont's gun.

"That did it. Fayette was hot. He'd squeal to save his hide so it was decided to kill him and frame Alburg and Dixie with the crime, leaving them with an impossible story. You upset the apple cart by digging out the one weakness in the scheme, something they'd even forgotten about themselves— Hoxie having been rushed to Mexico City so he wouldn't see Claremont's picture in the papers.

"Of course, since it was a big racket in a big payoff, the head of the deal had plenty of people he could call on, people who had to help in the deal but who would be strangers to all concerned."

"The real owner of the hotel?" Mason asked. "The real head of the payoff?"

"Why make me go into that?" Tragg said savagely. "You want to crucify me! You want to . . ."

"I don't want anything of the sort," Mason interrupted. "I just want to get the case cleaned up."

"It's cleaned up. You know who it was," Tragg said. "It was Sergeant Jaffrey of the Vice Squad. He owned the hotel lock, stock and barrel. He owned half a dozen other places, and he had three or four safe deposit boxes. It remains to be seen what's in them."

"Where is he now?" Mason asked.

"He's dead."

Mason came halfway up out of his chair. *"Dead!"*

"That's right. He was shot while resisting arrest."

"Good Lord," Mason exclaimed. "Who killed him?"

Tragg got up from his chair, stood motionless for a moment, then his right hand tightened, crushing the cigar he

225

had been smoking into crumpled bits of charred tobacco leaves.

"Who the hell do you think? I did," he said, and walked out.

About the Author

Erle Stanley Gardner is the king of American mystery fiction. A criminal lawyer, he filled his mystery masterpieces with intricate, fascinating, ever twisting plots. Challenging, clever, and full of surprises, these are whodunits in the best tradition. During his life time, Erle Stanley Garnder wrote 146 books, 85 of which feature Perry Mason.